SPECIAL MESSAGE TO READERS

THE ULVERSCROFT FOUNDATION
(registered UK charity number 264873)
was established in 1972 to provide funds for
research, diagnosis and treatment of eye diseases.
Examples of major projects funded by
the Ulverscroft Foundation are:-

- The Children's Eye Unit at Moorfields Eye Hospital, London
- The Ulverscroft Children's Eye Unit at Great Ormond Street Hospital for Sick Children
- Funding research into eye diseases and treatment at the Department of Ophthalmology, University of Leicester
- The Ulverscroft Vision Research Group, Institute of Child Health
- Twin operating theatres at the Western Ophthalmic Hospital, London
- The Chair of Ophthalmology at the Royal Australian College of Ophthalmologists

You can help further the work of the Foundation
by making a donation or leaving a legacy.
Every contribution is gratefully received. If you
would like to help support the Foundation or
require further information, please contact:

THE ULVERSCROFT FOUNDATION
The Green, Bradgate Road, Anstey
Leicester LE7 7FU, England
Tel: (0116) 236 4325

website: www.foundation.ulverscroft.com

Anna Jacobs is the author of over 60 novels and is addicted to storytelling. She grew up in Lancashire, emigrated to Australia in the 1970s, and writes stories set in both countries. She loves to return to England regularly to visit her family and soak up the history. Anna has two grown daughters and a grandson, and lives with her husband in a spacious home near the Swan Valley, the oldest wine-growing area in Western Australia. Her house is crammed with thousands of books. In 2006 one of her novels, *Pride of Lancashire,* won the Australian Romantic Novel of the Year Award.

You can discover more about the author at www.annajacobs.com

THE HONEYFIELD BEQUEST

Wiltshire, 1901: Young Kathleen Keller is being forced by her cruel father into marriage with a man she despises. In an act of desperation, she runs away in a bid for a safer life, although one she might not otherwise have chosen. But when tragedy strikes, Kathleen is left vulnerable, and one man threatens the fragile peace she has made for herself . . . Meanwhile, Nathan Perry works for his father's accountancy firm but yearns for something more satisfying. He is brought in to help with the purchase of Honeyfield House, established by a charitable benefactor as a safe house for women in trouble, and there he encounters Kathleen. Their lives are set to intertwine, and neither will be the same again . . .

ANNA JACOBS

◆

THE HONEYFIELD BEQUEST

Complete and Unabridged

CHARNWOOD
Leicester

First published in Great Britain in 2016 by
Allison & Busby Limited
London

First Charnwood Edition
published 2017
by arrangement with
Allison & Busby Limited
London

A catalogue record for this book is available
from the British Library.

ISBN 978–1–4448–3355–3

Published by
F. A. Thorpe (Publishing)
Anstey, Leicestershire

Set by Words & Graphics Ltd.
Anstey, Leicestershire
Printed and bound in Great Britain by
T. J. International Ltd., Padstow, Cornwall

This book is printed on acid-free paper

135302184

Part One

1901–1907

1

Wiltshire
Autumn 1901

Kathleen had never seen a customer look so unhappy. Avoiding other people, the man went to a small table in a back corner of the tea room and sat down with a heavy sigh, staring at his clasped hands. She felt so sorry for him she said to the other waitress, 'I'll serve that one.'

'You're welcome. He comes in sometimes and always looks miserable!'

'Don't be unkind. Someone he loves might have died, for all you know.'

'Oh! I never thought of that.'

No, you never think of anything but yourself! But Kathleen didn't say that. It'd just go in one ear and out of the other; the other waitress was such a scatterbrain.

She went across to the man and he stared at her blankly when she asked what he would like. When he didn't respond, she repeated, 'May I get you something, sir?'

'Oh. Sorry. A pot of tea, please.'

'And something to eat? You look tired and we have some delicious scones.'

Then he looked at her, really looked, and gave her a faint smile. 'You're very kind. You couldn't join me for a few moments, could you, and cheer me up? I'd buy you some tea and scones, too.'

3

'I'm sorry, sir. It's against the rules, and anyway, I have other people to serve.'

But she made detours to pass his table when she didn't need to, smiling at him each time. It upset her to see anyone look that unhappy. He was well dressed, couldn't be more than thirty, if that, so it wasn't likely to be a money worry. Unless he'd lost his job, of course, which could happen to anyone.

When he walked out, he left a sixpenny coin under his saucer for a tip. She appreciated such generosity because her father took all her wages, only letting her keep her tips, and he'd not have done that if he'd realised how much the tips added up to.

She put most of the money in a savings bank and kept her bank book well hidden, leaving a few small coins in a jam jar she left openly in her bedroom and called her tips jar.

Her father had never raided the jar, she had to give him that. Her mother had tried it once, but Kathleen had created such a fuss that her father had backed her up for once and her mother hadn't tried it again.

When she finished work at two o'clock for her afternoon break, Kathleen found the unhappy customer waiting for her outside and stopped in surprise.

'I asked the other waitress what time you finished and she said you had a two-hour afternoon break,' he explained. 'I hope you don't mind me waiting to speak to you.'

'Why do you want to do that?'

'I wondered if I could walk with you, just for a

4

few minutes? I won't pester you if you say no, but you have such a cheerful face. Your smile really lifted my spirits today.'

And she did something she had never done before when other men asked her out walking — she felt so sorry for him she said yes. 'All right. But just round the park.'

'Thank you, miss . . . ?' He looked at her questioningly.

'Kathleen. And you are?'

'Ernest Seaton.'

'I don't usually accept invitations from customers, but you look very unhappy today, Mr Seaton.'

He shrugged.

'Would you like to tell me about it?'

'Not really. I'll just say that I work in my father's business and he . . . isn't easy to deal with.'

'What exactly do you do?'

'My father owns a carting business. I do whatever's needed, work in the office or go out with deliveries. I don't like working in the office, though. He shouts if I so much as lift my nose from the account books or letter copying.'

Then she realised: this must be the son of Jedediah Seaton, her father's new employer. She shouldn't be speaking to him, she should walk away at once. Only . . . Oh dear, he was looking at her even more unhappily.

'You've heard of my father, haven't you?'

'Yes. *My* father has just started working for him as foreman of the yard. He says Mr Seaton's very strict, wants things done just so, but he knows what he's doing.'

And her father was also good at what he did, looking after horses and managing a big stable. He had never been out of work that she could remember. If her mother wasn't such a bad manager, and her father didn't drink heavily, the family would have been comfortably off.

Ernest snapped his fingers. 'Fergus Keller. He's very good with horses and a capable organiser of the stables, too. My father's really pleased with him.'

She stopped walking. 'Da could lose his job if your father saw us together. I'd better leave you. I wish you well, Mr Seaton, and I hope you find something to make you happier.'

But as she turned away, he grabbed her arm.

She stiffened, looking down at it and then at him. 'Let me go!'

He did so at once. 'I'm sorry, Miss Keller. But *please* won't you come for just a short walk? Because chatting to *you* is the first thing that's made me feel happy in a long time.'

She hesitated, remembering how miserable he'd looked when he came into the café. 'Oh . . . Very well. Just for a few minutes. We'd better stay at the top of the park, though. The paths are rougher and not many people go up there. And we'll be out of sight of anyone passing along the street.'

As they continued walking slowly round the top area, she asked, 'Can you not find somewhere else to work?'

'No. Carting is all I know, and anyway, when I suggested it, Father said he would not only cut me off from the family without a penny if I tried to leave, he'd see I didn't get another job in carting.'

'Oh dear. But perhaps he was just threatening it to keep you there.'

'My father never makes idle threats. He always does exactly what he says he will. When my younger brother left home against his wishes, Father cut him off without a penny and forbade Mother and me to have anything to do with him. Alex isn't very strong and working with horses makes him wheeze, but Father kept insisting he'd get over it if he set his mind to it. Only the wheezing got worse. It was so bad some days, Alex couldn't breathe properly. That's why he left.'

'Is he all right?'

'Oh, yes. Alex only wheezes when he's near horses. It turned out he'd been planning to leave for a while and had been saving his money. He's much cleverer than me. He has a stall in the market now and is making a good living, selling quality second-hand household goods. He calls it *Old Treasures*.'

'I've seen it. He has some nice things for sale.'

'Yes. He's clever at finding them. I couldn't run my own business, though. I'm not good with bookwork and accounts like Alex is. That's one of the reasons my father gets so angry at me.'

He shrugged again. 'Let's not talk about that. Tell me about yourself.'

He offered her his arm, but she shook her head and continued on her own.

'There isn't much to tell. I'm the youngest of

7

five. I have two sisters and two brothers. They're all married and I'm the only one left at home. I work as a waitress but I'm going to classes in the evening and learning to type. I did accounts last year. Next year I'll learn shorthand. I'm going to be a secretary one day.'

'Couldn't your father send you to proper secretarial classes so you can get all the studying done in one year? He's on a foreman's wages, after all.'

Which showed Ernest wasn't as stupid as he made out, she thought. 'He refuses to pay for classes and he takes all my wages, except for the tips. He won't let me go to more than one evening class a year, even though I pay for it myself.'

'Can't your mother persuade him to let you do more?'

'My mother never goes against him. She's terrified of upsetting him.'

'My mother does what my father says too. Why is Fergus so against you going to classes?'

'He says women only get married, so educating them apart from the three Rs is a waste of time and money, because employers don't let married women carry on working. But I'm not going to get married and I *am* going to become a secretary, however long it takes me.'

'You're beautiful when your face lights up like that.'

She stopped dead. 'Don't.'

'Don't what?'

'Give me compliments. I'm *not* interested in having a young man or courting.'

He looked so disappointed she added, 'I'll be your friend, if you like, but nothing more.'

He smiled shyly at her, a smile that transformed his rather lumpy face. 'I'd love to be your friend, Miss Keller. I'm not good with people and I don't have any real friends.'

The church clock struck a quarter to three just at that moment and he dragged out his watch from his waistcoat pocket, looking panic-stricken when he opened it. 'I can't believe that's the time already. I'm going to be late back and my father will kill me. May I see you tomorrow?'

'No.'

'Please.'

He looked so upset she relented. 'Same day next week.'

'A whole week away!'

'Yes. I have classes and things to do.' She usually spent her afternoon breaks studying in the public library. At least her father didn't complain when she borrowed books, because that was free, though he laughed at what she chose and said she was only pretending to understand them to show off. She'd seen him reading them sometimes, though. He wasn't a stupid man, just pig-headed about certain things.

'Very well. Next week it is.' Ernest tipped his hat to her and hurried off down the slope to the street.

'I'm a fool,' she muttered. She didn't need more trouble. It was hard enough persuading her father to let her keep going to the evening classes. Of course, her mother agreed with him, she always did, but at least she kept telling her husband it did no harm.

Once Ernest Seaton was completely out of sight, Kathleen walked briskly down the hill and went into the library, forgetting her new acquaintance as she chose another book about running a shop and hid it under a silly novel about a young maidservant who married a prince.

The librarian frowned at the business book. 'Books on this topic are only usually borrowed by men. Are you *sure* you can understand it, miss?'

He made similar comments every week. He was as bad as her father. 'I find them extremely interesting, thank you.'

He shook his head but didn't try to stop her borrowing it.

She smiled as she walked out with it on top of her pile. Actually, she didn't understand some of the words and ideas in the business books, but she would one day. Whatever her father said or did. She enjoyed learning new things.

When she went home, her father wasn't there, of course, but her mother glanced at the top book. 'What rubbish you read, to be sure. You'll forget all that sort of thing when you're married.'

'I don't want to get married.'

'Of course you do. All young girls do. Your brothers and sisters are all married now.'

Well, I'm not going to, thought Kathleen rebelliously. But she didn't waste her breath saying that again.

★ ★ ★

Nathan Perry was born in 1884 to a comfortable life as an accountant's son. By 1901 he had shown that he was going to be tall like his father, which he was pleased about. He had a shock of wavy, light-brown hair, which didn't please him, because it would never stay tidy and that got him into trouble with his father. Even his face was wrong and he often heard people say it looked too old for a child.

When he grumbled about this, his mother always told him he'd grow into his face, but that was no consolation because she couldn't say when that would happen. Every time he looked in the mirror and saw that sharp profile with its scimitar of a nose, he wished desperately that he was more normal-looking.

The strangeness wasn't just on the outside; it was inside his mind too. He found out by chance that he had a gift for finding lost people and objects. If he'd known how angry it'd make his father, he'd have kept quiet about it the first time it happened, but at eight years old who was wise enough to understand that people didn't like those who were too different?

He'd simply blurted out that his father's favourite penknife had fallen out of his pocket in the back garden, and when challenged, led his parents straight to it. As he hadn't been out in the garden all day that earned him a frown.

He followed up this success with several others over the next few months and one day his father took him into his study. 'From now on, son, you're to hide your ability to find things.'

'Shouldn't I help people who've lost something?' Nathan asked in puzzlement.

'No. Better leave them to do that themselves. How else will they learn to be more careful in future?'

Nathan frowned, not understanding the reason for yet another rule that seemed designed to hem him in.

His father harrumphed and said, 'Look, other people don't know where to find lost things. It's . . . unusual and it makes you look strange when you take someone straight to the object they're searching for. Your life will be a lot easier if you fit in and do as others do. Trust me on that.'

As Nathan started to protest, his father held up one hand. 'I have said my last word on this. Kindly do as you are told.'

Whenever his father spoke in that staccato tone, Nathan knew that beating his head against the wall would be easier than trying to change his father's mind. He'd watched his mother sigh and give in to her husband many a time, and had gradually worked out that life would be easier for him if he did the same. So he simply said, 'Very well, Father.'

The voice softened. 'Good lad.' A flap of his father's hand sent him out of the room.

The new orders didn't make sense, so Nathan sought out his mother, who was far better at explaining the complications of daily life.

She sighed when he asked her. 'Oh dear. I was afraid of this.'

'Afraid of what, Mother?'

She bent her head and he waited, realising she

was thinking what to say.

Then she looked up and gestured to the seat beside her on the sofa. 'Close the door and sit down, dear.'

He did as she asked and she took his hand, patting it absent-mindedly, which meant she had something important to say.

'What I'm going to tell you must be kept to yourself, Nathan. You're not to speak about it to anyone, especially not to your father. Promise me.'

'I promise.'

'You got your gift for finding things from my side of the family, more specifically from my maternal grandmother. Occasionally members of her family have a . . . a mental gift, though you can never tell what it'll be until it suddenly, well, appears one day.'

He knew the family's genealogy but he hadn't heard about anyone else with strange talents before. 'Go on.'

She explained about the Latimers and their big country house called Greyladies. 'And . . . ' She hesitated and looked over her shoulder before she continued, even though the door of her small sitting room was closed. 'The house is haunted and the women who inherit it see the ghost of the first Anne Latimer from time to time. They think she still watches over her descendants and the house she loved. Sometimes we — they know things they can't possibly know.'

'You started to say 'we', Mother. Are *you* able to know things in that way?'

She stared down at her lap. 'Sometimes, yes. But I promised your father when we got married that I'd try not to do it any more and that I'd not tell anyone about the Latimers. He thought I was making things up at first, about knowing things, and when he found I wasn't, he grew angry with me. As if I had any choice in the matter! I was *born* like that but I've been able to suppress it, thank goodness.'

He knew why she had said 'Thank goodness'. Because she always did as her husband wished. It seemed a strange way to live to him.

'And now it seems you too have a gift of some sort. You're part Latimer, after all, even if it's only a distant connection. Your gift is for finding things.'

'I can't help it any more than you can.'

'No. I can see that. I feel you need to understand the . . . the situation, which is why I've broken my promise to your father never to speak of it. *Please* don't tell him and please try to stop doing it.'

She looked so uncomfortable he decided not to mention the other things he had experienced, like sensing the presence of a ghost in one house they'd visited or occasionally knowing when something bad was going to happen.

'And you won't try to discuss it with your father, will you?'

'No. What good would that do?'

She sighed. 'No good at all.'

'I'm not going to make a fool of myself or upset Father, but I'm very relieved to know that I'm not alone in being different. What's more, I

14

don't think it's a bad sort of difference, so thank you for telling me about your family, Mother.'

Her gentle smile told him he'd said the right thing. 'If you try hard, I'm sure you can learn to . . . to ignore it.'

Why? he wondered. Why should he deny this ability if it helped people?

One day he'd go and visit this Greyladies place and perhaps speak to someone there about the strangeness in the family.

But he knew how angry it would make his father, so he'd not mention it. And he was quite sure his mother wouldn't talk about it again either.

His mother never spoke of it again but as the years passed Nathan's gifts remained as strong as ever. He didn't want to ignore them. Watching his parents, he decided that if *he* ever got married, it'd be to someone who didn't want him to hide these strange abilities. They were part of him, after all.

It might be best, he decided, not to marry at all. Because his mother wasn't really happy, and his father was always too watchful about what his wife and his son were doing.

Trying to live with someone else seemed to cause so many complications that it wasn't worth it.

What's more, as soon as he was grown up and was earning his living, he'd move away from home. He liked the idea of living quietly on his own, liked it very much.

2

After their first meeting, Kathleen met Ernest in the park several times, at first only once a week, then she relented and agreed to meet him twice a week. He seemed a kind man and she was touched by his air of unhappiness, but she didn't find him at all attractive and didn't want to be more than his friend.

He told her what life was like in his home. Very comfortable physically, it sounded, with two maids and a cook, and everyone with their own bedroom and plenty to eat — but it must have been uncomfortable in mood, because his father sounded to be worse than hers about bossing people around.

The Seatons didn't keep a carriage, but then they rarely went anywhere except to St John's parish church on Sundays, and they walked there, even when it was raining, so that didn't matter.

'My mother insists we all go together. It's very boring,' Ernest said.

'That's Church of England, isn't it? We're Catholics.'

'Oh yes. I suppose you are. I remember, now, my father mentioned it when he hired Keller. He doesn't usually hire Catholics or the Irish, but he said there was no one else at all suitable and your father came highly recommended.' He hesitated. 'Um, I don't know much about Catholics.'

'I wish I wasn't one. The Church is run by the priests and they're always interfering in people's lives. And the nuns teach the girls at school. They wanted me to go to college and become a teacher, but Da wouldn't hear of it. He's — ' She broke off. Best keep her worries to herself.

He looked at her and stopped. 'It's you who sound angry now.'

'Father Michael came round to see my parents last night and I overheard them talking. Well, actually, I eavesdropped. Da was saying I turn twenty-one next week and the priest said they should get me married off before I become an old spinster — or go to the bad. How dare he say that about me?'

'You're not the sort of girl who goes to the bad. Anyone can see that.'

'No, I'm not. But I'm not the sort to get married, either, thank you very much. Once a woman does that, she's a slave to her husband — and to the Church. Our priest only thinks of women as breeders of children and housekeepers.'

He blinked as if she'd shocked him with such frank talk, so she changed the subject, telling him about a book on London she'd borrowed from the library. 'Such lovely photos, it had. I'm going there one day. I want to see the new King and Buckingham Palace and the Tower of London. And the big stores. Not that I'd have any money to spend, but at least I'd be able to look and dream.'

'I've never been to London, either.'

'But your family could afford it any time you wanted.'

He smiled at her. 'My father would throw a fit at the mere idea of wasting time on gallivanting round London, or taking a holiday of any kind, except for Christmas and Easter.'

'He sounds as much a bully as my father.'

Ernest's face became unhappy again. 'More, I should think.'

★ ★ ★

The following Saturday Kathleen turned twenty-one. Her mother wished her happy birthday, the manageress at the café gave her a small iced cake to mark the occasion and that was it.

This birthday was a magic number, she thought bitterly, supposed to make you an adult and independent, but if you didn't have any money, how could you be independent? As far as she could see, women were never able to order their own lives. They didn't have the vote, their wages were lower than men's and their fathers bossed them around till they passed them on to a husband, who did even worse things to them.

When she got home from work on the Saturday afternoon, her mother looked nervous. Her father wasn't back yet and tea was already on the table: ham, with a boiled egg as well for her father, bread and butter, apple pie and custard to follow.

In the evening, her father stayed home and wouldn't let her go round to her friend Jenny's, as she'd planned. 'We've got the priest coming tonight,' he said curtly. 'You'll stay home and listen to what he says.'

The sharp tone of his voice made her heart sink. Had he found out about her afternoon walks with Ernest?

After tea she waited for them to tell her exactly why the priest was coming, but they didn't. She got out one of her library books but her father told her to put that rubbish away and talk to her mother.

After that he ignored them and read his newspaper, but her mother hardly said a word. Her mother never did say much when her father was around.

It was a relief when there was a knock on the door. *Let's get it over with*, Kathleen thought, bracing herself.

Father Michael came in, not smiling this evening as he usually did.

'Will I get you a cup of tea, Father?' her mother asked, voice shaking with nervousness.

'No, Mrs Keller, not today, I thank you. I just had one at the last house. Let's have our little chat, shall we?'

So they all sat in the parlour, which smelt of furniture polish and the new linoleum.

Her father said by way of introduction, 'I've asked the good father to speak to you about your future, Kathleen Frances.'

She said nothing, waiting for the blow to fall. Her father was the only person to use her full name, and today he'd said it sharply as if he was angry with her.

The priest took over. 'You're twenty-one years old now, Kathleen, a young woman in her prime. It's a good age at which to marry, but your

19

parents are worried because you've shown no interest in any of our young men.'

'I don't want to get married, thank you, Father.'

He sucked in his breath. 'How can you say that? It's a young woman's Christian duty to marry and have children.'

'Some of them don't.'

It was her father's turn to breathe deeply.

'Ah, and it's sorry such young women are about not being able to get married. They talk to me about it, you know. Except for those who have a calling, of course, and you've shown no interest in wanting to become a nun.'

'No, I'd not fancy that.'

'I didn't think so. Now, I want you to have a good long think about it and then do your duty, find a young man and raise a family. You'll be the happier for it, I promise you.'

She didn't say anything, but she hadn't changed her mind and she didn't agree with his view of what made a woman happy.

Her father cleared his throat. 'I put the word about at church and I've been spoken to by Desmond Mannion, Father. He'd be interested in courting Kathleen, he says. I've told him I'm agreeable because he's got a decent job.'

She stared at her father in shock. 'But he's a bully and everyone knows all the men in his family beat their wives.'

'Then the wives should behave themselves better, shouldn't they?'

'Well, I wouldn't touch Desmond with a barge pole let alone marry him. He's a horrible man and he doesn't even keep himself clean.'

'It's up to a wife to keep her family clean. Anyway, *you* haven't found yourself a husband so I took it on myself. The Mannions are doing well. Desmond's in steady work on the railways and will be a good provider, and you, young lady, are far too fussy about keeping clean. You cost me a fortune in soap.'

She leant forward and said loudly and clearly, 'I will not even consider courting a man like that.'

'You are living in my house and you will do as I tell you or get out.'

The priest intervened. 'Shhh, now, gently does it, Fergus. Kathleen, my dear, couldn't you just give it a try? Walk out with Desmond and see how you go.'

'No, I won't. I can't stand him.'

Her father clouted her on the side of the head, sending her spinning across the room.

'Fergus Keller, what do you think you're doing hitting our Kathleen like that!' her mother said. 'In front of the father, too. You know I won't have violence.'

It was the one thing her mother would stand up to him for. And he only threatened violence when he was drunk, usually.

'She deserves it, Deirdre. She'd make a saint furious, that one would.' He came across and yanked his daughter to her feet. 'I am the master of this house and I have spoken, Kathleen Frances Keller. You will marry Desmond Mannion.' He shook her like a dog shakes a rat, then flung her away from him.

He rarely got that angry but when he did, you had to be careful what you said and did. She kept silent but promised herself she'd not give in. She'd rather run away than marry a man like that. Far away.

'Let us all pray for the Lord's guidance about this,' the priest said hastily.

Her father thrust her to her knees in front of Father Michael who began a long, rambling prayer. By the time it was over her knees were aching and her cheek was throbbing.

Her father looked to have calmed down a little, or at least the wild light had gone out of his eyes. But he still gave her a grim, determined look, as if challenging her to defy him.

Kathleen hadn't changed her mind, though, and she never would. She could be as stubborn as him about this.

She would run away this very night, she decided.

* * *

To her dismay they locked her in her room when she went to bed and the following morning her father told her she'd be walking to church with Desmond.

He waited by the door for her suitor to arrive.

'Can't you stop Da doing this?' she whispered to her mother. 'It's wrong.'

'I agree with him. You need to be married.'

She threw her mother a reproachful look and touched the bruise on her cheek. 'And do you agree with this, too?'

'No. You know I don't. And he doesn't usually beat people. But you do need bringing into step, Kathleen. You've grown too uppity, working in that fancy tea room. A woman needs a husband. Look at your sisters. Nice little families they've got.'

Families that were getting bigger all the time, she thought. So far, Josie and May had become pregnant with a new baby each year, so their families wouldn't stay little for long. Unless they died in childbirth, as her mother's next sister had.

No. The last thing Kathleen wanted was to get married. And she wouldn't do it. They couldn't make her say the words, after all, even if they dragged her to the church.

A knock at the door revealed Desmond, big jowly face shiny with washing and his weekly clean shirt making the skin on his neck look even redder. He was slightly shorter than she was, because she was tall for a woman, but he was broader and very strong with it. She shivered. She'd not stand a chance of fighting him off.

'Kathleen's a little shy about walking out with you,' her father said. 'So you'll need to hold on to her tightly till she gets used to a man's touch.'

Desmond came across to her, frowning as she turned round to display her bruised face. He looked at her father for an explanation.

'She had a little fall yesterday,' he said.

From the look Desmond threw him, he understood exactly how she'd got the bruise and wasn't pleased by it. He studied her as if assessing her worth before saying, 'Good morning to you, Kathleen Frances.'

She thought it best to mutter, 'Good morning,' back to him.

'We'll be off, then.' Her father scowled at her again. 'I'm hungry. I don't like waiting for my breakfast till after the later Mass. Don't make me have to do it again, miss!'

As they walked out on to the street, Desmond took her arm and didn't let go of it. Worse still, his eyes hardly left her body. It was as if he was assessing what she was like without her clothes on. It made her feel humiliated, even though he hadn't touched her body, except for her arm.

How quickly could she run away, she wondered? And where would she go? She couldn't run away from work because she'd not be able to take her spare clothes with her, but if they kept locking her up at night, she'd not be able to leave.

She didn't say a prayer in church because she was done with a deity whose priest and worshippers treated her like a slave without a mind of her own.

After Mass was over, she was marched home and then her father said, 'We'll see you on Tuesday evening, Desmond lad. You can sit in the front room and chat to her, do a bit of courting.'

'Yes, Mr Keller. I'll look forward to that.'

He sniggered and she guessed he'd be doing more than talking, and what's more, they'd let him maul her around.

'Goodbye, Mrs Keller, Kathleen Frances.'

When he'd gone she rushed for the back

scullery and vomited her sick disgust into the sink.

Her father came and leant against the doorpost. 'Vomit as much as you like, girl. It's your own fault. You should have found yourself another husband if you don't fancy my choice of man. Trouble is, most of the ones your age are taken now.'

'I don't want a husband at all and I won't marry *him*.'

His hands bunched into fists, but he didn't hit her again. The expression on his face said it wouldn't take much to make him lose control, though.

He'd been angry for days, because his wife had lost the housekeeping money and had to ask him for more. He'd had to give her his drinking money, and that meant him staying at home in the evening. Well, serve them both right. It just showed you shouldn't marry someone you didn't even like.

★   ★   ★

On Monday morning Kathleen's father got ready for work and as he was picking up his lunch box, he studied her face. 'You'd better stay home from work today. That's a bad bruise. I didn't mean to hurt you so badly.'

It was as near as he'd ever come to an apology, but he was still intending to marry her to a brute, so she didn't care what he said. She was going to run away. She'd already thought what to say to that. 'I can't stay at home. I'd lose my job and then how would I save for my wedding?'

'Hmm. I'm glad to see you're starting to think straight. You'd better tell that manager you had a fall.'

She inclined her head but couldn't force her mouth to agree with him.

He turned to her mother. 'You'll walk with her to work and escort her home again in the evening from now on.'

Her mother made one of her rare protests. 'But I need to cook tea and — '

'Tea can wait. We need to keep her safe till she's wed. It'll only be for a month or so.'

'Yes, Fergus.'

★ ★ ★

At the tea room the manager gasped in shock at the sight of her face. The other waitresses sniggered but didn't look surprised. One of them had seen her on the way back from church yesterday and must have told the others.

'I had a bad fall on Saturday,' she said but made sure her tone said otherwise.

'Well, we can't let our customers see you like that. And if you come in again with a bruised face, I'll have to replace you with someone more presentable.'

'I've got some face powder,' one of the other waitresses offered as they got ready. 'That'll hide it a bit.'

But it didn't hide much and Kathleen hated the itchy feel of the horrid stuff on her skin.

At first they kept her in the back room,

helping put food on the plates and set out the tea things on trays, but a rush of customers meant she had to go out and serve. That took all her courage.

Ernest came in and she saw the exact moment he caught sight of her face. He took a hasty step forward and she shook her head slightly. He stopped moving towards her, thank goodness.

When she went to serve him, he whispered, 'What happened?'

Only to him did she tell the truth. 'My father thumped me.'

'Your father did this!'

'Yes. It's his way of trying to persuade me to marry a man I detest.'

'*Marry!* Are you going to do it?'

'Not if I can find a way to escape.'

As another waitress passed by he said loudly, 'And a piece of apple pie as well, miss.'

She took the food to him and he caught hold of her arm. 'Will you meet me in our usual place during your afternoon break? Please.'

She nodded and went to get another customer's order.

Neither her father nor her mother seemed to have remembered her afternoon breaks and she prayed it'd stay that way.

3

When she left the tea room, Kathleen walked straight past Ernest, saying in a low voice, 'I'll follow you to make sure no one sees us together.' Then she stopped to look in a shop window and let him overtake her.

He walked briskly along the street and turned into the park. At the top of the hill, he sat on one bench and she chose another one nearby, where she was hidden from the road by some bushes.

For a moment he was silent, then he said, 'What happened?'

So she explained in more detail what her father was doing to her and her plans to run away.

As the minutes ticked by without him commenting, she wondered if this would be the last time she saw him.

Finally, he made a little noise in his throat and said, 'I think you'd be better marrying me than running away. I'd never beat you and I earn a steady living in my father's business.'

She was so shocked she could only gape at him.

He smiled across at her sadly. 'I know you're not in love with me, Kathleen, and you don't want to marry anyone. But you'll be safe with me, at least. I promise you.'

There was another reason she didn't want to be married and it burst out now. 'I'd still be tied to our children, though. The Kellers usually have large families and the women do nothing but have babies and run round after them.'

'The Seatons don't usually have large families and anyway, there are ways to limit families in this modern world. One of the grooms told me about it. I'd want two or three children, but not a dozen.'

She stared at him. 'It's a sin to stop the children coming.'

'Only in your church.'

'Oh. Yes, I suppose so. And if I marry you and join your church, will you promise you'll do that? Keep the number of children down?'

'Yes. I promise.'

And she believed him. He was like a child in a man's body, blurting things out without thinking. But if he was telling the truth, he'd be able to keep her safe. A great weight slid from her shoulders. Something had gone wrong in her mother's body and she'd borne a dead child after Kathleen, then been unable to have any others. So she'd only had five children. But other women from church had ten or more. She didn't want to be trapped like that.

'How can we get married, though? Da won't give permission for me to marry anyone who isn't a Catholic.'

'You're over twenty-one now. You don't need his permission. My father won't want me to marry you, either, so we must do it secretly. I shan't say anything to him till after we've tied the knot.'

He frowned, clearly thinking hard, and she waited patiently.

'Can you get hold of your birth certificate, Kathleen?'

'Yes. Ma keeps all the family's papers in the top drawer of the sideboard in our front room, the rent book and so on.'

'Good. And can you get out of the house after everyone's asleep?'

'I can try. I'd need to get away tonight, though, or I'll spend tomorrow evening fending off Desmond Mannion. He ... um, started bumping into me when we walk together and tries to touch me where he shouldn't.'

Ernest looked across at her sympathetically. 'I've met him. He worked at our yard for a few days but my father sacked him. He boasted about the women he'd had. I didn't like him. What time can you leave the house?'

'My parents are heavy sleepers. They never stir once they're asleep. But my father locked me in my bedroom last night and I should think he'll do the same every night from now on till they marry me off. I'll have to try to climb out of the window. I've read in storybooks about people knotting sheets together to escape.'

Ernest shook his head. 'It'll be easier if I bring a ladder, won't it? Can you get the window open and climb through it or does he lock that as well? And dare you climb down a ladder?'

She returned his smile. 'It wouldn't occur to Da to lock the window. And I wouldn't be at all afraid to climb down. I was a tomboy when I was little and I used to love climbing trees till Ma stopped me playing with the lads.'

'Midnight it is, then.' He stood up. 'I have to get back to work now, but I won't let you down, Kathleen.'

Again she believed him, she didn't know why. He might speak and think slowly, but he seemed honest.

Was she doing the right thing? She didn't know. But it would be better than running away on her own. She'd never even been out of Swindon, so she wouldn't have any idea where to go.

★ | ★ | ★

That night after she was locked in her bedroom, Kathleen put her plan into operation. There were no gaslights up here, only downstairs, and they hadn't given her a candle, but she was able to see clearly enough to pack her clothes by the light from the gas street lamp outside, whose top was just level with the bottom part of her window.

Trying to move silently, she stuffed as many of her spare clothes as she could into her pillowcase, used safety pins to help keep it closed and put it under the bed. Then she put on her best skirt under her working skirt, and two extra blouses, as well as extra underwear. She felt like an overstuffed doll, but she wanted to take as many clothes with her as she could.

Afraid of falling asleep, she sat bolt upright, her back against the wall and listened carefully to what was happening downstairs.

It seemed a long time till she heard her parents come upstairs. Soon their bedhead began bumping against the wall in a regular rhythm. Her father snorted and moaned as he had his way with her mother. He was like an

31

animal, Kathleen thought, doing that nearly every night and not caring who heard him.

She'd asked her mother once if that sort of thing was normal and if it hurt. Her mother had shrugged and said you got used to it because men insisted on it and no, it didn't usually hurt.

Desmond Mannion would treat his wife the same way, Kathleen was sure, and she didn't intend to get used to it, thank you very much. Ugh. The very thought of him doing that to her made her feel sick.

But what would Ernest Seaton be like in bed? Would he keep his word and be gentle with her? Doubts were creeping in now because he was right about one thing: she didn't love him, didn't think she ever could, and didn't really want him to touch her, either.

He was such a pale, plump man with thin stringy hair whose brown colour already looked faded, though he was only twenty-eight. He seemed kind and decent, though, if not very clever. She prayed she wasn't mistaken about that. Kindness made a lot of things more bearable in this life, even small kindnesses from your workmates.

If the two of them could manage to get married without her father stopping them — or Ernest's father — she'd be free and her parents could disown her all they liked.

She knew that their main reason for pushing her into marriage was to get all their children tied to 'good providers' so that when her father was old and unable to work, there would be money to spare to look after them. You'd think they could save enough to look after themselves, because he earned more than most men round here, but her father liked to buy his friends a drink and her mother was a poor manager so the money, including Kathleen's wages, was often frittered away.

There had been no noises from the next bedroom for a long time, so when she heard the church clock chime midnight, she put on her shabby boots and went to look out of the window. Her Sunday shoes were safe in the pillowcase and she'd managed to fit most of her decent clothes in it too because she didn't have all that many.

She sighed in relief as she saw Ernest waiting near the corner. It was a good sign that he had kept his promise and was on time, surely?

As she slid the bottom half of the window open slowly and carefully, he looked up and waved, bringing the ladder closer. She'd greased the pulley cords of the window tonight with a dollop of dripping she'd scooped on to an old rag when she was washing the dishes. To her relief the window didn't squeak at all. Another good sign.

She'd easily got hold of her birth certificate because her mother insisted that she keep her library books in the front room, except for the one she was reading. Her mother was terrified of them getting damaged, for some strange reason, and a fine being applied, even though Kathleen had been borrowing books for years without that happening.

There was a faint clunk and the top of the

ladder appeared against the bedroom windowsill. She took a deep breath and gestured, before throwing her bundle of clothes down to Ernest. He caught it deftly and set it to one side, then held the bottom of the ladder and signalled her to climb out.

She crossed herself automatically before she did this, then got annoyed with herself for doing something religious when she'd vowed to be done with the Church. Taking a deep breath, she eased out on to the ladder. After a couple of rungs, she closed the window.

It was all happening so easily and smoothly she couldn't believe it.

'I was worried you'd change your mind,' he whispered as she reached the ground.

'No. Not at all.'

Ernest took the wooden ladder away from the windowsill, hefted it into a comfortable position and began walking.

She walked beside him, clutching her pillow-case tightly and wondering where they were going.

He took her to the yard at Seaton and Son, unlocking the gate and putting one finger to his lips. He trod lightly when he walked, as some plump men did, and she watched him stow the ladder away neatly. Was he going to hide her here? Surely not when her father worked for Seaton's and was sleeping in the house at the other side of the yard?

But Ernest led the way out into the street again and locked the gate.

'Where are we going?' she whispered, worrying now.

'I'm taking you to stay with our old housekeeper till you and I can marry, but I can't get you there till tomorrow because she lives outside Swindon to the west, in a village called Monks Barton.'

'I've never heard of it.'

'It's a small place, about ten miles from here. That's too far for me to walk because I'd have to come back home afterwards.' He gave her a wry smile. 'I'm not good at walking long distances. Even half that distance would make me too tired to think straight and I'm going to need all my wits about me to get us safely married.'

'So what shall I do tonight?'

'There's a shepherd's hut just outside town that no one uses now. You'll be safe there. It's not too far. I've got a load to deliver near Monks Barton tomorrow afternoon and I'll pick you up as I pass the hut. You should hide on the cart under the tarpaulin till we get there, if you don't mind. It'll be better if no one sees you till after we're married.'

When she didn't answer straight away, he asked, 'Will that be all right?'

'Yes, of course. Only . . . what does your housekeeper think of this? Does she know I'm coming?'

'No, she doesn't but she'll make you welcome for my sake. I can always rely on Rhoda to help me. She's the only person who's ever really cared about me.'

'What about your brother?'

'Alex? I've only spoken to him once or twice since he moved away from home. My father would throw a fit if he saw us together.'

'You seem very sure of this housekeeper.'

A smile lit his face briefly, making it suddenly seem less dull. 'I am sure of her. You see, my mother left me in Rhoda's care most of the time when I was younger, because Mother doesn't like children and I was rather sickly. So Rhoda's my real mother, as far as I'm concerned.'

Ernest took the pillowcase from her and they walked in silence for a while. He looked happy, much happier than she felt about this whole thing. All she knew was that marrying this man was her best, and perhaps her only, chance of staying out of Desmond Mannion's clutches without having to tramp the roads and end up who knew where. So she was going to seize it with both hands.

She hoped she and Ernest would manage to build a decent life. His family were well off so there ought not to be any money problems. But what if his father disowned him as he had Ernest's brother? How would they live then? She'd not think of that; they would face the problem if they met it.

Perhaps she could repay what Ernest was doing for her by helping him get away from his father one day. She certainly didn't want to live in the same town as her own family.

If the two of them saved hard they might buy a little shop or a lodging house somewhere far away from Swindon. At the seaside, perhaps. She'd be good at helping Ernest run a business, she was sure. She was clever with money. She'd had to be because she'd had to make a farthing do the work of a penny all her life.

She stumbled and nearly fell. Ach, this was no time to be dreaming! She had to stay alert.

As they left the built-up areas behind without meeting anyone, she began to feel more hopeful that they really would succeed in getting away. She looked round with increasing interest because she'd not been far out of town in this direction before and the moonlight was bright enough to let her see the countryside they were walking through.

Her weekend strolls with the girls from church were quite short and they did more talking than walking. Their main topics were clothes and finding husbands. The group of young women had got smaller every year as one by one they got married.

She'd only gone out with them to get out of the house and didn't have much in common with them. She'd rather have stayed at home and read a book but her father wouldn't have let her waste her time on that sort of thing. She could only read when he was out at the pub or when she bought a candle and sneaked it up to her bedroom.

After about a mile, Ernest stopped next to a gate leading into a small field and pointed to a rough wooden hut in the far corner. He was panting slightly, which surprised her because they hadn't been walking fast.

'There's the shepherd's hut. No one uses it now, so you can wait for me there quite safely. I've eaten my midday sandwiches in it a few times when it was raining, so I know the roof is still sound, and there's a little stream nearby with clean water, so you won't go thirsty.'

He opened the gate and led the way across the field to the corner. 'No one will see you if you stay inside the hut. If you need a drink you should make sure no one's around before you go to the stream. And I bought you this in case you got hungry.'

He took out from inside his jacket what looked like a packet of buns. They were a bit squashed, but she'd be glad of them later, she was sure.

'You've hardly spoken, Kathleen. You're not . . . having second thoughts, are you?'

'No, no. But I don't know whether I'm on my head or my heels, it's all happened so quickly. I'm deeply grateful to you for helping me, Ernest, and I promise I'll do my best to be a good wife to you.'

'I'll do my best to be a good husband, too.' He indicated the yellowing bruise on her cheek. 'And I'll never hit you, I swear. Never.'

He showed her the stream then said he had to leave in order to get home before anyone was stirring. 'I don't know what time I'll get here. Just before noon, I hope, but sometimes the delivery schedules change, so don't worry if I'm later than that. I won't let you down.'

'I know.' She set her bundle down in the hut, which had a small bench across the back, just long enough for her to lie on. Suddenly she felt very tired indeed.

'Goodbye, Kathleen.'

When she turned round Ernest was already crossing the field, and as she watched, he closed the gate and walked away.

She was left alone with her tangled thoughts.

In the end she lay down, using her bundle of clothes as a pillow, and told herself to go to sleep, because she was utterly exhausted. She was glad of the extra clothing now because it kept her warm. She hoped she could make a good impression on this housekeeper Ernest thought so highly of; she hoped she was doing the right thing. Life could be so hard for women on their own if they didn't have families, so she hadn't really wanted to run away by herself. Only desperation would have made her do that.

The trouble was, if this Rhoda cared about Ernest so much, she might not like him marrying a girl from an Irish Catholic family. Kathleen had seen the signs outside lodging houses and places offering jobs: 'No Irish Need Apply' or 'No Catholics'. She could never understand why they spurned people like her.

Worrying about the future kept her awake for a while, as did the night noises, but in the end she could feel herself getting sleepier and gave in to the urge to close her eyes.

★　★　★

In the morning Deirdre Keller unlocked her daughter's bedroom door and was so shocked to find no one there, she screamed for her husband.

Fergus came running in half-dressed and cursed violently, shoving his wife out of the way to look under the bed as she had already done. 'I locked that door myself. Was it still locked?

39

You're sure? Well, then, how the hell can she have got out? There's only one key.'

On that thought he went to the window and found the catch unlocked. 'She must have got out this way, damn her.'

'How could she get down without hurting herself?'

'Someone must have helped her, brought a ladder.' He thumped the wall with his fist, then cursed because he'd hurt himself. 'She's got a fellow, that's what, and it'll be someone we wouldn't approve of. I told you to get her married off as soon as she turned eighteen.'

She might have known he'd find a way to blame her, Deirdre thought resentfully. 'But how could she have met someone? She's either been at work or at home in the daytime and we don't let her out on her own in the evenings.'

'She has those breaks in the afternoons, doesn't come home then, does she? You should have gone and kept her company.'

'I didn't have time, Fergus. The housework doesn't do itself. Anyway, Kathleen goes to the library most days, so I thought she'd be all right there. I've *seen* the books she borrows.'

'Those sodding books have addled her brain. I should have stopped her borrowing them.'

Deirdre checked the drawers. 'She's taken all her clothes with her. She mustn't intend to come back.'

'I'll get her back, just you see, if only to show her who's master here.' He kicked the bottom drawer shut and pushed his wife aside, clumping down the stairs. 'Make yourself useful and put the bloody kettle on, woman.'

She hurried to do his bidding.

'I'll make her sorry she crossed me,' he said several times as he gobbled down his breakfast and drank three cups of hot, sweet tea. 'Very sorry. You'll see.'

Deirdre had an idea, but waited till her husband had left for work before she checked it. And yes, Kathleen's birth certificate was missing from the drawer. Her daughter must be intending to get married, thank the Lord.

She'd not tell Fergus about that but leave him to find out for himself, or else he'd blame her.

Sitting down at the table, she started weeping. She'd never see her youngest daughter again, she knew it.

Then she changed her mind and hoped she wouldn't see Kathleen, because Fergus would half-kill the poor girl if he caught her. He hated to be crossed, especially in his own home. And lately he'd been drinking more and getting angry more easily.

It wasn't good to drink so much, but there was no way *she* could stop him.

4

When Kathleen woke the sun was high in the sky and she guessed it was around noon. She ate the squashed, messy buns and scooped up some water in her hand. After using her hairbrush she fastened her long hair back in a bun and tidied her clothes as best she could. Then she sat down again, wondering how to pass the time because she'd left her library books behind.

The minutes seemed to pass slowly and she listened to the birds and insects busy around her, wishing she were busy too. She didn't enjoy being idle.

The road carried very little traffic and only three vehicles passed. Each time she heard one coming she jumped to her feet, hoping it was Ernest. There were chinks in the thin planks that formed the walls of the hut and she could see through them without being seen.

But none of them was him.

She couldn't help worrying. It seemed to be later than he'd expected to get there. What if he didn't come? What if he'd changed his mind about marrying her?

It began raining, a damp, chilly drizzle that made her shiver. She wished she could have brought her coat, but her family kept their coats on hooks in the hall and her mother would have noticed if hers had been missing.

Huddling down in a corner she waited . . .

and waited . . . trying to believe Ernest had meant what he said and wouldn't let her down. She didn't know him well enough to be sure of him yet.

★ ★ ★

Eventually, she heard the sound of horses' hooves and the rattling of a large cart and let out a groan of sheer relief when she saw Ernest perched up high on the driver's bench. The man beside him was driving and she wondered what was happening, why Ernest wasn't in charge of the vehicle.

She heard him say clearly, 'Stop here.'

The cart came to a halt. He jumped down and hurried into the field, running across to the entrance of the hut, heedless of the rain. 'Are you all right, Kathleen?'

'Yes, of course. Just a bit cold because I couldn't bring my coat. Who's that man? I didn't think you'd be bringing anyone with you.'

'No. Nor did I. But it's a heavier load so they wanted two men on it. I've told Wally I'm doing a favour for Mrs Newman, taking a niece of hers across to stay with her. So it'd be best if you talk about your Auntie Rhoda.'

'But now someone will know where I've gone.'

Ernest nodded unhappily. 'But if I call you Mary, Wally won't know your name. Maybe I should slip him some money to keep quiet.'

'No. He's bound to mention it sooner or later if you do. How about . . . ' She thought hard for a moment, then had an idea that might work better. 'We could say I'm escaping from an employer who tried to molest me, and if he finds out where I am, he'll kill me? That'll explain the bruise and why I need to hide under the tarpaulin.'

Ernest's heavy face lit up. 'Good idea! I'll go back and tell Wally, then when I signal, you come across to join us.'

She made sure the other man saw her badly bruised face and when he looked at her pityingly, she dabbed at her eyes.

'Don't worry. I'll not say anything about where you're going, miss,' he called to her as Ernest helped her up on to the back of the cart and covered her carefully with the tarpaulin.

As they set off, she heard him say to Ernest, 'Men who beat women should be took out and hung. If anyone touched my sister, I'd beat them twice as hard. I would indeed.'

'You're right, Wally. But her auntie will look after her.'

'Aye. You need your family when you're in trouble.'

Kathleen had found a space between two boxes where she could sit and not be jerked about too much, but she was still cold.

Ernest hadn't had any idea what to say about her. He didn't seem to be very clever.

He'd said his father shouted at him a lot. Perhaps that was why. She'd have to be careful how she treated him — she must never call him stupid like his father did. Poor Ernest. He seemed so unhappy.

He definitely wasn't the sort of man she'd have chosen to marry.

The cart slowed down as it passed a sign saying Monks Barton. Kathleen peeped out from under the canvas as they stopped in front of a neat cottage in a street of similar dwellings. Everything she could see looked tidy, not just the houses and front gardens but the small church, the inn, the village green and even the duck pond in the centre.

The village seemed welcoming, if that wasn't being too fanciful. Then she remembered why she'd come and sighed. What had got into her father lately? He'd never hit her like that before. He hardly ever spoke to his wife in the evenings if he didn't go out, just sat reading the newspaper from cover to cover.

She looked out of the other side of the canvas cover and saw Ernest slip a coin to his driver, heard him suggest Wally buy himself a drink at the Merry Ploughman and come back in an hour. This suggestion was greeted by a beaming smile.

Then Ernest came round to help her down and escort her to the front door. Kathleen thought it best to stand a little to one side, leaving him to do the talking.

The door was opened by a tiny woman, slender and white-haired, with twinkling blue eyes, who flung her arms round Ernest and stood on tiptoe to give him a smacking kiss on each cheek. 'Why didn't you send word you would be passing through? I'd have made you a cake and — Oh!' She noticed Kathleen and looked at him questioningly.

'This is my friend Kathleen Keller and I wonder if I could ask your help for her?'

'Of course, dear. Any friend of yours is welcome here.'

As Kathleen stepped forward, Mrs Newman saw the bruise and gasped.

Inside the house Ernest tried to explain why they'd come and got tangled up within a few sentences, so Kathleen put her hand on his arm and took over, describing her predicament and what Ernest wanted to do.

'*You two are going to get married?* Does your father know about this, Ernest?'

'No. And he mustn't until it's done.' He put an arm round Kathleen and spoke more firmly, 'I couldn't bear it if he stopped us.'

'Well, I never!' But she had been studying Kathleen as they spoke and must have liked what she saw, because she said quietly, 'I'll help you in any way I can, dear boy. And your friend. You know that.'

Kathleen felt him sag against her in relief.

'You did right to come to me. Your young lady can stay here till you're wed and I'll keep her safe. The world can be cruel to young women. I've seen it time and again and it always pleases me to be able to help someone.'

Kathleen surprised herself by bursting into tears and Mrs Newman put an arm round her shoulders and gave her a firm hug, even though she was a much smaller woman. She couldn't remember the last time anyone had hugged her and that made her sob even harder.

By the time Ernest left, it had been decided

that he wouldn't visit them until Friday when he'd come for the evening meal, which he often did, so his father wouldn't wonder at it. Mrs Newman would make arrangements for them to speak to the curate afterwards.

'We don't often see the vicar here, just the curate, who lives next to the church,' she explained. 'It's rather a small congregation, even with the families from nearby farms. But the curate is a really kind man and I'm sure he won't object to marrying you two.'

'I don't think Kathleen should be seen until we're married,' Ernest said again.

'She can't stay in the house all the time, or it'd cause comment. And she'll have to attend church on Sundays because they'll be calling the banns.' Mrs Newman clicked her fingers as inspiration struck. 'I know. We can pretend she's just lost her mother, which will explain why she's had to come to me for help. It was a good idea to pretend I'm her auntie, Ernest dear. Well done. My friends know I have one or two nieces who live in other parts of the country.'

His pleasure at this praise shone from him.

Mrs Newman wrinkled her brow in thought. 'What's your real mother's name, Kathleen? It'll be on your birth certificate, so I'll need to know.'

'Deirdre.'

She repeated it. 'Right. We'll say she was my half-sister. You can wear black and a hat with a veil to church, so your face won't be very clear to anyone.'

'I'm sorry, but I don't have any black clothes, Mrs Newman.'

47

Her kind hostess smiled. 'I can help there. I look after the charity box at church and some of the better-off families round here are very generous with their cast-off clothes. I don't know what the villagers with big families would do without their help.'

She took a step backwards and studied her guest. 'You're quite tall, aren't you? But nice and slim. We can alter something for you, if necessary.' She turned back to Ernest. 'Now, dear, I'll tell the curate you've loved my niece for a while, but she had to look after her poor sick mother so you couldn't get married. Now that she's alone and penniless, you want to get married straight away to look after her. Have you got that?'

He repeated the basic facts and she nodded. 'Well done, dear. Is that story all right with you, Kathleen?'

She didn't like the idea of building a new life on lies, but what choice did she have? 'I'll do whatever you think best, Mrs Newman.'

'Remember to call me Auntie Rhoda from now on.'

The little clock on the mantelpiece struck the hour and Ernest sighed. 'I can't stay much longer. You'll keep Kathleen safe for me, won't you, Rhoda?'

She kissed his cheek. 'Of course I will.'

Because he was looking at her hopefully, Kathleen kissed his other cheek and he gave her a quick, shy hug. After he'd left, she looked at her hostess a little nervously.

Rhoda smiled at her. 'I haven't seen my lad

looking so happy for a long time. That father of his has a lot to answer for, always shouting at him, and it sounds as if your father is as bad with you. Now, let me show you to a bedroom and you can unpack your things, then we'll have a nice boiled egg for tea and some of my gingerbread to follow.'

She patted Kathleen's arm. 'Things will work out, you'll see. I hope you'll make my Ernest happy. He isn't hard to please and is always grateful for kind words.'

She turned round at the door to add, 'You seem like a bright young woman and you must realise he's not very clever. But he's a dear, kind boy, always has been, and he'd do a lot better if his father treated him lovingly instead of criticising him all the time.'

She frowned and said, 'Ernest sometimes drinks too much when he's unhappy, but I don't think he'll do that after he's married to you. I saw the way he looked at you and I saw you help him out when he got confused.'

'I'll do my best to make him happy — and to help him whenever he needs it.'

Rhoda gave her another long, searching look, then nodded. 'That's all I ask. Just do your best and be kind to him. There's many a married couple managed, for all their differences. It just takes a bit of kindness.'

★ ★ ★

Ernest came to tea on Friday, enjoying the fussing and attention from the two women, and

49

exclaiming in pleasure at his favourite cake for afters.

It took so little to please the poor man, Kathleen thought.

When the meal was cleared away, they all went along the road to see the curate, a scrawny young man with thick spectacles.

'You didn't tell me your sister had died, Mrs Newman,' Mr Pether said reproachfully.

'Not my sister, my half-sister. Deirdre was much younger than me and we weren't close. I didn't find out she was dead in time to go to the funeral.'

'It was a very simple affair,' Kathleen said quickly. 'I didn't have the money for anything fancy.'

After a quick glance at her birth certificate, he handed it back to her. 'I'll call the first banns on Sunday. You must both be in church for that.'

Ernest nodded and squeezed her hand, looking blissfully happy.

'And when you've called the banns for the third time, perhaps you could marry them straight after the service, Mr Pether?' Mrs Newman suggested. 'Just a simple ceremony because of Kathleen's bereavement.'

'Of course. Of course. I enjoy marrying people, I must confess. So much hope goes into a marriage, well, into most of them, anyway.'

That made Kathleen feel sad. It would be a relief to be out of her father's hands, but she wasn't sure how it would be to be married to Ernest Seaton. She'd tried out her future name in her bedroom, whispering, 'Mrs Seaton. Mrs

50

Ernest Seaton.' But it had sounded strange.

Not until they were back at 'Auntie' Rhoda's house did she realise something. 'Mr Pether didn't ask me if I was Church of England.'

'I noticed. Let's not mention that. I can lend you my prayer book and teach you what you need to know so that you don't show yourself up in church on Sunday. We worship the same god, after all. I'm sure *he* won't mind which church you say your prayers in.

'And bless him, Mr Pether always has his head in a book, so he won't think to ask any probing questions. He's a gentle soul, but not very practical. People round here keep an eye on him and try to see he isn't cheated.'

5

When Ernest had taken his leave that first Sunday, Kathleen sat lost in thought, still wondering if she was doing the right thing.

'If you don't want to get married, speak out now or forever hold your peace,' Auntie Rhoda said suddenly. 'My lad is already building his hopes on you.'

'It's all happened so quickly,' Kathleen explained. 'I don't want to back out now, I wouldn't do such a thing to him. I just wish we didn't have to be so secretive.'

'Well, *I* think you'll make poor Ernest a lot happier than he has been lately and he won't make you *unhappy*. He hasn't been happy for most of his life, poor lad, and I'm sure he won't start drinking again, not if he's married to you.'

Kathleen didn't like the sound of a husband who drank too much. Her father had been drinking too much lately and always got loud and bossy after a few pints of beer. 'How can you be sure of that?'

'I'm over sixty years old, child. I think I've learnt a thing or two about people in those years. And I know my Ernest better than anyone else does. Now, let's go through your clothes and see what you need. I have some clothes in the poor box which we can alter for you. You'll need a winter coat, for a start.'

'If they need altering, it'll be a problem. I'm

not very good at sewing, I'm afraid.'

'Then I'll teach you to sew while we're at it. That'll pass the time very pleasantly, you see if it doesn't. And it saves so much money to make and mend your own clothes.'

She produced a skirt from the charity box which was far nicer than anything Kathleen had ever owned before and it had a lovely jacket to match. They were both in a khaki colour.

'Why would someone give such a good outfit away?' Kathleen asked in surprise.

Auntie Rhoda sighed. 'Dear Mrs Carringham-Griggs at the manor house gave me this. She bought it during the war in South Africa when the colour became very fashionable, but khaki didn't suit her and then she had a baby and grew plumper, so it no longer fitted, either. I've been saving it for someone special, because it's too good for everyday wear. Try it on.'

The skirt fitted perfectly, but was too short.

Auntie Rhoda picked up the hem. 'Aha! Lucky for you it has a good deep hem. If we let it right down and buy some braid to cover the mark on what used to be the bottom edge, it'll be perfect for you.'

The jacket was tailored with wide lapels in contrasting dark brown velvet. It came down over the skirt to about twelve inches below her waist. Kathleen stared at herself in the mirror. 'It's the most beautiful thing I've ever owned. My family didn't have much spare money for clothes, you see, and my mother can't sew.'

'Well, the jacket could have been made for you. And I've found another skirt and a couple of blouses from the same lady. Oh, we'll have you looking really elegant for your wedding, my dear.'

Auntie Rhoda had the skirt hem unpicked before teatime and took the opportunity to demonstrate to her guest how to sew a seam with small, even stitches. She set Kathleen to practising on a piece of fine cotton, which would make a good handkerchief when hemmed.

'I'm making a lot of work for you,' Kathleen said guiltily.

'I shall enjoy having you here, dear. As for extra work, I never like to sit idle.'

'I don't, either. I used to borrow books from the library and I was going to classes to become a secretary one day. I could only read when Da went out for a beer because he didn't like to see anyone wasting their time on books.'

That earned her a sharp glance from those bright blue eyes and Auntie Rhoda made a tsk-tsking sound. 'Well, I have plenty of books and I would never stop someone reading once their day's work is done.' She gestured towards a bookcase crammed with books of all colours and sizes. 'You're welcome to borrow any of them, my dear.'

'Really?' Kathleen fell to her knees in front of the bookcase, reading the titles and wondering which to choose first.

Only as they were putting their sewing away ready for a quiet hour with a book did Auntie Rhoda say suddenly, 'I wonder what Mr Seaton will say when he finds out. I should warn you that he won't be best pleased.'

'Ernest said that. What is his father like?'

'A bossy, grumpy man. He was a hard master, but I did my work well and didn't have much trouble with him. Then I inherited this cottage and a nice little nest egg from a spinster cousin, so I was able to leave his employ and make a happier life for myself. I wish Ernest could do the same. That boy will never make a good businessman, not if he tries for a hundred years, he won't. Though he's good with horses and other animals.'

A few moments later she sighed and added, 'I think we'll be able to keep your wedding secret for a while, but eventually Mr Seaton will find out. Little escapes him and poor Ernest is bound to give something away. Then we'll have to tread very carefully, because believe me, there will be a big fuss made.'

After some more thought, she added, 'It would be best if you could be expecting a child by then. Being disappointed in his sons, Mr Seaton is looking for grandchildren, but so far Ernest has managed to annoy the young women his father thought suitable. Fortunately he's so shy in company, he hardly says a word, so they don't take to him if they can find someone else.'

She gave a sudden grin and for a moment Kathleen could see what she'd been like as a child when about to get into mischief.

'I told Ernest what to say to upset the young ladies — when his father wasn't in the room, of course. Well, we servants knew the families of Mr and Mrs Seaton's friends, and they'd made enough money to spoil their daughters, turn them into lazy flibbertigibbets. None of those young ladies would have made him happy and they'd have scorned him, too.'

Which gave Kathleen even more to think about when she went to bed in the cosy little room under the eaves.

But she still came to the same conclusion: she'd had no other real choice if she wanted to get away from her father and Desmond Mannion. Heroines in books could do all sorts of daring things and it'd turn out well, but this was real life.

So she must just make the most of her marriage to Ernest.

★ ★ ★

The wedding day was the first Sunday in November and it dawned cool, with a morning mist over the fields. Kathleen felt nervous as she got ready, but Auntie Rhoda — how natural it seemed to address the old lady that way now — noticed and soon made her feel calmer.

The clothes helped, too. The new skirt and jacket had carried her through the Sundays and now gave her heart for the wedding. She was wearing a neat little felt hat that had been a bit battered when donated to the church box. But by the time Auntie Rhoda had steamed and reshaped it, and added new trimmings of silk flowers and a feather, it looked very smart.

Ernest was so late they began to worry, and he barely got to the village in time for church. When he came into view, they both sighed in relief.

They watched him leave the horse and trap at the inn and come rushing across the green and along the short street to the cottage.

'My father wanted me to attend church with him today,' he said breathlessly. 'He keeps asking me why I'm spending so much time here.'

'Oh dear, that means he's starting to get suspicious. He hates to let you out of his control. We'll talk about it later and decide what to do. In the meantime, let's go and worship our Maker, then get you two married. We'll walk to church in style, one on each of your arms, Ernest dear.'

To Kathleen's surprise a few people lingered after the service to watch the wedding, as well as one of Auntie Rhoda's friends, who had agreed to stand with her as the second witness.

The marriage ceremony went smoothly, except for Ernest stammering as he made his responses and having to be prompted. Then suddenly the curate was saying, 'I now pronounce you man and wife. You may kiss your bride, Mr Seaton.'

Which Ernest did with new confidence.

But Kathleen didn't enjoy his mouth on hers any more than she had on the few occasions he'd kissed her goodbye.

What would tonight bring? She'd been dreading it all week, remembering the grunting and groaning, and the banging bedhead at her parents' home.

Auntie Rhoda had provided a wedding cake and a glass of her primrose wine for each of the neighbours invited to her cottage afterwards to drink to the health of the bride and groom. But she didn't encourage them to linger and sent

Ernest and Kathleen out for a nice brisk walk once the guests had gone.

'Don't waste the sunshine. We won't get many more fine days like this.'

Ernest didn't say much but he smiled a lot and held Kathleen's hand as they walked. He seemed to know the area well and took her to see some of the local landmarks, including a view of a hillside with a big white horse carved into it.

Anything to do with horses pleased him, so she got him talking about them. He seemed to enjoy himself and she knew enough from what her father talked about to ask the right questions and keep the conversation going.

It was a relief to get back to Auntie Rhoda's house again. She didn't mind talking about horses but there were other things in life.

Then, as they cleared their tea things away, Auntie Rhoda said abruptly, 'I'm staying with my friend Jeanie tonight. Did you tell your father you were staying with me, Ernest, as I suggested?'

'Yes, but he said he wanted me back under his roof by nine o'clock sharp.'

'Oh, dear. What did you say to that?'

'I said I'd try to get back. But I told the innkeeper to look after the horse and cart tonight as you said I should. I could go back quite late, though.'

She stood thinking, then shook her head. 'No. You must stay with your wife tonight and you must love her as a husband should. Remember what I told you. It's very important indeed, Ernest.'

'Father will be angry if I stay.'

'He's often angry. But you don't want to give him a chance to say you're not properly married, do you? He might try to take Kathleen from you.'

He grabbed her hand. 'I won't let him.'

But his bride could feel his hand trembling in hers.

When Auntie Rhoda had left, Kathleen decided to get the consummation of their marriage over and done with. 'Let's go to bed early, Ernest. You haven't seen my bedroom. It's very cosy and you'll like sleeping there, I'm sure.'

When he'd admired the room, she suggested they get undressed with their backs to one another, for modesty, and he nodded.

'I haven't done it before,' he blurted out as they stared at one another across the bed, clad now in a nightshirt and flannel nightdress respectively. 'Alex is younger than me and he's done it, but I haven't.'

After a pause, he added, 'I used to pretend I had because my father always said I'd never manage to pleasure a woman. So I listened to what the other men said about women and said the same sort of thing.'

'Good heavens!' This was the last thing she'd expected to hear. 'And did he believe you?'

'Yes. Because I went drinking as well and I get drunk very easily so he saw me when I staggered home. It seemed to please him that I was 'behaving like a man at last'. It made life easier.'

'Oh. I see.'

Ernest was looking ready to panic, and she

realised she'd have to take charge of what they were doing. That made her feel more like a mother than a wife, but at least she wasn't afraid of him hurting her. She doubted anyone could be afraid of such a timid man.

'It doesn't matter to me what you pretended to your father, but please promise me you won't lie to me.'

He nodded several times. 'I promise. Yes, I do.'

'Now, I haven't done it before either, Ernest dear, so we'll have to find our way together. If we do it carefully and don't hurt one another, I'm sure things will be all right.' She blew out the candle, took a deep breath and got into the bed.

'I think I know what to do,' he said into the darkness. 'One of the drivers told me all sorts of things — and I've watched animals do it. They seem to like it a lot.'

Dear heaven! she thought. What had she got herself into? Thank goodness Auntie Rhoda had explained to her in detail exactly what had to happen.

It took a lot of coaxing and gentle persuasion to get Ernest to the point of the marriage act, so she was surprised that he'd convinced his father he was playing the man. But in the end they managed to consummate their marriage. And if she didn't enjoy it particularly, at least it didn't hurt, and he seemed to enjoy their brief encounter.

It felt very strange, though, to have someone invade her body, and equally strange to lie next to Ernest afterwards.

He fell asleep almost at once but she lay

60

staring at the last flickers of the little fire Auntie Rhoda had lit in the bedroom. It took her a while to realise that tears were trickling down her cheeks. She might be Ernest's wife now, in every way, but this wasn't what any normal young woman expected from her marriage.

She tried to console herself with the thought that this husband wouldn't try to boss her around, but she'd have liked to spend her life with someone she could talk to properly, someone who wasn't afraid of so many things. Poor Ernest was more like a child who responded to any small word of encouragement or kindness. It was as if he was starved of praise.

She prayed her father wouldn't find out where she was or what she'd done for a very long time. Let them settle down together first.

But what would Ernest's father do when he found out? Auntie Rhoda seemed very sure he would find out quite quickly. Would he come after them and separate them by force? Could he do that?

Would it really make a big difference to Mr Seaton if she was expecting a child? Women in her family seemed to get pregnant quite easily. She probably would too.

Well, if she did have a child, it would be loved and properly fed and educated. She wasn't going to bring one up in fear and ignorance, as her mother had done with them. If Kathleen hadn't had teachers who took an interest in her and praised her intelligence, she didn't know what would have become of her.

Ernest had promised not to give her a lot of

children but, oh dear, they needed to make this first one as quickly as possible.

★ ★ ★

It was decided that Ernest would come to visit his wife in Monks Barton every Friday or Saturday from now on, taking a pony and trap from his father's stables and staying overnight at the cottage. He already had an arrangement with the local pub for them to look after the pony and trap when he came to visit Rhoda, so the practicalities worked out very nicely.

Rhoda spread the word among her friends in the village that Mr Ernest didn't want it known to his family that he was married because his father wouldn't approve, so people kept quiet about it. They were kind people, she assured Kathleen, who could mind their own business and keep a secret better than most.

Every Sunday after Ernest left she said, 'Well, there's another week gone without Mr Seaton trying to interfere.'

And every Sunday Kathleen felt nothing but relief that her tedious ordeal in bed was over.

She loved living with Auntie Rhoda and helping her in the house, though. The two of them got on so well together, almost as if they were mother and daughter. Kathleen was learning to do housework properly and after her own mother's slapdash ways, it was a revelation to her how other people lived. Everything in the cottage was clean, not just the house but the people and all their clothes. She loved the way the parlour smelt of potpourri and furniture polish.

The first weekend Ernest gave her the two pounds that his father paid him as wages.

'I can't take all your money,' she protested.

He thought about this. 'I shall need some for buying a pot of tea sometimes when I'm out and about, but you can keep the rest. I want you to live comfortably.'

'We'll ask Auntie Rhoda how much would be right, shall we?'

'Yes. She'll know.'

In the end, they arranged for him to keep ten shillings for his own spending money and as Auntie Rhoda would accept only ten shillings a week for their food, Kathleen was able to save the rest and add it to what she'd already got in her savings account. What a marvel it seemed to have money mounting up so quickly!

After much consideration, she bought some navy blue woollen material from the shop in the next village, which was much bigger than Monks Barton, to make a new winter outfit. Auntie Rhoda came with her and wouldn't let her buy the cheapest material, insisting that good quality paid for itself in the long run because it lasted.

Kathleen made it up into a skirt under her kind hostess's guidance, learning to cut out and tack the pieces together, then, when the skirt fitted properly, use Rhoda's little sewing machine. She treadled away on it happily, feeling as if she had unlimited energy.

The jacket was of a simple design but was much more difficult. In the end she got it right, though, with the older woman's help. She was determined to learn to sew.

Apart from buying clothes, of which she was desperately short, she refused to waste even a penny and her frugality pleased her kind hostess, she could see.

Auntie Rhoda made her a present of a new blouse, ordered ready-made from the shop. It had a lace collar and cuffs. 'A young wife should look her best for her husband. You can keep this for best and I'll teach you to wash it very carefully so as not to damage the lace.'

'It's beautiful. Thank you so much.' Kathleen dared to hug Auntie Rhoda.

'You deserve a few pretty things,' the older woman said. 'You're only young once.'

Kathleen sneaked into her bedroom to stroke the soft creamy lace several times that first day. She'd never owned anything with lace on it before.

★ ★ ★

When Ernest made his second visit after their marriage, he seemed relieved to hand over most of his wages to her. 'Could I bring the rest next time as well?'

'The rest? What do you mean?'

'I've got some other money in my room at home. It gets heavy if you leave it in your pockets and if my father knew I had some left, he'd say he was paying me too much.'

Ernest turned up next time with several old envelopes in his little suitcase, some containing coins, some banknotes.

Kathleen stared at them in shock, then saw him looking at her apprehensively, so quickly praised him for being careful with his money.

She emptied everything on the table and made a game of counting it, but when she asked him to check it, she was shocked at how poor he was at working out the total amount.

'I don't like doing sums,' he confessed, seeing her surprise. 'My father gets angry with me but when I look at them, the numbers jiggle about in front of my eyes and I get confused.'

'It sounds as if you need spectacles.'

'My teacher said that once but Father got angry with her, said no son of his was walking around looking like a damned owl.'

Ernest looked so anxious, she let the matter drop and went back to counting. The more she heard about his father, the less she liked the sound of him. They both had uncaring fathers, it seemed.

When she'd finished counting, she stared down at the piles of crumpled notes and coins in astonishment. They came to over a hundred pounds. Heart pounding, she counted them all over again, to be sure. She'd never had so much money in her whole life and felt rich.

'That's wonderful, Ernest! How clever of you to save all that money.' She tried to give him a quick hug but he clung to her tightly for a minute or two, so she stroked his hair gently and he made happy little murmuring noises. He didn't often attempt to touch her in what she thought of as *that other way* and left her to initiate the bed play. Mostly he just wanted to cuddle.

'What shall I do with all this money?' she asked Auntie Rhoda after he'd left.

'Put it in your savings account. They'll pay you interest on it, so it'll grow bigger.'

'Shouldn't this money be in an account in Ernest's name?'

'It'd be better to keep it in your own account, dear. He won't care and that way his father won't be able to take it off him. Visiting the post office in the next village makes a pleasant walk on a fine day, even in winter, and you can put your own spare money into your account every week as well.'

Kathleen had never expected to be able to save money. It made her feel far more secure.

6

The two women celebrated Christmas Day quietly because Ernest's father had insisted so strongly on him spending the day with his family that he hadn't dared refuse.

Kathleen had bought a book for Auntie Rhoda, one which she'd mentioned wanting to read: *Lord Jim* by Joseph Conrad. The pedlar who came regularly to the village had got it for her in Swindon because she was still afraid to go there.

They laughed when they found that Auntie Rhoda had bought her a book too, *Love and Mr Lewisham* by H. G. Wells, because Kathleen had been fascinated by that author's *The War of the Worlds* when she'd borrowed it from the bookcase in the parlour.

Until then it hadn't even occurred to Kathleen that there might be other worlds, and that led to a discussion about their own world, its sun and moon, and other planets. 'I have so much to learn. I hate being ignorant.'

'You're a quick learner, dear. Think of all the lovely books you'll need to read to learn things.'

Kathleen could only sigh happily at that bright shining thought.

★ ★ ★

Then it was 1902. The year dawned with a light dusting of snow and a chilly wind. Kathleen had found a warm coat in the church box and had had a pair of boots made by the shoemaker in the next village, so she was cosily dressed. It was the first time she'd had brand-new boots made in her whole life and she couldn't believe how well they fitted, how comfortable they were to walk in.

She had never been so happy, she thought, never! Oh, no! She clapped her hand to her mouth. It was tempting providence to be so smug. She put a penny in the church poor box to make up for that lapse and went home to read one of the newspapers which Auntie Rhoda bought occasionally, devouring every page to find out what was happening in the wider world.

Kathleen knew reading newspapers made you think. She read about the royal family. In January last year, Queen Victoria had died and her sixty-year-old son had come to the throne. It still seemed strange to talk about 'the King', though. He was going to be crowned King of England later in the year. King Edward the Seventh. That would be a fine spectacle, from the details given in the newspapers.

Auntie Rhoda pointed out one article that said there were now over two hundred female doctors and a hundred female dentists practising in Britain. She was angry about the writer's patronising tone. 'Why shouldn't women make good doctors? Tell me that, Kathleen! The man who wrote this wouldn't say no to one of them saving his life, would he? So why is he scornful when he writes about them?'

The Boer War was still being fought in South

Africa, but that was so far away it didn't seem important to Kathleen, and anyway, she found the details of it confusing. Of more concern was the fact that a four-pound loaf now cost fivepence and she knew how difficult that would make life for her mother.

She thought about her mother sometimes, what a hard, narrow life she'd led. But she was afraid to get in touch with any of her family, because of her father. Besides, she wasn't close to her brothers and sisters, who would no doubt have sided with her father about the marriage of their sister.

Then, in February Kathleen forgot the wider world, because Ernest didn't come to see them for over a week. He didn't send a postcard letting them know he couldn't come, either, which he had done the only other time it had happened. A postcard could get to you in one of the later posts of the same day, even in a small village like Monks Barton.

Kathleen was worried. 'Should I write to him, do you think?'

'His father used to open all the letters that were delivered to their house and I expect he still does, even his wife's letters.'

'Then how do I find out what's happening? Ernest may be ill. He may need me.'

'If he doesn't come this weekend, I'll visit him. I don't often do that, so we'll wait a little longer.'

A second weekend passed, and still there was no sign of Ernest. On the Sunday evening Rhoda put into words what they were both thinking. 'His father must have found out about you and be preventing Ernest from visiting us. It's the only explanation.'

'Oh dear.'

Rhoda looked at her guest's stomach and spoke more bluntly than usual, 'You haven't used your monthly rags recently. Do you think you might be expecting?'

Kathleen could feel herself blushing. 'Well yes, I may be. I feel sore here.' She touched her breasts.

The older woman closed her eyes and let out a long sigh of relief. 'Thank goodness! I'll go into Swindon on Wednesday. I can travel in with Farmer Johnson when he goes to market. I'll call at the Seatons' house and see if I can find out what's happened to Ernest. This uncertainty can't go on.'

★ ★ ★

However, on the Monday afternoon there was the sound of wheels and harness jingling outside the cottage. They both rushed to the window and saw a pony and trap.

'That's Mr Seaton,' Rhoda said. 'And Ernest isn't with him. I'd better speak to him first.'

Kathleen shook her head. 'No. I don't want him to think I'm afraid of him. Whether he likes it or not, I'm his daughter-in-law.'

'Are you sure you can face him? He won't try to hit you, but he shouts a lot and has a temper. He uses words as weapons. I'm hoping the idea of a baby will help win him round, but he likes to get his own way and he didn't arrange this marriage, so it won't be easy.'

'All men like to get their own way I've found — except for Ernest.' It made her feel sad that she always had to stop herself from saying 'poor Ernest'.

Mr Seaton was a burly man and got down with difficulty, leaving his pony and trap in the hands of the young fellow who'd driven him. He came striding up the path to the cottage looking furious.

Rhoda opened the door before he could use the knocker, not stepping aside to let him in and keeping Kathleen standing slightly behind her as if for protection. 'Good afternoon, Mr Seaton.'

He didn't reply, simply stayed where he was, eyeing the younger woman as if she was an animal he was thinking of buying.

He reminded Kathleen of an ageing bull one of the nearby farmers had, thickset with grizzled hair and a short neck. Ernest would probably look like that when he grew older, but without the fierce expression.

She stared right back at him and he raised his eyebrows as if surprised by this reaction.

'This is — '

'We'll go into your parlour before you start introducing me, Rhoda,' he said. 'I don't want to put on a show for your neighbours.'

He would have led the way in, treating them both as if they were servants but Kathleen knew that gentlemen were supposed to let ladies enter a room first, so she moved quickly to take the lead. 'This way please, Mr Seaton.'

She heard Rhoda let out a faint gasp but that

71

didn't deter her. After thinking long and hard about this confrontation, knowing it was inevitable, she'd come to the conclusion that if she gave ground at the start, Ernest's father would trample all over her from then onwards. He behaved like that to his son, his wife and everyone else within his orbit.

Well, he wasn't going to bully her. She'd had enough bullying from her father over the years to last her the rest of her life.

When their visitor sat down on the sofa, she remained standing by her chair, saying nothing till it dawned on him that she was expecting to be treated more politely. After one frightened glance at her, Auntie Rhoda also remained standing.

He stood up again and gave them a mocking bow. 'Do sit down, ladies.'

Kathleen inclined her head and took the armchair opposite him while Rhoda took the smaller armchair between them.

He flung himself down on the two-seater sofa again, not waiting for an introduction. 'Your name's Kathleen, isn't it? Well, at least you have spirit. I like to see it in a horse; I'm not so sure if it suits a young woman, though.'

She didn't rise to the baiting, merely giving him a half-smile and waiting to see what he was going to say and do.

He turned from her to his hostess. 'I hadn't expected you to betray my trust like this, Rhoda. I thought my boy would be safe with you.'

'I did what I thought best for both you and Ernest, Mr Seaton. You've said several times that

72

you want grandsons, but *you* haven't been able to persuade your son into marriage.'

Silence, then he jerked one thumb in Kathleen's direction. 'How did this one bring him to the point when no one else could? She's quite pretty but so are other women. What's so special about her?'

'She's kind. Ernest needs kindness.'

Annoyed to be left out of the conversation, Kathleen joined in. 'I didn't have to bring your son to the point, Mr Seaton. *He* had to persuade me. I met Ernest several months before I married him. I was a waitress in a café he liked to visit. He seemed very lonely, so I used to walk in the park with him now and then during my afternoon breaks, just chatting quietly, nothing more.'

Mr Seaton winced and closed his eyes as if in pain. 'A waitress! Damned fool of a boy! Could he do no better than that for himself? And from the way you talk, there's Irish in your family.'

'Yes.'

'I think he's done very well marrying her,' Rhoda commented quietly.

He glared at her. 'That is a matter of opinion, madam. Go on then, Kathleen. Tell me how it happened.'

'Ernest admired me from the start, I could tell, but I wasn't in a hurry to get married. We were just . . . friends.'

He let out a derisive snort.

She scowled at him. 'Friendship is not something to be sneered at, Mr Seaton. It was easy to tell that your son was unhappy.'

'That's because he's a lazy young devil.'

'I disagree. If someone treats him kindly he'll do anything for them. But he thinks slowly and nothing *you* say or do to him will ever change that.'

'So you took advantage of his stupidity to trap him! Well, I'll find a way to overturn your marriage, see if I don't.'

'And make your first grandchild a bastard?'

Her words seemed to hang in the air for a long time before he spoke again, his voice markedly quieter. 'You're with child? Already? *Ernest's* child?'

'Of course it's his.'

'When is it due?'

'Ten months after our marriage. And I came to Ernest a virgin, Mr Seaton, in case you're wondering. I'll swear that on the Bible, if necessary.'

'Words are easy.'

'I believe her,' Rhoda said. 'She's a decent young woman and has been good for your poor son.'

'She can be as decent as you please but she brings nothing to the marriage, nothing! And she's *Irish*, of all things. What will people say about that, eh? It's not money that's important in my world, but social and business connections. Dammit, I wanted better for Ernest than someone like her.'

The words stung but they also stiffened Kathleen's backbone. 'I'm giving him a child and that isn't *nothing*. And as the women of my family bear children easily, this one won't be the

74

last, I'm sure. That's something important to bring to a marriage, don't you think?' She laid one hand on her belly, the first time she'd done that publicly. The small swelling felt good. As if she wasn't alone any more.

'Hmph! Who are your family? What do they do besides spawn waitresses?' His words might be quieter but they were still laced with scorn.

Here it was, the question she'd been dreading, but she didn't intend to lie to him. 'You already know my father ... Fergus Keller, your foreman.'

Mr Seaton closed his eyes again as if in pain, then opened them to glare at her. 'Does he know about this marriage? Has he been deceiving me, laughing at me behind my back?'

'No. And I hope you won't tell him where I'm living. I never want to see him again. I married Ernest because my father was trying to force me to marry a brute who would have knocked me about and made me unhappy. My father had thumped me to try to persuade me and when Ernest saw how badly bruised my face was, he said I should marry him instead. And before you ask, that was his idea, not mine.'

For the first time her voice faltered. 'I was at my wits' end, so I accepted. I felt your son would be kind to me, at least, and he has been. Very. I'm fond of Ernest, Mr Seaton, which is more than you seem to be.'

'Who was this man they wanted you to marry? Do I know him as well?'

'He's called Desmond Mannion.'

His expression changed from anger to disgust.

'That lout. He worked for me once. Ill-treated the horses, skimped on the cleaning. I sacked him within the week. I don't blame you for not wanting to marry *him*.'

He sighed and rubbed his forehead as if he didn't know what to say next.

Rhoda stepped in. 'Shall I make us all a pot of tea, Mr Seaton?'

'Good idea. But you've not won me over, Rhoda Newman, and don't think you have.'

'You'll make up your own mind, sir. You always do. But *I* won't desert Kathleen, whatever you say or do. She's a fine young woman, healthy and a hard worker. She'll make a good mother and is already a good wife.'

He stared at Kathleen as if seeing her for the first time, muttered something and turned away to stare into the fire. When Rhoda had left the room he spoke without even looking at his companion. 'I'm not having you and Ernest living in my house.'

'I wouldn't want to. You make him nervous and we'd be too near my father as well. I still live in fear of him finding me and beating me senseless . . . making me lose the child, perhaps. He hates to be crossed.'

'Oh, I'll make sure he doesn't hurt my grandchild, believe me.'

'Thank you. That would be a load off my mind.'

'There's another reason for keeping you out of the way and the marriage secret for a while yet. I'll tell you about that another time.'

She waited a moment then asked, 'What have

you done with Ernest?'

'Had him locked up till he told me why he'd been coming here so often. That took a few days. Surprised me. He doesn't often defy me. Then I had to decide what to do about you.' He glared at her. 'One thing you can be sure of: *I* don't beat my children senseless, whatever they do.'

'No, but you cut them out of your life if they displease you. You have another son, I believe.'

'I'll have you know that I offered to let Alex return if he'd only do as I asked, but he said he preferred his new life. He now keeps a stall on the market selling second-hand bits and pieces, only he calls them antiques. How do you think I feel about that?'

'If he's successful you should be proud of him.'

'Pfff! He could be helping me run the business. He has a fine brain when he bothers to use it.'

She sighed. Then the brother wasn't at all like her poor husband.

'What will you do if I cut Ernest off without a penny?'

'Move away from here and help him find another job. We've saved enough money to tide us over for a while and Rhoda says he's good with horses.'

'Have you indeed got some money put by? That'll be the first time he's ever saved anything.'

'He'd saved quite a lot but didn't know what to do with it and I'd been saving my tips for years. What's more, I've saved most of the housekeeping money Ernest has given me since we married because I have no rent to pay here. I'm good with money, Mr Seaton. That's another thing I've brought to the marriage.'

'So you say. You're good with words, too. Not stupid, no, definitely not. At least that's in your favour if we're to consider you breeding my grandchildren.' Another pause, then, 'I'm damned if I know what to make of you.'

She risked echoing his words. 'I don't know what to make of you, either, Mr Seaton.'

When he let out a crack of laughter, she felt she was making progress, winning him over just a little. And for the sake of her child, that was necessary, however little she liked him.

After he'd drunk three cups of tea and eaten several scones, he said abruptly, 'We'll keep the marriage secret for the time being and see how you go with the childbearing. If you can give me a grandson to raise, one who's got more brains than his thick-skulled father, well, I shall not be displeased.'

'Give *you* a grandson? This is *my* child and I won't hand it over to anyone else to raise.'

'Oh, won't you? Not even if I pay you well?'

'No. You'll only make it as unhappy as you've made Ernest and probably your other son. Why, you won't even let him wear spectacles, so it's no wonder he has trouble doing the accounts.'

He gaped at her. 'Who's talking about spectacles?'

'I am. Ernest needs them.'

'We were discussing my grandchildren.'

'Who will be *my* children. I intend to raise them with love and educate them as best I can.

They won't be beaten for nothing or have their books taken away from them.'

He cocked his head on one side and studied her. 'You like reading, do you?'

'Yes. Very much indeed.'

'So do I.'

She was surprised at this admission.

'Is that what Fergus did, took your books away?'

'Yes. If they hadn't belonged to the library, my father would have burnt them when he got angry at me, I'm sure.'

'Hmm.' Mr Seaton made up for his moment's weakness by speaking more sharply as he delivered his ultimatum. 'This is how we'll arrange things, then. I'll let you and Ernest stay together on condition you keep the marriage secret and don't come near my home or business.'

Kathleen inclined her head, keeping her hands out of sight because they'd suddenly started to shake. It was a moment or two before she could pull herself together. She didn't tell him the marriage was known about in the village already. She wasn't going to tell him anything she didn't have to.

'I'll raise Ernest's wages now he's a married man, and you need better clothes than those you're wearing if you're to appear one day as my daughter-in-law.' He turned to Rhoda and took out his wallet. 'Is twenty pounds enough to get her started with better clothes?'

'Yes, sir.'

'*You* are to keep this money, Rhoda, and use it only to buy her clothes. Keep careful accounts of what you spend it on. I like to see where my money goes. I trust you, but *she* will have to prove herself. If you need more money, come and tell me why.'

'I'll be happy to see to that, Mr Seaton because she'll be a pleasure to dress. She's a fine-looking young woman.'

He stared at Kathleen for a moment or two in silence then shrugged. 'Handsome is as handsome does.'

Gulping down the last of his tea, he heaved himself to his feet. 'I'll send Ernest over to stay with you two for a few days. Maybe you can calm him down, Kathleen. I certainly can't. He keeps weeping and calling your name. I never thought I'd breed such a damned weakling.'

She hated to think of Ernest so upset. How badly had Mr Seaton treated his son?

'Don't look at me like that. I'm not your father; I didn't beat him.'

'There are other ways of ill-treating someone.'

'Ernest is a fool and if he didn't look like me, I'd wonder whose son he was.' He gave them a nod and left the cottage, raising one hand to signal to his driver who was walking up and down near the pony trap.

Kathleen watched Mr Seaton climb up into it. His face grew ruddy with the effort. He ate too much, probably. You could do that if you were rich, and compared to the people she'd grown up among, he was very rich indeed. And yet, he seemed almost as unhappy as his son. She had thought having all the money you needed must make you happy, but clearly it didn't.

She heard him tell his driver to take him home

but he didn't wave goodbye or even look round at them.

She looked at Auntie Rhoda. 'He didn't mention his wife, not once. Do they not get on?'

'Not at all. She's a foolish woman interested only in her social life, always worried about what people will think about her and what she does. They meet at meals and go to church together and that's about it.'

As she went back into the house, Kathleen's nerves got the better of her and she had to rush into the scullery to be sick.

When she'd finished, Auntie Rhoda handed her a damp cloth and a towel. 'You did well, Kathleen.'

'Did I? I'll have to do better in future, though, or Ernest will suffer. He must have led a terrible life with that man. He needs handling gently, not bullying.'

'It wasn't easy for the poor boy, I will confess. It was Alex who got the brains in the family, but Alex wheezed if he went near horses. Mr Seaton acted as if he was doing it on purpose, which is ridiculous. You'll no doubt meet Ernest's brother one day. You'll like him.'

'If you say so.'

'Ernest was always being scolded and told he was stupid. He was never good enough for his father. And as you'll find, your husband can indeed be infuriating and stubborn. He's not always meek. A few years ago he fell in with some bad types who started him drinking heavily. But his father didn't seem to mind that, which surprised me. Hah!'

'Ernest doesn't drink now, does he?'

'No. I persuaded him to stop, because it doesn't take much to make him drunk. I told him it upset me and cried. He'd never seen me cry before. So he promised me he wouldn't drink any more. He didn't really like the taste or the way it made him feel, anyway. It was the company he enjoyed, flattering him they were, pretending to be his friends.'

'And it sounds like his mother wasn't much better, was she?'

'No. Selfish. Stupid. A social climber, though she hasn't managed to climb very far because people don't take to her. She left me to raise both her sons.'

'I'm glad Ernest had you.'

'He's the son I never had and I love him. My husband died young and left me to make my own way in the world. Life is never easy for long, Kathleen. I think you're going to have a peaceful few months, but always be prepared for things to change suddenly. Keep that money to yourself and the bank book safely hidden.'

'Ernest hasn't even asked how much we have in the bank.'

'No. He wouldn't. Unlike his father, he doesn't care about money.'

Which made Kathleen wonder why Auntie Rhoda was warning her so strongly about all this. Did she think Mr Seaton would change his mind?

She hadn't cared whether the baby was a son or a daughter before, but now she thought a son might be better, for all their sakes.

* * *

Two men brought Ernest to them that evening after dark and he seemed disoriented, having to be helped into the house.

When he saw Kathleen he flung himself into her arms and burst into tears.

She left Auntie Rhoda to see the men out and took her husband into the little parlour, shushing him and patting his back.

It was a while before she could calm him down. And as she held him, she realised then more clearly than ever before that to all intents and purposes she already had a child. The baby in her belly would be her second one.

What a mess her life was in! Was it to be like this for ever, tied to a man who was so weak, wasn't very clever and couldn't even read easily?

Then she thought of Desmond Mannion, with his brutal face and big, bunched fists, and told herself not to be stupid. Compared to him, Ernest was a wonderful husband. And stupid or not, he'd saved her, hadn't he? She owed him a lot for that.

But she'd have to pay for it for the rest of her life. Every single tedious day.

* * *

The following day Jedediah Seaton summoned his foreman to his office. 'Close the door and sit down. What I have to say to you is to go no further.'

'Yes, sir. I mean, no sir.'

'I've found out where your daughter is.'

Keller leant forward. 'Where?'

'None of your business now. I want you to — '

'Excuse me, sir, but my daughter ran away, as you know. Goodness knows how she's living. She needs bringing into line. I'm not having one of my family behaving immorally.'

'Needs a good beating, does she?'

'If necessary. She's a stubborn bitch, impudent too.'

Seaton looked at him thoughtfully. He sounded to hate the poor young woman. What a way to treat your daughter! 'Well, she's not your concern now so you'll do no more beating.'

'I don't understand.'

'She's married my son, so she's *my* concern from now on, and you'll kindly remember that.'

Keller gaped at him. 'Kathleen? My Kathleen? She's gone and married Mr Ernest?'

'Didn't I just say so?'

'I hope *you* gave her a good beating then, sir.'

'Certainly not. She's carrying his child and I want a grandson. If you so much as lay a finger on her, you'll lose your job here. And if you do anything whatsoever to harm that unborn child, I'll have you put down like a mad dog.'

Keller stiffened. 'I was right, though, wasn't I? She had been behaving immorally.'

'No. You were wrong. She went to live with a decent woman I know and respect, who wouldn't lie to me, and Kathleen was married from her house. The child isn't expected until ten months after their wedding date. Your daughter ran away from *you* and I'm only letting

84

you stay on here as foreman because you're the best I've seen with horses and because I want to keep an eye on you. A very close eye.'

His foreman scowled down at his boots, then sucked in a sudden sharp breath and looked up. 'But you're not Catholics. The child will be brought up a heathen.'

Seaton threw back his head and laughed. 'The child will be brought up in the Church of England. That's not heathen. Dammit, man! We worship the same god, use the same Bible.'

There was a long silence, then Keller said sullenly, 'I suppose so, sir.'

'Get about your business, now. And remember, you're not to try to find your daughter or go near her, let alone touch her. She's my business now. And you're not to mention this to anyone, not even your own family.'

'Yes, sir.'

He didn't tell Keller or his son and wife that one of the reasons for keeping the marriage secret was his nephew Godfrey, who had changed over the past few years, ever since Jedediah had disinherited Alex. It was as if Godfrey felt himself to be the rightful heir now, and although Ernest wasn't nearly as clever as Alex, he was the only remaining son and he would be the heir, as far as his father was concerned, not his nephew.

Godfrey tried to hide it from his uncle but he now seemed so jealous of Ernest inheriting the family business and fortune that Jedediah was beginning to suspect that he'd do anything, legal or not, to get his hands on it. Godfrey's own father had been a failure who had lost most of his money in poor business ventures, and then grown stranger and stranger, eventually killing himself.

The older he got, the more like his father Godfrey seemed to become. Perhaps he didn't like working in his wife's family's business. Being an undertaker wasn't everyone's idea of a good way to earn a living. It was as if some sickness was festering in his mind.

Damnation! Jedediah thumped the edge of his clenched fist on his desk. Why couldn't Ernest have married someone of his own class, someone with a family powerful enough to protect her and, more importantly, protect her children?

This situation was like a bomb waiting to explode, and he didn't know what to do for the best. Some problems weren't easily solved. If Ernest had been a clever man, he'd have been able to protect himself, but he wasn't, so Jedediah had to do that and pray that this Kathleen had a son, who could be trained by his grandfather and inherit the business. In the meantime, it would be best to keep them out of sight and conceal the fact that they were married.

To make matters worse, Godfrey had been sucking up to Jedediah's wife and she was treating him like a favoured son. She had always been a fool. Now, she had to be watched as well.

★ ★ ★

Outside, Fergus Keller went across the stable yard into the hay store and sat down to have a

86

think. After a while he smiled and nodded a few times. He'd wanted children able to support him and Deirdre in their old age, hadn't he? Most men did. Well, Kathleen would be able to do that easily.

And when Mr Seaton died, Ernest would inherit and they'd need someone to look after the business. Ernest wouldn't be able to do that without help. Jedediah Seaton was growing old and looking increasingly unhealthy, but Fergus was still in his prime and one day Kathleen was going to need him.

He continued to smile as he went back to work. Some things were worth waiting for. Fate had been kind to him and Kathleen had done better for herself than Desmond Mannion, a lot better.

But while he waited for his time to come, he'd find out where Kathleen was and keep an eye on her. He'd know where to put his hand on her when the old man died.

And in the meantime he'd pray that she didn't die in childbirth, that she would bear sons who would charm the old man.

7

In July the Midwives' Act received royal assent, and after that midwives were only allowed to practise if they were certified. Mrs Todd, who had been bringing babies into the world in and around Monks Barton for thirty years, was able to satisfy the criteria but even so, Kathleen's son would have to be born under the supervision of the young doctor who had just set up in the village.

This would be the first child Dr Lowcroft had helped bring into the world in the district and the women of the village were not at all sure they liked the idea of having a man interfering.

It felt strange to Kathleen to have a man see her like that, but as the labour progressed quickly she forgot her embarrassment and concentrated on the hard work of birthing the baby. She knew what to expect from her own family but welcomed the guidance and help of Mrs Todd. Not that much help was needed. Her body did what it had to.

Dr Lowcroft watched over the whole process carefully, ignoring the midwife's muttering and obvious resentment of his presence.

'It's a boy,' she told Kathleen quickly as the baby was delivered.

'Oh, I'm so glad.'

The infant was already crying good and hard.

Dr Lowcroft stepped forward to supervise the

cutting of the umbilical cord, then took the baby from the midwife and examined him carefully, much to the young mother's annoyance, because she was longing to hold him in her arms.

'You have a fine strong boy, Mrs Seaton. Your father-in-law will be delighted.'

Kathleen suddenly realised what had made a doctor trained in London choose to practise in a small village like Monks Barton. She held out her hands for her son, and blurted it out. 'Mr Seaton helped you set up here, didn't he? Be sure to tell him how straightforward the birth was when you report to him.'

Dr Lowcroft stared at her in surprise. 'I thought you knew that he'd helped me set up here and why. Didn't he tell you?'

'No. He wasn't concerned with me. He wants grandsons more than anything else on earth.'

'Ah, I see. That was why he was so pleased that I had made a special study of childbirth.' He smiled at Mrs Todd. 'You're obviously very experienced, ma'am, and I'm sure there will be much that I can learn from you. In return, I'll share the latest medical findings on childbirth, if you like.'

She smiled at him, annoyance forgotten. 'I would like that, Doctor. I care very much about my mothers and babies, and if there's a better way to do something, I want to know about it.' Then she added slowly, 'Doctors don't usually do that. Share, I mean.'

'There is a new generation of doctors being trained and we want the whole system to be more efficient, which you don't get by keeping medical knowledge to yourself.'

He turned back to Kathleen. 'Well, you've just provided Mr Seaton with a fine, healthy grandson. Let's see how much this little lad weighs . . . Nine and a half pounds! A big first child. And listen to him yell. Fine pair of lungs he's got, eh?'

After he'd left, Mrs Todd muttered, 'He seems better than most doctors. Whatever that stupid act of parliament says, they don't usually want to get involved in childbirth, not the ones I've met, anyway. I'd give the devil his due if he did something well, and I'll do the same for this doctor. I've heard nothing but good things about him so far, I must say.'

She continued to talk as she cleared up. 'He doesn't turn away the poorer patients or charge them if they have to choose between food and his fees. I still don't understand what the government was thinking, passing that stupid act about midwives, but perhaps we've fallen lucky with this man. Anyway, never mind that now. Let's finish getting you cleaned up and settled.'

When she'd finished, she wagged one forefinger at Kathleen. 'Mind, you're to stay in bed for a week.'

'What? I'd go mad.'

'You'll be the better for a good long rest. Most women are glad of the excuse.'

Kathleen could see it'd be no use protesting, so decided to ignore the order and just take things more easily for a few days.

Then she looked into the cradle and forgot about everything else. Her whole body felt warm with love at the sight of the little red face. And her son — *her son!* — had already got one arm loose and was waving it at the world.

Mrs Todd came to stand on the other side of the cradle. 'He's a lively one, isn't he? I think you should feed him now.'

It seemed a long time till Mrs Todd left her in peace.

Soon afterwards Auntie Rhoda peeped into the bedroom. 'Shall we send word to Mr Seaton? He wants to see the child straight away.'

'Well, *I* want to show Ernest his son first.'

'He and his father will probably come to see the baby together.'

'Did you know that Mr Seaton had helped Dr Lowcroft set up here in order to have a doctor who understands childbirth to hand?'

Auntie Rhoda stared at her open-mouthed. 'He never did! The cunning old devil.'

'Yes. But I didn't need a doctor's help.'

'Mrs Todd said you were made to bear children.'

Not one a year, though, Kathleen thought rebelliously. She'd seen how that wore down her sisters.

But her father-in-law must have had someone keeping an eye on them, or the doctor must have sent word, because Mr Seaton was at the house within two hours of the birth.

When she realised from the voices in the hall that he hadn't brought Ernest with him, Kathleen locked her bedroom door. Auntie Rhoda knocked on it and called, 'Mr Seaton is here to see his grandson.'

91

'He'll have to knock this door down if he wants to see the child before its father does,' Kathleen yelled. Then she set her ear to the door to see what they said about that.

'Whatever's got into her, Rhoda?' Mr Seaton asked.

'She wants to show the child to his father first. It's what normally happens, you know. And it's best to humour a woman who's just given birth. Where is Ernest?'

'Out making a delivery.'

'And when did you send him out?'

Silence, then Rhoda's voice again. 'That wasn't kind, Mr Seaton.'

'To hell with being kind, tell her to let me in or I *will* knock the door down. I've been very forbearing about this marriage. The least she can do in return is show me my grandson.'

'You'll have to drag me out of the way to force your way in,' Rhoda replied.

Tears welled in Kathleen's eyes at this support, because she knew how nervous the older woman usually was when dealing with her former employer.

Then there was the sound of a horse and cart pulling up outside and she wished desperately that she had the front bedroom and could see who it was.

Someone burst into the house and she heard Ernest call out, 'Where is she?'

'She's locked herself in the bedroom,' his father said. 'Childbirth does strange things to women's brains. It's why they weren't made to be masters or to vote.'

Kathleen stuck her tongue out at him, even though he couldn't see her. How could he say that when he knew how slow-witted his son was compared to her? If Ernest deserved a vote, so did she. Though she'd not go as far getting herself arrested for protesting about it.

She heard Rhoda speak soothingly. 'She's waiting to show you the baby first, Ernest dear. Come along, Mr Seaton. You can sit in my parlour and I'll make you a nice cup of tea, after which you can see your beautiful grandson.'

He grumbled all the way down the stairs but he went, thank goodness.

★ ★ ★

Kathleen waited to unlock the bedroom door until she'd heard them going into the parlour, then she flung her door open and smiled at her husband. 'Come and meet your son, Ernest.'

He seemed to be holding his breath as he followed her across to the bed and stared down at the crumpled red face of the infant in the cradle.

'My son.' It was little more than a whisper, but she thought she'd never seen such awe and love on a man's face, and she felt the same. She couldn't believe how strong her feelings were for the tiny creature in the cradle, even after only a few hours of having him out in the world with her.

She linked her arm through her husband's. 'The midwife says he's a big baby and going to be tall, though how she knows, I can't tell.

93

Perhaps she's seen that you're tall, Ernest. You should stand up straighter and not slouch. It's good to be tall.'

He was hardly listening, his eyes still devouring the child. 'What shall we call him?'

'We had thought John, remember?'

He wriggled uncomfortably. 'If that's what you want.'

'I want us both to choose the name and be happy with it.'

'John is a very short name, isn't it?'

'We could have it as a second name.'

He was looking down at his feet as he muttered, 'I like the name Christopher. Do you?'

'Yes. Very much.'

'You do?' He looked up at her again.

'I really do. Christopher John Seaton would make a fine name.'

'I like that.' He reached out to touch his son's hand with one gentle finger. The baby grasped his finger tightly, making Ernest gasp in delight and hold his breath for a moment.

A voice from the doorway broke the spell. 'Very touching. Am I allowed to see my grandson now? Rhoda tells me he's a big baby.'

Kathleen hadn't even heard her father-in-law come back up the stairs and felt annoyed. Couldn't he even give them a few minutes to savour this important moment?

He came across to the cradle and stared down. 'He looks healthy, anyway. Well done, Kathleen.'

'I couldn't have done it without my husband.'

He studied his son, then his grandson. 'Well done, Ernest. You're a father now and you know what, you looked just like that when you were born.' He reached out to touch the baby's soft little hand. 'Aha!' He showed them a small mark at the wrist then bared his own wrist. 'That's the Seaton birthmark. I have one and so does Ernest.'

She knew without further explanation what he was telling her, that he accepted the child as his descendant. 'We're calling him Christopher John.'

He nodded approvingly. 'My father was Christopher James.'

'Then the choice of name should please you.' Her eyes challenged his.

'Yes. I must say, you look surprisingly well for a woman just out of labour. Shouldn't you be resting in bed?'

'No. I feel fine. Having a baby is a perfectly natural thing, you know, not an illness. And the doctor said it happened very quickly, so it didn't tire me out.'

He looked as if his smile was reluctant, but it was a smile nonetheless. 'Good. And do you want to come and live in my house now, Kathleen?'

'Thank you, but no. I think we'd be happier with a place of our own and you and your wife would be happier without us under your feet all the time, not to mention how loudly a baby can cry. Is she coming to see the baby?'

'I haven't told her about the marriage or the baby.'

'What? Are you so ashamed of me?'

'No. I'm ashamed of *her*. And I'm worried

that she'd tell my nephew, Godfrey about you. He's trying to poke his nose into my business.'

As she opened her mouth to protest, he held up one hand. 'Leave that to me. And stay out of sight. Just be glad you can have a few peaceful years before you have to face up to my family's conflicts.' He hesitated, then added, 'I don't trust him. He might find a way to harm the child.'

She sucked in her breath. 'Surely not?'

'He's changed. I don't trust him at all. Let me keep you safe here.'

'Very well. There's a rather nice cottage a few doors away from this house that would suit us just fine if we had the furniture for it. And it'd be easier to have other children if Ernest lived with me all the time.' She held her breath. Had she asked for too much?

'All right. I'll pay the rent for the cottage.'

'Thank you. I'll see about getting some furniture. You can buy some quite good pieces second-hand.'

'There's a lot of furniture in our attic, good quality but old-fashioned. You can have your pick of that. I'll send a carriage for you next week to come and choose the furniture. I'll let you know the day.'

'Can it be a time when my father isn't there?'

'You don't want to show him his grandson?'

'He's not interested in babies. He cares more about drinking.'

'He's never turned up at work drunk. I told him he'd lose his job if he ever did.'

She felt ashamed to have blackened her father's name. 'He wouldn't do that, anyway. He only drinks of an evening, but he does like a few pints.'

'Most working men do.' He shrugged. 'Well, it's your choice about him seeing the baby. But you'll not keep *me* away from my grandson.'

'I'll not try. You do care about him.'

Rhoda's clock chimed the hour and he took out his big gold hunter watch to check the time. 'I have to get back now. Mrs Seaton is giving a dinner party tonight and will be fussing like a mad hen.'

When he'd gone, Ernest sat down on the bed with a happy sigh. 'I'm glad you don't want to live with him. I don't want him watching everything you do and shouting at you like he does me.'

'You'll not be living with him, either. You'll be with me in what was Lizzie Talbot's cottage. You'll be coming home every night to sleep there from now on.'

'Father will find a way to stop me.'

'He'd better not.' But she guessed that he would still limit the visits. He had to if he was to keep the marriage a secret. She wasn't sure she believed him about fearing what his nephew might do, but for the time being she'd enjoy raising her son in peace. And even if Mr Seaton didn't allow Ernest to live as he pleased, he'd surely allow him more freedom and more time with his wife, because he'd want more grandchildren.

Well, she intended to find out more about limiting the number of children. She'd heard women whispering about 'voluntary motherhood', as they'd called it. After she'd had another child, she intended to take a year or two off childbearing. She wasn't going to wear herself out. Who wanted eight or ten children anyway? It'd be too many to look after properly, unless you were rich.

★ ★ ★

On the day they were taken into Swindon to choose furniture, Mrs Seaton was not at home, nor was Kathleen's father to be seen in the stable yard attached to the house.

They didn't see any servants about the place either, but as the former housekeeper, Rhoda knew her way round well enough to guide her young friend up to the attics.

After they'd chosen some furniture, the cart driver who had brought them to Swindon and a man she'd never seen before joined them to carry pieces of furniture out to the cart.

But she now had a very good reason to worry about Ernest's cousin Godfrey. If Seaton feared what his nephew might do, the man must be dangerous.

Ernest wouldn't even talk about his cousin. He scowled when she mentioned his name and said several times, 'Don't ever let him come into our house, Kathleen. He's a bad man, a very bad man.'

She wouldn't let Godfrey try to hurt her son. She'd protect that child with the last breath in her body.

★ ★ ★

98

One of the maids kept an eye on what the strangers were doing which was easy as they'd been ordered to stay in the servants' quarters until the master told them they could continue their day's work. Cook and the housekeeper grumbled. The other servants enjoyed an hour or two of freedom.

Flora slipped out to watch and try to overhear what these people were saying.

Godfrey Seaton had told her that he would pay her well for any information about what her master was up to. He'd warned her not to tell her mistress about anything she found out. Mrs Seaton would be happier if she was left in peace.

Flora managed to overhear the strangers talking and work out that Mr Ernest had got himself married. She was delighted to have something to tell Mr Godfrey. She was planning to leave this job and get married herself as soon as they'd saved enough money. She didn't like working for the Seatons. They were not a happy family and that made for unhappy servants.

8

Little Christopher thrived, growing plump and rosy. But as Ernest had predicted, his father still insisted on his son spending most week nights at the family home, allowing him to come to the cottage only on Saturday nights until Kathleen pointed out to him that this reduced the likelihood of him fathering more children.

'Very well. I'll allow him the occasional midweek night at the cottage too, but if he tries to sneak out to see you at other times, I'll withhold his wages.'

She was angry but they had no choice except to do as he ordered.

She didn't find out for a few months that her father-in-law was hinting to people that Ernest had a woman somewhere whom he visited at weekends.

She wept about that. But when she told Auntie Rhoda she was going to take Ernest away from his father and move to another part of the country, the older woman persuaded her not to do it.

'You know you're married, Kathleen dear. That's what matters. And your friends in the village know too.'

'But why can't Ernest and I be openly married? He can't marry anyone else now, after all.'

'Mr Seaton hasn't confided in me, but it's to

do with Godfrey Seaton, I'm sure. That man gives me the shivers and I'd not like to cross him. It's best not to anger Mr Seaton either, dear. Just put up with it and enjoy your life here.'

'That's all very well, but some people new to the village believe the rumours, even though we were married here, and they won't speak to me — treat me like a fallen woman. The new curate doesn't correct them, either, and even the doctor seems to think I'm living in sin. Can't *you* tell them differently?'

She sighed. 'Mr Seaton has warned me not to correct the rumours either.'

There was silence as Kathleen looked at her in shock, hurt to the core that she had agreed to this.

'Why does it suddenly matter so much to you? You have a few friends here who do know the truth. You have your son, your library books, a pleasant home. Can you not be satisfied with how things are?'

'I'm hoping to have another baby and I hate the thought of my children being called bastards.'

'Well, just think how you're able to save money as long as you live here. That's important too.'

It was important but so was the presence of a good friend like Rhoda two doors away. Ernest wasn't an interesting companion; Rhoda was stimulating, teaching her so much.

When Kathleen suspected she was expecting another child, she made the effort to change Mr Seaton's mind. But he was adamant that she continue to live quietly in Monks Barton. He even threatened her that he'd lock Ernest up in a lunatic asylum if she didn't do as he ordered.

So Kathleen had to put up with the arrangements. All she could do was save her money, keep her bank book safely hidden and hope that one day she'd find a way to escape.

And if no opportunity arose, well, her father-in-law couldn't live for ever, could he? After Mr Seaton died, she'd persuade Ernest to sell the business and that'd give them enough money to buy a boarding house. At the seaside, perhaps. She'd make a simpler, more peaceful life for her poor husband, who was easy enough to please.

But she could never love her husband as a man. Because he wasn't, not really. He was more like an overgrown child. That made her sad sometimes.

* * *

When Kathleen was certain she was expecting another child, she set aside her worries and waited patiently for the child to grow in her, enjoying the company of Auntie Rhoda, who really did feel like an aunt now, and watching her sturdy young son learn to crawl, walk and say a few simple words.

Ernest loved the boy so much it was beautiful to see, and he seemed able to interact with the child much more easily than he did with adults.

Mr Seaton came to see them every month, doing it secretly by leaving his own pony and trap at a livery stables in Swindon and using one of their vehicles and drivers. He boasted that he paid the owner five shillings each time and gave the driver an extra shilling, so that they would forget who had hired the vehicle and where he'd been in it.

This all seemed ridiculous to Kathleen but she said nothing. She was always polite to her father-in-law, even though she still felt angry at the way he was treating her.

'That's a fine lad,' he said grudgingly when Christopher turned one. 'I hope the next one will be a boy as well.'

'With babies you get what you're given and I shall love all my children,' she snapped.

'Well, this is a man's world and women are the weaker sex — everyone knows it.'

'You underestimate what women are capable of.'

'*You* are the one who overestimates women because most of them aren't nearly as clever as you,' he said sourly.

'What's your mother like?' she asked Ernest later. 'Do you think she loves you?'

He looked at her as if she was speaking a foreign language. 'No. Mother shouts a lot when Father isn't at home. She goes out with other ladies and that's all she cares about. I stay away from her if I can. And I haven't told her about our Christopher. I don't want her coming near him.'

Of course Ernest let slip to his father that Kathleen had been asking about his mother.

'Stop asking about my wife,' Mr Seaton

ordered on the next visit. 'I haven't told her about these children and I'm not going to. She's a fool and will tell everyone else, and blacken your name into the bargain.'

'You're doing that already.'

'Partly to protect you from her spite and partly to protect you from Godfrey. I'm beginning to wonder if he suspects something, though I don't see how he can have found out about you. How many times do I have to tell you to be careful and live quietly? You'll have to take my word that it's the best way to go. Your children will have a peaceful, happy childhood living here. You're a good mother. Oh, and one other thing: don't go near my younger son. I threw Alex out and I'm not having him involved in family matters. He's disloyal, that's what he is.'

Books helped Kathleen pass the long, lonely evening hours. She had a woman now to do all the heavy housework. Mr Seaton had insisted she hire someone and he was paying for the help, so why not? No woman she knew enjoyed scrubbing floors or doing the weekly wash.

She visited the library in the next village every week, sometimes twice a week. She also found an elderly lady in Monks Barton who could finish teaching her to type and who was glad of the extra money. She bought a second-hand type-writer with her teacher's help.

Later her teacher introduced her to another lady who was able to teach her more about keeping accounts.

It wasn't that Kathleen intended to be a secretary now. No, her ambitions had grown wider than that. She was definitely going to run her own business one day.

One of the pieces of furniture they'd brought from Mr Seaton's attics was a little desk that she used for her studies, setting it in front of the window. One day when she was polishing it, she found a secret drawer by accident. From then onwards, as a precaution, she made sure her marriage lines and all their birth certificates were safely hidden there instead of among her underclothes.

She might need to prove that she'd been legally wed and her children legitimate. She'd not forgotten how easy it had been for her to get hold of her birth certificate when she ran away from home. No one was going to steal these documents from her. She didn't even tell Rhoda about the secret drawer.

★   ★   ★

Kathleen's second baby was born even more quickly than the first, taking only two hours from start to finish to make its entry into the world. The doctor seemed to find this rather unladylike but admitted that her nine-pound daughter was as healthy an infant as her son.

'We're going to call her Elizabeth Ann,' Ernest told Dr Lowcroft. 'We decided on names a while ago. She's going to be pretty like her mother and Christopher is going to be tall like me.'

The doctor nodded, always seeming impatient if he had to talk to Ernest. 'I'll leave you to rest now, Mrs Seaton.'

Kathleen gave him a half-smile and hoped he'd take that for acceptance of his instructions. She was tired of people, usually men, telling her what to do.

The midwife watched him go, then chased Ernest and Auntie Rhoda out of the room while she made Kathleen more comfortable. 'Men. What do they know? Though our doctor isn't as bad as I'd expected.'

As she smoothed the bedcovers, she smiled at Kathleen. 'You're a lucky woman, Mrs Seaton, to have babies so easily.'

'Well, I don't want any more. Two are enough.'

'You fall for them easily.'

'Unfortunately.' She hesitated, then asked, 'I've heard about a lady called Annie Besant who was put on trial for writing about birth control. What exactly did she mean? How do you control the having of children except by not having relations with your husband?'

Mrs Todd looked at her, opened her mouth as if to answer then shut it again. 'It's forbidden to teach people about it.'

'Do you know?'

'I can't help knowing in my job.'

'I daren't ask Dr Lowcroft because he tells old Mr Seaton everything that happens here.'

The air seemed charged with tension and Mrs Todd bent her head for a moment, then looked up. 'I could explain it to you, but if you told anyone where you found out, I'd lose my licence to practice as a midwife.'

'I'd never betray you. Never.'

'I'll think about it. There are other people who

106

know. I'll talk to them about you.'

It was a week before Kathleen saw Mrs Todd and raised the subject again, still determined to get the information.

'Ask Mrs Newman,' was all the midwife would say. 'She believes women should be allowed to choose voluntary motherhood and she helps poorer women sometimes when it's dangerous for them to have more children. Which is more than that arrogant young doctor will do.'

'Auntie Rhoda does?'

'I'm not saying another word. It's for her to tell you, or not.'

★　★　★

That evening Kathleen broached the idea of not having another baby for a while. 'Someone told me you might know how to prevent a woman falling for a baby.'

Auntie Rhoda looked at her sharply. 'Don't you want any more children?'

'Yes, but not yet. And never at the rate of one a year, like my sisters.'

Auntie Rhoda bent her head over her embroidery, brow wrinkled in thought, and Kathleen waited, trying not even to breathe loudly.

'Very well, dear, I'll tell you all I know. I work with some other ladies who believe in helping our poorer sisters, you see. We meet every month to make plans or we get in touch with one another directly if we see a need to help someone.'

'That's where you go on the last Thursday of the month.'

'Yes.' After another silence, she said, 'The work is supported by the Greyladies Trust. There is money available from it to help poorer women.'

'I've heard the name Greyladies, but I can't remember where exactly.'[1]

'It's a very old house south of here. It's been passed down the female line of the Latimer family since the Dissolution of the Monasteries, which Henry VIII began in 1536, if you remember your history.'

Kathleen didn't remember ever learning about that, but nodded.

'The house is called Greyladies because it was a former abbey and the nuns wore grey habits. It's situated in the village of Challerton. The owners have been helping women in need for centuries.'

'How wonderful!'

'I think it is. I feel honoured to have been chosen to help.'

'How did that happen?'

'I was helping someone when I met Mrs Latimer. I'll tell you about it another time. Weren't you wanting to find out about preventing too many babies?'

'Yes. Do go on.'

Auntie Rhoda explained carefully the various methods and promised to provide Kathleen and Ernest with the necessary equipment for the rare occasions when he wanted his wife.

'Thank you.'

'If you ever get a chance to share the knowledge with other women and help them in their turn, then please do that.'

Kathleen looked at her thoughtfully. 'I've never really been in a position to help other people. It's always been such a struggle to get what I needed for myself.'

'Not so much of a struggle nowadays.'

'No. Only . . . I might have good food and shelter, but I'm still living a very restricted life.'

'Your time to do more will come, dear. I'm quite sure of that.'

'How? I have three children now, to all intents and purposes.'

She didn't have to explain that. Auntie Rhoda nodded and her expression was sad. 'Ernest is a kind boy, though, when he can be.'

'Yes. I know. And I'm fond of him.' But oh, she'd wanted so much more from a husband. And from life.

9

In November 1905, Ernest failed to arrive on the Friday evening, which was not like him. In fact he hadn't missed a weekend since his daughter's birth.

Kathleen grew increasingly anxious as the hours passed and by ten o'clock that night she was sure something must be seriously wrong to have kept him away.

If he doesn't arrive in the morning, she thought as she got ready for bed, *I'm going to visit Mr Seaton and find out what's going on.*

She was woken at daybreak by the sound of someone hammering on the front door and went rushing downstairs, wriggling into her dressing gown. She flung open the door to see a young man she didn't recognise holding out a letter while with the other hand he steadied a bicycle.

It was cold and light rain was falling. His black waterproof cape was dripping with moisture and he was huddling under the eaves for shelter.

'Message from Mr Seaton, ma'am. He says it's important and I'm to wait for a reply.'

Rhoda came hurrying along from her cottage two doors away, as neatly dressed as ever but with her long grey hair simply tied back, instead of rolled into a bun. She had her grey winter shawl round her shoulders and seemed oblivious to the rain as she closed her umbrella.

Kathleen stood back to let her into the house.

'I saw young Jimmy arrive from my bedroom and I knew he worked for Mr Seaton. Is something wrong?'

'I'm about to find out. Jimmy has brought me a letter from Mr Seaton but I haven't opened it yet.'

The two women looked at one another, both knowing that something must be very wrong for him to send a messenger openly like this.

Kathleen took a deep breath to calm herself. 'Lean your bicycle against the wall, Jimmy, and come inside. You can wait in the hall while I read it. No need to stand out in the rain. It's a cold day.'

He wiped his feet carefully and came in. 'Thank you, ma'am. Um . . . I was to say that Mr Seaton wants me to get back with your answer as quickly as possible.'

'I'll go and read it at once.'

She didn't want to read it in front of the messenger, so beckoned to Rhoda and led the way into the parlour. As soon as she'd shut the door, she tore open the envelope and went to read it near the window where the light was better.

Kathleen,
I'm sorry to tell you that Ernest died suddenly yesterday afternoon. The doctor says it was his heart. He just keeled over as we were talking and was gone.

She gasped and stopped reading for a moment.

'What is it?' Rhoda asked.

'Ernest is dead.'

'But . . . he can't be! He's only a young man and he hasn't been ill. Why, he was here only recently and we were all laughing together.'

Rhoda fell silent, then asked more quietly, 'What happened, dear?' She put an arm round Kathleen and they read the rest of the letter together.

This makes no difference to your position in the family, but it will still be safer for you and your children, and I really do mean safer, for you to stay out of sight of my wife and my nephew.

He's now my closest blood relative, apart from my son Alex, who still refuses to return to the business. Godfrey has taunted me for years that Ernest will never be able to father children, unlike his own sons. He wouldn't let you and your children stand in his way for long if he knew about your marriage.

I intend to write a will which specifically cuts him out, but if I had no heirs Godfrey might be able to claim my money after I die, because Alex isn't married, so isn't likely to produce any heirs.

I beg you to please stay out of sight. I've given it a lot of thought and I want those two children of yours to be given every chance to grow up happily, so please do as I ask and stay out of sight for a few more years till the children have grown more mature in their understanding of the world — and its villains. Young Christopher can join me in the business one day.

I'll come to see them when I can and will continue to keep an eye on you all.

Do not attend the funeral. If you even try, I'll have you taken away from the church forcibly.

Yours in haste,
Jedediah Seaton

Kathleen clapped one hand to her mouth in an attempt to hold back her tears. 'I can't believe Ernest is dead.' But Rhoda was sobbing so uncontrollably, she had to look after her companion before she could even think about writing a reply.

It didn't take long to scrawl a response.

Thank you for letting me know that my husband is dead.

I won't be kept away from the funeral, but to respect your wishes and fears about your nephew, I shall be heavily veiled and will stay at the rear with Rhoda. It will seem as if I'm there to support her.

Kathleen Seaton

She sealed the envelope carefully and took the time to light a candle and put a couple of dabs of sealing wax across the flap. She didn't need Mr Seaton to tell her that no one else must see her letter at this point.

But it wouldn't be right to stay away from her

husband's funeral. It just . . . wouldn't.

She stood at the door watching the young messenger pedal away into the grey, rainy day, then went back inside and turned the damper up on the kitchen fire. Thank goodness the children weren't awake yet.

She waited for the fire to burn up again, not weeping but feeling cold and heavy with grief for a life cut short. Poor Ernest. He had been such a kind man.

Rhoda mopped her eyes and looked at her sadly. 'I should have been comforting you. Only you haven't been weeping. I know you didn't love him, but — '

'I'm still too shocked,' she said hastily. 'It doesn't seem possible.'

Rhoda's voice was bitter. 'I'm old enough to know that death can surprise you at any time. What did you say in your reply?'

'I said I was definitely going to the funeral but would respect Mr Seaton's wishes by wearing a heavy veil and staying at the rear with you.'

'I agree you ought to be there, but should you disobey Mr Seaton? After all, he's trying to protect you.'

'In this matter, I can't obey him. Ernest is — was my husband, the father of my children. I owe him that last respect.' She waited a few moments then added, 'Is this nephew of Mr Seaton really that bad?'

'Yes. Godfrey Seaton seems made of stone. He has the most chilling grey eyes I've ever seen. In fact, he doesn't usually show any emotion, but occasionally he can fly into a fearsome rage. It doesn't happen often but people are terrified when it does. It's a wonder he hasn't killed someone when he's been like that. I know he maimed one man, and his wife's family had to pay the poor fellow off.'

'Oh dear. I was hoping Mr Seaton was exaggerating the danger.'

'No. I'm afraid not. He's right to warn you. I'd never have taken a job in his nephew's house, however much he paid me. I'd rather go into the poorhouse.'

This response from her usually calm friend gave Kathleen something else to worry about besides how she'd live without Ernest's wages.

Most of all, she'd miss the simple protection of being his wife. Just by existing, he'd protected her and the children.

Who would help her to protect them now?

She couldn't run away or she'd be denying her children their birthright, but oh, she wanted to.

★ ★ ★

Later that day another letter was brought by the same tired, wet messenger.

You may attend the funeral, Kathleen, as long as you make it seem that you're there as Rhoda's companion. People know how much she loved Ernest so won't wonder at her presence.

The funeral is on Thursday at ten o'clock in the morning, at All Saints Church. Neither you nor Rhoda are invited back to

115

the house afterwards, mind.

When all the fuss has died down, I'll visit you to discuss new arrangements for the support of yourself and the children.

J. S.

Without a word, Kathleen passed the note to Rhoda, who read it, wiped away more tears and said, 'Thank goodness he's come round about the funeral. It's better that you don't upset him because you'll be dependent on his help from now on.'

'I suppose so. What shall we do about the children on Thursday? My father may be attending the funeral and I don't want him to see them. I'm hoping he won't even recognise me if I wear a thick veil.'

Rhoda thought hard for a few moments, then nodded as she got an idea. 'We can ask my friend Felicity Dalton to keep an eye on them. I'm sure she'll be happy to do that. She loves children and she's played with yours a few times at my house. She can come round here and — '

'I'd prefer us to take them round to her house, and to do it as secretly as possible.' Kathleen saw Rhoda's surprise and added, 'I'm not only afraid of the nephew but of Mr Seaton too. He might try to take his grandchildren away from me while I'm at the funeral.'

'I doubt Mr Seaton would do that. His wife didn't even look after her own children, so she'd definitely not look after yours, particularly if they're cutting Godfrey out.'

'Well, to be double sure they're safe, do you

think Mrs Dalton would take them the night before so that no one sees where they go?'

'Are you that worried?'

'Yes. I love them too much to risk losing them.'

Mrs Dalton was clearly surprised at their request but looked at the young widow pityingly and said she was happy to help in any way. She would love to take the children for the night so that Rhoda and Kathleen could get an early start.

★   ★   ★

On the afternoon before the funeral, Kathleen waited until it was dark, glad that the early dusk of winter would hide what they were doing. Then she carried Elizabeth and made a game of creeping out through the back garden without any noise to keep little Christopher quiet.

They made their way along the back lane to Mrs Dalton's house without meeting anyone, thank goodness.

'They'll be all right with me, dear,' Mrs Dalton assured her yet again.

'I know they will. I'm very grateful.'

'They're too small to understand what's happening anyway. Are you all right? It's hard to lose a husband so young.'

Kathleen shrugged and was glad when Mrs Dalton didn't seem to expect a proper answer. She had felt weary and unhappy since she heard the news, but that was natural when your husband died. What wasn't natural was that she hadn't been able to weep for Ernest, not a single tear.

The cottage seemed strangely quiet without the children, but even so, Kathleen refused Rhoda's offer of a bed for the night, wanting to think things through on her own.

As she lay in bed, comforted by the warmth of an earthenware hot-water bottle at her feet, she remembered how Ernest had always refused to walk long distances, saying it tired him too much. Even when he was helping her to run away, he'd asked her to wait in the hut until he could arrange transport to Monks Barton.

And his face had always been pale, his lips too. Could that have been because of a problem with his heart? Had he always had a weakness?

Oh, who knew what went on inside people's bodies? Human life was uncertain at the best of times. She might enjoy good health, but look how her life had twisted and changed so abruptly.

Poor Ernest!

Poor fatherless children, too. He had loved them so much.

At the thought of him cuddling their children, smiling tenderly, the tears came at last, a river of regrets and sadness.

★ ★ ★

The following morning was showery so it was a good thing Rhoda had hired a carriage to take them to the church. It was a small, shabby vehicle and the horse looked weary even before

118

they started. However the patient creature clopped along steadily enough and they were the first to arrive at the church.

Rhoda gave the driver some money for refreshments and arranged to meet him afterwards at the local inn just down the road. Then she took a deep breath and led the way into the church, holding Kathleen's arm and having to pretend that she needed the younger woman's support.

Two men in black were waiting at the church door to act as ushers. The older one nodded to Rhoda and stepped forward. 'Good morning, Mrs Newman. Mr Seaton said you'd be coming. I'll show you to your place.'

'Thank you, Mr Balham. This is my niece, Jeanie, here to lend me support.' To explain Kathleen's heavy veil, she added, 'We've had another death in the family recently, so it's a sad time for us both.'

He gave Kathleen a cursory nod but didn't really look at her as he showed them to a pew near the rear. 'Mr Seaton says you're not to go up to the coffin. It's already sealed anyway. There's not been a viewing.'

Rhoda sighed. 'I'd have liked to have seen my dear Ernest's face again.'

'Mr Seaton didn't want everyone gawping at his son.' He waited for that bald statement to sink in before continuing. 'After the service is over he says you can attend the consignment of the coffin to the grave, but . . . um, he wanted me to remind you to stand at the rear and also that you're not invited back to the house

119

afterwards.' The usher seemed embarrassed as he relayed these instructions.

'Of course not,' Rhoda said calmly. 'As the former housekeeper, I didn't expect to be invited. But I was very fond of Ernest and very much wanted to attend the boy's funeral, which Mr Seaton has kindly allowed.'

'Of course.' The usher inclined his head and went back to stand at the entrance, leaving them alone in the echoing emptiness of the church.

Kathleen shivered and bent her head in a prayer for Ernest's immortal soul.

Shortly afterwards, mourners began to come in and the two ushers showed them to their pews, speaking in hushed voices.

An organist began to play quietly.

At one point, Rhoda nudged Kathleen and said, 'That's Alex. I'm glad he's been allowed to come.'

Ernest's brother looked nothing like him. He was a slender gentleman of middle height, with an intelligent look on his face and a full head of hair.

'Look at that!' Rhoda whispered indignantly a moment later. 'They've not seated Alex in the family pew. What a shame! This is a golden opportunity for a reconciliation, but Mr Seaton is known for holding grudges. And if Alex won't go back to work in the family business, his father won't reconcile.'

'Can't Mrs Seaton persuade him to forgive and forget?'

'I doubt it. She never goes against her husband.'

120

That sounded like Kathleen's mother, too. So many women acted subserviently towards their husbands. But Kathleen didn't comment on that and kept the heavy veil over her face and the brim of her simple black straw hat tilted forward to further conceal her features.

Peering through the dark mesh of the veil made everything around her seem unreal and distant. Well, things had felt strange since she had heard the sad news. When three-year-old Christopher had asked for his father yesterday, she had put off trying to explain death to such a small child. And Elizabeth was only two. She wouldn't even remember her father.

How would Kathleen make them understand that they'd never see their father again? Death was so final, beyond a small child's comprehension.

There were rustlings and murmurs as people turned to watch the family enter the church and walk slowly down the aisle towards the coffin at the front.

Mr Seaton looked powerful and confident in these surroundings, Kathleen thought with a shiver. What if he changed his mind and tried to take her children away from her? Or tried to discredit her and them, and rely on his younger son to provide him with an heir? Would she be able to stop him?

She was interested to see her mother-in-law at last. Mrs Seaton was richly dressed in black silk but with a sour expression on her face rather than grief. She appeared to be weeping into a handkerchief as she walked slowly along on her

121

husband's arm, but if Kathleen was any judge, there wouldn't be any tears to moisten the delicate linen and lace square with which she was dabbing her eyes.

Rhoda nudged her suddenly. 'That's Mr Seaton's nephew Godfrey just starting up the aisle. He and his father-in-law will have done this funeral, I'm sure.'

Godfrey Seaton was so like Ernest in spite of being older that Kathleen gasped in shock.

Rhoda guessed what had upset her and leant closer to whisper, 'I'm sorry. I should have warned you how like him Ernest was.'

'He too was a sickly child, like my poor Ernest. That seems to run in the family, though your Christopher shows no sign of it. Godfrey and Mr Seaton might detest one another but they also have one thing in common and you should always remember that: it doesn't do to cross either of them.'

Kathleen watched the bereaved parents incline their heads towards the coffin on its elaborate bier, then take their places in the front pew. Godfrey didn't even nod towards the bier but followed the usher's pointing hand to sit down in the second pew next to Alex Seaton. Strangely, Ernest's brother moved as far away from his relative as he could and didn't even look in his direction after the first glance.

A group of people filed in and took their places at the rear. They looked like servants and one or two nodded a greeting to Rhoda.

Kathleen stiffened as she saw her father lead another group in: the employees from the carter's yard. To her dismay his eyes seemed to settle on her almost immediately but though he stared from across the aisle for several moments, he didn't make any gesture of recognition or greeting.

She knew he'd been warned not to contact her by Mr Seaton, but did he not even care enough to nod? Apparently not. Oh, she was stupid to care still. Her father had never shown much affection to his children.

When no more guests had arrived for a while, the music changed to a sad, slow tune that Kathleen didn't recognise, and the minister came out to the front.

The service seemed to take a long time. She was unused to the way things were done in Church of England funerals, so Rhoda had to prompt her to sit and stand.

She listened to the eulogy given by Ernest's father, which seemed to be endowing his son with virtues the young man hadn't possessed.

Well, you didn't say bad things about the dear departed, did you? You tried to remember their good points. Ernest had been kind and loving, a besotted father to his two little children. That's what she would remember about her husband.

Throughout the service Mr Seaton looked angry rather than grieving. Kathleen could see him quite clearly if she looked diagonally towards the front, because there were gaps between the sparsely filled pews of well-to-do mourners.

At length the service ended and the pall-bearers came to lift up the coffin and carry it out to the churchyard. The family followed them and as they passed, Mr Seaton glanced sideways and gave Rhoda a brief nod, then gave the servants and employees another nod.

Mrs Seaton, draped in rustling black silk, was making play with her handkerchief again and though she had nodded to friends near the front, she ignored the servants and employees completely.

Kathleen and Rhoda were among the last to leave the church and make their way to the rear of the group standing round the open grave. This group didn't include the servants but it did include two or three of the employees from Seaton's. Her father was one and he was standing directly opposite her on the other side of the group.

Kathleen lowered her gaze hastily, but she could sense that he was staring at her. She and Rhoda lingered till the words of committal had been spoken and the main mourners had thrown handfuls of dirt on the coffin and left.

Rhoda grasped Kathleen's arm. 'We'll wait till they've all left, shall we?'

When the two women were the only mourners standing beside the gaping hole, Rhoda signalled to the gravediggers to wait and moved forward. She bent to pick up a handful of the damp earth and gestured to her companion to do the same.

Kathleen let her own handful of dirt fall slowly on to the highly polished coffin with its elaborate brass furniture and murmured a simple prayer for her husband, then tossed in the remaining earth and turned in obedience to Rhoda's tug.

It was over.

10

As the two women walked out of the churchyard, a figure stepped out from behind a tree, barring their way.

For a moment he stared at her. 'You're a widow now, Kathleen. You'll need your own family's help again one day, I'm sure, given the circumstances.'

He didn't wait for an answer but strode away, weaving in and out of the graves.

Rain hissed down in a sudden downpour.

'Are you all right, dear? You've gone white.'

She looked at Rhoda. 'I think my father realises I'm in danger from Cousin Godfrey and will be planning how to profit from what he sees as my good fortune.'

'Mr Seaton won't let him.'

'And what will happen when Mr Seaton dies?'

'He'll leave you well protected.'

'Will he even know that my father is planning something?'

'Of course he will. He told me once that he's keeping an eye on your father. He's instructed him not to come near you.'

'It didn't stop my father speaking to me today.' Suddenly her future seemed full of potential dangers. Not for the first time, she wished she could whisk her children away from Monks Barton and never come back again.

But how to get away without leaving a trail?

And anyway, Christopher had a right to his family inheritance, not so that he could become a carter but so that he could train for a profession, a lawyer perhaps. She might not have been able to make her simple dreams come true, but she hoped to give her children far better chances in life. It was worth staying in Monks Barton for that.

The elderly usher was again waiting for them at the entrance to the churchyard. 'I'll escort you to your carriage, Mrs Newman.'

'Thank you, Mr Balham. It's waiting for us at the inn.'

He didn't speak as he walked beside them and helped them into the carriage, then he closed the door and stepped back, raising one hand in farewell.

But he waited for them to leave before he moved back towards the church.

Neither woman had any doubt that Mr Seaton had told him to make sure they left.

* * *

Kathleen didn't try to chat and nor did Rhoda. The only sounds on the journey back were those of the falling rain pattering on the carriage roof and the soft, tuneful whistling of their driver.

After a while Kathleen wondered whether he was whistling hymns out of respect for the sadness of the day or because he was religious.

Just before they got to the village Rhoda said, 'I know you long for independence, Kathleen, and I can understand why, but is it possible for

126

any of us ever to be completely independent? We all need help from others from time to time. As you were helped by Ernest.'

Kathleen felt ashamed that she'd needed that reminder. Oh dear, life was such a tangle of needs and obligations at times.

She was glad when they got home. The first thing she did was hurry through the back garden to Mrs Dalton's house to pick up the children. She'd missed them so much.

But she slept badly that night, worrying about her father now as well as Ernest's family.

And Rhoda had been right. Godfrey might resemble Ernest but his expression was very different. If ever a man looked evil, he did.

★ ★ ★

It was three days before Mr Seaton came to see Kathleen. He didn't give her any warning of his visit, just turned up one afternoon in a hired carriage, not his own vehicle.

Continuing to be secretive, Kathleen thought, as she watched him make his way to the front door, scarf hiding the lower half of his face and hat pulled down over his eyes.

This was the sort of struggle for power that she'd read about in Miss Corelli's novels, which she couldn't put down once she started reading. *The Sorrows of Satan* was still her favourite and she'd bought herself a copy after she got married, the first of ten books she now owned and could read any time she wished.

She'd found out about Miss Corelli's books in

the newspaper originally, with a critic condemning the author as a writer of 'popular rubbish'. He'd made it sound as if there was something wrong with a writer being popular, as if you could only become popular by writing rubbish. The idea that only unpopular books had any value still puzzled her.

She realised she was standing daydreaming and Mr Seaton was knocking at her door for a second time, so hurried downstairs to let him in.

'Go and fetch Rhoda!' he ordered. 'I'll keep an eye on the children.'

But as usual Rhoda had heard a vehicle turn into the street and peeped out to see it stop outside Kathleen's house, so had thrown a shawl round her shoulders and come hurrying along to join them.

The children were clinging to Kathleen, nervous of the big, loud man they saw only occasionally.

Rhoda picked up Elizabeth and let her sit on her knee and play with her doll.

Mr Seaton studied the child, head on one side. 'She's a pretty little thing. Takes after her mother, not her father, luckily.'

That was a left-handed compliment if she'd ever heard one, Kathleen thought. 'Excuse me a moment, Mr Seaton. Christopher, dear, why don't you bring in your toy farm and play with it behind the sofa?'

As the child trotted off to fetch the box, Mr Seaton couldn't hide the pride in his eyes. 'He's a fine lad, and has a look of his Uncle Alex, thank goodness. Anyway, we'd better get down to business now. I've come to explain the new arrangements I'm making for your keep.'

And to check on me, she thought, *or you'd have sent word that you'd be coming.*

'Since Ernest isn't here to support you, I'll do it. But as he won't be here to eat your food, either, you'll need less housekeeping money than he gave you.'

He looked round slowly as if assessing every single item in the room. 'I shall continue to pay the rent on this cottage, because it's a sound little place and I won't have my grandchildren housed like paupers. I'm not happy to see you wearing black. You shouldn't wear mourning from now on if you want me to go on supporting you. It'll give you away. But don't wear fancy clothes. I still expect you to dress modestly.'

She felt angry at this restriction, and she'd never in her life worn fancy clothes. But if there was one thing she knew how to do after the last few years of taking care in his presence, it was hold her tongue.

He turned to the older woman. 'You can supervise the purchase of some suitable clothes for her, Rhoda. Not mourning.'

'I'll be happy to do that, Mr Seaton.'

He turned back to his daughter-in-law but was distracted by his grandson's game with the little wooden animals. He watched Christopher carefully and listened to him chatting to the toys as he moved them around.

'The lad speaks well for his age.'

'They both do, because I talk to them a lot.'

'It shows. Now, I'll give you half the wages

Ernest was taking home each week to cover your housekeeping. If you need anything extra for the children, Rhoda will write to me about it. Put R. N. on the back of the envelope, Rhoda, so that I'll know it's from you and open it in private.'

Kathleen saw he was waiting for her to speak and forced herself to say thank you, but thought he was being rather mean, not to mention controlling.

'I'll send you the money by postal order once a month and I'll come to see the children when I can. They'll get more interesting as they grow older, and I particularly want to keep an eye on them once they start their schooling.'

The words escaped before she could hold them back. 'I find them extremely interesting now.'

'You're the mother, so naturally you do. I'm a busy man and child-rearing is women's work. Not that you don't look after them well, and the house, too, I'll grant you that. I came without warning on purpose and I can see that you keep everything clean and tidy.'

As if she hadn't guessed that!

He got up to leave, so she went out with him. But he stopped before he opened the front door. 'I want to emphasise that you are not to have anything to do with Godfrey Seaton and are never to let him into this house. He mustn't find out that Ernest has left legitimate children.'

'I would never do anything that endangered my children, Mr Seaton, and you should know that by now.'

He stared her, then gave a little nod.

'What about my father? How much does he know about the situation?'

'Not much. I told him to stay away from you if he valued his job. Have you heard from him or seen any sign of him?'

She didn't like to tell him about the encounter in the churchyard in case it cost her father his job. Better that he kept his job and remained under the watchful eye of Mr Seaton. 'My father has never come here, thank goodness.'

'Not a loving daughter, are you?'

'No. He didn't have much to do with us children, though he thumped us if we angered him. But he always put bread on the table and a roof over our heads.'

'Aye well, he's wonderful with the horses but he's hard on the men, lashes out with his fists without thinking. I've had to speak to him about that a couple of times.'

He heaved himself up into the carriage and it set off as soon as he'd closed its door.

She went back inside with a lot to think about.

After a restless night, she came to the conclusion yet again that her children would best be served by staying here, which meant strict compliance with Mr Seaton's rules.

She'd think about their future when they were older. She wasn't at all sure that she wanted a harsh man like Mr Seaton shaping their attitudes to the world. He'd failed to bring out the best in both his sons, or to understand them and their needs. She wanted so much more than that for her children.

Without the need to pay rent, she could still

save steadily on the sort of money he'd be allowing her, even if it wasn't as much as before. She'd stop the woman doing the heavy cleaning and that would save a few shillings a week.

She felt as though the next few years would be a time for laying foundations in her children's lives.

She didn't know why she was so sure, but she was: nothing bad was likely to happen for years. This would be a growing time.

And later . . . well, some of the people involved in her life might not even be alive then.

11

Nathan did well at school but he didn't have a special friend and he continued to enjoy his own company more than other boys seemed to.

That was a good thing in the long school holidays, because his father didn't like the disruption of going away to the seaside, so they stayed at home and his father went into work most days anyway, 'just for an hour or two to check that everything's all right'.

Luckily they had a big old house with plenty of room for a boy to stay out of sight, especially if he played quietly. The attic was Nathan's favourite place. It was full of what his father called rubbish but Nathan thought of as treasures. He'd recently come across a pile of old *Strand* magazines, as well as boxes of books.

He started reading the magazines when looking for something to do during a long week of summer rain. All his friends were away and his mother had a summer cold, so she was staying in bed.

The magazines contained stories about a fictional detective called Sherlock Holmes and Nathan enjoyed them very much indeed. It seemed to him that Mr Holmes also found out things that other people didn't. Only he used the power of his mind to analyse situations, not a weird gift that still led Nathan to lost objects, whether he wanted to find them or not.

He came to the conclusion that it would be exciting to be a detective but he doubted his father would agree, or even his more tolerant mother. Well, his father thought adding up rows of figures was interesting!

As his boyhood drew to a close Nathan thought a lot about the world and his place in it and formed his own conclusions. He didn't see why it was a bad thing to help people find things they'd lost and one day he would stop pretending about that.

In the meantime he occasionally helped someone out, but only if he could make it look like sheer chance or luck that he'd found what they were searching for.

Once he met a young woman in the street who had dropped a locket her sweetheart had given her and was almost hysterical with grief. Nathan managed to persuade her to walk back the way she'd come and they easily 'found' the locket.

What was wrong in doing that? he wondered afterwards. Nothing that he could understand. It was a turning point for him.

It made him feel good to see how happy the people were to retrieve their possessions. He'd go on helping people, he decided, even if it was only in small ways.

He had other unusual reactions to the world, too, besides his ability to find missing objects. Sometimes, when he went into an old building, cold shivers would run down his spine and he'd know that something bad had once happened there. He didn't actually see ghosts but he sensed their presence. Oh yes he did, whatever his father said about them not existing.

There was, Nathan was sure, a great deal more to the world than what people could see, something *beyond* the everyday human experience. Well, the Christian religion insisted on that, didn't it? Other religions did too, so it wasn't necessarily wrong or evil.

Because he was almost at the end of his schooling now, he began to plan for a future he'd enjoy. And as soon as he was earning a living, he'd leave home, even if he could only afford to rent one room.

He'd once mentioned that he'd be leaving home when he was older, and his mother had grown quite agitated, begging him not even to think of it.

When she calmed down, she said confidently, 'Anyway, you can't do that till you're married, dear. Your father simply won't allow it.'

But he still wasn't sure he wanted to marry, not if it meant living a duplicitous life.

The trouble was, Nathan knew his mother shook with terror on the rare occasions when she annoyed her husband, and wept in secret afterwards. Sometimes he was able to divert his father's attention elsewhere.

On his optimistic days he felt there had to be some way to persuade her to let him go, some way to encourage her to stand up for herself. At his more realistic moments he understood that she would never willingly let him go.

Nor would his father.

★ ★ ★

At the age of seventeen, as he was about to start his final year of grammar school, Nathan was summoned to his father's study. Unusually, his mother was there as well, but she avoided his eyes and concentrated on her needlework, so he knew this wasn't about something pleasant.

'Sit down, lad. We need to have a serious talk with you about your future.'

He didn't like the sound of this. His father never said 'discuss' or asked his family what they wanted; he just ordered them all around. Saying nothing, Nathan took a seat and waited.

'After you leave school, you'll need to find a job.'

'I was hoping to go to university to study science.' That was another way of finding things, he felt, making discoveries about the world.

'What? No, no! I'm not having that.'

Nathan's dreams crashed in flames at the staccato certainty of his father's tone. He'd been planning to get his teachers' and his mother's help during the course of the year to persuade his father to let him study science.

'Apart from anything else, I don't approve of what goes on in universities. Students lead an idle life for several years when they should be learning good working habits so that they can support themselves and their families after they marry. And now that women are allowed to study there, it's even worse. Who knows what such females get up to?'

He waited a minute but Nathan knew better than to interrupt or comment at this stage.

'No, in my opinion, universities are a waste of

time for all but the idle rich! Better for people like us to start as we mean to go on, my boy, by working hard at a *real* job.'

'I do work hard at my studies, Father.'

'Yes, your school reports have been excellent, I'll grant you that. I'd not have let you stay on till eighteen otherwise. But we must look to the future now and plan what you're going to do for the rest of your life. Therefore, when you leave school next summer I've arranged for you to start work in my friend Frewen's accounting firm.'

His father still had *that look* on his face and *that tone* in his voice, so Nathan knew his dreams were going to be dashed whatever he said or did. He kept silent only with great difficulty, for all his years of practice, because this was so important to him.

'You'll inherit our family firm one day, so you'll need a thorough training in accountancy. I don't believe that this training should be done initially by a family member. No, best you experience other ways of doing things before you come to work at Perry's and learn *our* ways. At the same time, you'll make various useful contacts at Frewen's. It's important to know the right people.'

As his father outlined the steps by which his son would gradually rise to become a chartered accountant like his father and grandfather before him, Nathan fought to control his anger and sorrow.

He succeeded, but vowed that one day he would find a way to be free and do as he liked with his life. In the meantime he was, he realised suddenly, enough like his father where money was concerned not to throw away what would be a very comfortable inheritance one day. And if that meant he was mercenary, so be it. Being sensible was a better way of describing it, wasn't it? Especially when your mother needed you so desperately.

His father looked at him across the big desk in his study. 'Well? You're very quiet. Have you nothing to say about what I've arranged?'

Nathan forced suitable words out. 'I'm still taking it all in, sir. I'm . . . um . . . grateful for your help.'

His father gave a tight little nod. 'Good. You will start work at Frewen's on the Monday after you finish your last year of school. And, of course, you'll also start studying to become a chartered accountant. It'll be a busy few years for you but well worth it. Oh, and I'll warn you now not to plan to get married until you're fully qualified, because I won't have it. Later on your mother and I will help you find a suitable wife. But not yet.'

The fire of rebellion flared up again for a few moments at this further, quite gratuitous edict, but Nathan fought it down once more.

Thank goodness his thoughts were his own. Even his father couldn't control those.

But when he was safe in bed, he couldn't hold back a few tears, even though men were not supposed to cry. He had wanted so much to go to university, to explore the foundations of the physical world, to learn interesting facts about the universe, to meet other people.

To get away from his father.

★ ★ ★

That final year at school seemed to fly past. As the months ticked by, Nathan became quieter than before, standing at the edge of groups, not rejected but not fully a part of them, either, because they were making all sorts of exciting plans and no one considered accountancy exciting.

He didn't have the carefree confidence in life that his classmates did. Couldn't feel like that after his big disappointment. Especially when he heard them discussing universities and which ones to try for.

He summed up his achievements and capabilities to himself one day. He was quite good at sport and very good at mathematics and science. He had a few friends, though no one really close, had no enemies that he knew of and was praised lavishly by his teachers for his hard work and his potential for academic success.

At the formal school dances, held in conjunction with the sixth form of the nearby girls' grammar school, he'd met girls, pretty ones too. Dancing with them was pleasant, but none of them ever sighed over him, he could tell that, and he wasn't strongly attracted to any of them, either.

He knew that he would get good results in his examinations, because he'd found the examination papers very straightforward. It was a bitter final blow that he could easily have got into a good university — Oxford or Cambridge, even.

Before he left school, his headmaster made one last attempt to persuade his father to allow this. Nathan could have told him it'd be useless.

All it achieved was to make the atmosphere at home very fraught.

And then suddenly school was over and the new clothes his father had bought him were brought to his bedroom on the Sunday evening. The school uniform was consigned to the attic.

There had been a discussion of whether he should wear a morning coat and top hat to work, as his father did, but his mother had prevailed by worrying gently that he'd look different from the other young gentlemen you saw in the various businesses, who all seemed to be wearing lounge coats these days.

Fortunately his father loathed the thought of his son seeming different in any way, so Nathan was allowed to dress as his contemporaries did. Thank goodness for that. It meant he would be wearing a bowler hat with a round crown and a narrow, curled up brim instead of a top hat, and a navy lounge suit instead of a frock coat.

On the Monday morning he got up early and put on the new clothes, sighing. They felt very different from his school uniform, especially the high, starched collar. It seemed as if he'd put on shackles.

He studied himself in the mirror, grimacing at the sharp-featured face that stared solemnly back at him. His mother had been right about one thing. He had grown into his face, and his nose no longer looked quite as big. But still, no one would ever call him handsome.

He picked up the small leather purse his father had given him and shook it, listening to the faint clinking sounds of the coins inside it. This allowance was to last him for the first month. At the end of that time, he would start receiving regular wages and would be expected to manage on his own earnings. That would be good for him, his father said, teach him the value of money.

The allowance wasn't generous. His father was never generous with money, except when *he* wanted something. But there was enough money for daily expenses with a little left over.

There was a tap on the bedroom door and his mother came in. 'My goodness, you do look smart, Nathan darling.'

'You're not usually up this early, Mother.'

'It's not every day my son starts work. I thought you and I could have breakfast together. Your father is still asleep.'

That was one small mercy, at least.

By the time the meal was over, his father had got up. As taciturn as always in the mornings, he only nodded to his son as he accepted a cup of tea from his wife.

Nathan put on his hat, kissed his mother goodbye at the door and walked briskly down the street. He'd already timed how long it would take him to get to work and had decided to set off earlier and walk there to get some exercise, instead of taking the tram into town.

His father's body was plump and soft, and he

panted if he had to walk up many stairs. Nathan did not intend to become like him, not in any way if he could help it.

Just before nine o'clock, he entered the building where Frewen and Sons was situated and reported to Mr Sanderson. His father said the chief clerk was a shrewd old fellow, who would teach Nathan far more than any book ever could. He hoped so. He still enjoyed learning for its own sake.

He didn't allow himself to sigh as Mr Sanderson got out some ledgers and began explaining how to make entries. Nathan already knew that from his occasional visits to Perry's to help out when the office boy was on holiday. The system at Frewen's was just as straightforward and could have been explained in five minutes, not fifteen.

He didn't want to spend his life adding up columns of figures and writing in dusty old ledgers. But if he had to become an accountant, then he'd learn to deal with the account books properly. He could never bear to do things sloppily.

There was enough rebellion still simmering in his mind for him to go out at noon and suck in great deep breaths of fresh air. All morning he had watched the dust motes floating in the air of the office he shared with the other clerks and wished they were allowed to open a window.

He could tell already that the next few years would not be very interesting.

Part Two

1907–1911

12

The seasons passed and Kathleen enjoyed her children's early years. She also enjoyed living in her own cosy cottage, if truth be told, without anyone to tell her what to do or take up too much space in bed. She felt guilty at how little she missed Ernest. She played with her children, read to them and taught them as much as she could about dealing with life. You were never too young to learn.

She saw Rhoda nearly every day, except when her neighbour would disappear for a whole day, sometimes for two or three. Kathleen longed to ask about this but Rhoda had only explained her absences vaguely. 'It's my ladies' group, dear. We're helping other women, but the work we do is often secret so I'm afraid I can't tell you any more.'

How did Rhoda help people? Kathleen would have liked to do something as worthwhile as that, because she felt she needed a purpose in her life other than caring for her children.

She had learnt to type and keep simple accounts, but had no way of using those skills. She felt so frustrated at times she could have screamed — if she'd been the screaming sort. Instead she told herself sternly to be glad of what she did have and stop wishing for the moon.

The trouble was the moon was so bright and beautiful, as were some of the places and activities she read about in the newspapers.

* * *

In almost no time, it seemed, Christopher was five and more than ready to start school. He was such a clever boy she'd have liked to send him to a better school than the one in the next village, with its two mixed classes, junior and senior, and its simple lessons.

She even got as far as asking Mr Seaton to pay the fees for a better school, but he refused point-blank to consider it. 'We're trying to keep your children's existence a secret, Kathleen. It's the safest thing to do.'

'But — '

'You must trust me on this. Anyway, how would you get your son to Swindon and back every day? Hmm?'

'We could move nearer to town, or to another town. Change our surname. There must be a way.'

'Well, I'm not risking it. We're trying to keep you hidden, not send you where a certain person might recognise you or where you'll stand out as a stranger. Besides, you have Rhoda just down the street here to keep an eye on things and send to me for help if you need it. Surely you wouldn't want to leave her?'

Kathleen could only sigh at his solution of burying her and the children in a quiet little village, which didn't even have a railway station. If there hadn't been a library in the next village, she'd have gone mad from boredom in the evenings.

Or run away.

She still thought of doing that occasionally, when the tedium of daily life got her down, but common sense prevailed because she couldn't think of any way to escape without being followed. It sounded easy in novels; it wasn't easy in real life. And Mr Seaton was right about one thing. She didn't want to move away from Rhoda.

However, she played her last card to see what he'd say. 'I'm afraid the village school isn't noted for giving a good education. I'm not at all happy about that.'

He sat frowning for a few moments, then said, 'I'll see what I can do to improve the local school. We don't want Christopher to be badly educated.'

She didn't believe him and thought that he was just pacifying her. And oh, she wished he'd sometimes mention Elizabeth when talking about her children's future, because her daughter was just as clever as her son. But Mr Seaton only mentioned the little girl in passing and his thoughts were mainly on Christopher's needs. The lad would, he assured her regularly, be his heir one day.

As if that was the only thing she cared about. She wasn't even sure she wanted him to work with his grandfather.

Mr Seaton would never change, she decided. Like so many men, he didn't see women as important in the wider world, even his own granddaughter. And he ran his business in an old-fashioned way. Even she could tell that.

The world was changing. Rich people were replacing their horses with motor cars. And even poorer people were managing to see more of the world, do more things.

★ ★ ★

To everyone's surprise, the schoolmistress in charge of the junior class at the school in the next village resigned and moved away during the summer holidays of 1907, and a much younger and livelier woman took her place in charge of the junior class.

Miss Tolver might not be the senior teacher at the school, but she certainly shook the whole place up, changing the books used to teach reading in the lower class to more modern ones. Where these came from, no one knew. But she wasn't content with that and solicited donations from the better-off members of the community to buy extra reading books for the brighter children to practise on.

That meant the senior teacher had to buy better books for the older pupils as well.

'And about time too,' Rhoda said. 'You must feel better about the school now.'

Kathleen had to wonder if Mr Seaton had had a hand in the abrupt arrival of Miss Tolver, but somehow she didn't like to ask him outright. She knew Rhoda reported back to him from time to time, but trusted her friend not to betray secrets like her savings account.

That year, without her even asking, Mr Seaton increased her allowance to what it had been when Ernest was alive, saying gruffly that growing children needed good food and new clothes.

He came every few weeks to check on them. The children were invariably nervous in his presence. They knew he was their grandfather, but he'd stressed emphatically that they were not to tell anyone about that, so they were scared to even mention his name to people.

He always commented that they looked to be a healthy pair, but didn't spend long with them and made no attempt to gain their affection or get to know them properly. In fact, he spent more time with Rhoda, with whom he seemed more comfortable.

Kathleen didn't think he'd ever played with a child in his life. Which was his loss.

★　★　★

In 1910, when Christopher was eight, Mr Seaton didn't turn up for the second month running. That wasn't like him, so Kathleen asked Rhoda if everything was all right.

'I'd have heard if there were any problems at Cumberland Villa, dear.'

'Are you sure? He keeps our existence a secret, so they might not know to send us a message.'

'He'd have found a way to let me know.'

'Not if he's dead.'

Rhoda stared at her in surprise. 'He's a busy man, dear, that's all. Now, if you don't mind, I have to get ready to go to my meeting. My lady friends and I have rather a lot on at the moment.'

That evening Kathleen was looking out of her front window when she saw her father outside, standing in the shadow of the huge old tree just down the street. That was unusual enough to make her heart skitter in her chest. She'd not seen him since the funeral and she knew Mr Seaton had forbidden him to come near her, so her father was risking his job.

He must have seen her at the window watching out for the children coming home from school, as she did every afternoon, but he made no attempt to signal to her. He just stood there, motionless, gazing round.

Had something bad happened to Mr Seaton? Was her father intending to push his way into her cottage and start telling her what to do again? Or had he come to see the children? His hair was more grizzled now, but he was still a big, strong man and no doubt still got his own way most of the time.

She moved to the back of the room, standing out of sight, watching him.

Why had he come? Why now?

When Ernest had failed to turn up, it had been because he'd died. Surely either she or Rhoda would have heard by now if her father-in-law had died? A chill ran down her spine at the thought, because if he had died, his nephew might hurt her children, who stood between him and the family fortune.

She'd grown too complacent, too comfortable in her little world, taking the easy way out, she admitted to herself. But the children had had some happy childhood years and she'd continued to save money, so it still seemed to have been the right thing to do.

But now she ought to work out an escape plan

because the children were old enough to understand the need and to keep quiet about it to their friends. She had money saved now and she would be able to —

She sucked in her breath and forgot everything as the shadowy figure in the periphery of her vision suddenly moved, taking a step forward. Holding her breath, she watched her father stare down the street in the other direction.

Were the children coming home from school? Was that what he was waiting for? If so, she'd run out and —

To her relief, when Christopher and Elizabeth came into sight, they were walking beside her kind neighbour Mrs Dalton, who was carrying a shopping basket and chatting to them.

Surely he wouldn't accost them where someone could see him? He didn't. He merely stood watching intently. As they got closer, he edged back until he was mostly concealed behind the tree trunk. She could see him, but they probably wouldn't notice him.

Still talking, the children passed the tree. At the gate they waved goodbye to Mrs Dalton who went on to Grandpa Brownley's cottage. She sometimes gave the old man a few groceries, Kathleen knew.

She had the door open before the children got there and after they came inside, she locked it, sagging against it for a moment.

'What are you locking the door for at this time of day, Mum?' Christopher asked.

'There was a strange man wandering round and I was worried he might try to get in and steal something. We'll go and lock the back door as well, then I'll get you something to eat and you can tell me what you did at school today.'

But when the children were safely seated with their milk and biscuits, she slipped into the front room and peeped out of the window again.

There was no one behind the tree now and her father wasn't anywhere in the street, either. In future she'd be careful to keep the front door locked all the time.

Maybe she should go and meet the children from school every day, even though it was a couple of miles away in the next village?

No, they'd feel humiliated by that. Other mothers didn't collect their children. Older brothers or sisters brought them home when they were little and as they grew older, they walked back with neighbours' children. Some, even quite little ones, walked at least part of the way alone, especially those from small farms outside the village.

She returned to the kitchen in time to see a man walk past in the back lane. She could only see the top of his head above the hedge, but she recognised her father's forehead and thick, coarse hair.

She pressed one hand against her stomach which suddenly felt as if it was full of lead. He was learning the lie of the land, she guessed. Why? Was he intending to break in?

Dear heaven, what would she have done if he'd tried? How could she possibly have stopped a strong man like him?

But he moved on and after that there was no sign of him at the front or back.

She forced herself to calm down. She would do what she had to, whatever it took to protect her children. And she'd finish making those plans. Oh yes, she would.

She still considered it better to stay here for a year or two longer if they could, but she was going to be ready to act.

★ ★ ★

In the morning, Kathleen walked as far as the edge of the village with Christopher and Elizabeth on the excuse that she was going to the shop. On the way they met some of the other children from school and when she stopped at the shop, the group of children walked off together, chattering away.

She didn't really need anything, but people might wonder if she didn't go in now she was here, so she bought some flour and three pieces of liquorice root for a treat tonight. They all loved to chew on the twig-like pieces and get a mouth full of the flavour.

That afternoon there was a knock on the front door and she checked who was there before she opened it, relieved to see Rhoda.

'Since when do you lock your door?' her friend asked.

'Since yesterday. I'll give you a key to let yourself in, but I'm keeping it locked all the time from now on.'

When they were both inside, she turned the key again.

'What's happened?' Rhoda asked.

'My father was in the village yesterday, standing across the road under that tree staring at this cottage. Then he watched the children come home from school. I was worried he'd try to talk to them but they were walking with Mrs Dalton, thank goodness. I saw him later walking along the back lane. Something *must* have happened to Mr Seaton.'

'I'm afraid it has.'

'He *is* dead, then?'

'No, no. But I heard today that he's been very ill. Pneumonia. They thought he was going to die. He's turned the corner now but it'll be a while before he recovers properly.'

'How did you find out?'

'One of the ladies I meet with in connection with our charity work told me about it.' Rhoda didn't tell Kathleen about her work in detail, because it was done secretly wherever possible. She greatly admired the young woman now running the Greyladies Trust and was happy to be involved.

Rhoda realised Kathleen had spoken and was waiting for an answer. 'Sorry. My thoughts wandered for a moment. What did you say?'

'That I was sorry to hear my father-in-law had been ill.'

'Yes. Apparently Mr Seaton's wife was frantically worried about him. Well, she would be. She doesn't love him, but she needs a husband to make money for her, because she spends it without thinking, and also, he gives her credibility in her social life. Widows don't get nearly as many invitations.'

'You don't sound as if you like her.'

'I don't. The thing is, Kathleen dear, this has made me consider what may happen to you if Mr Seaton dies suddenly. His wife won't help you. And though he keeps telling us he's going to make provisions for the children, bring them out into the open as his heirs, arrange a good education for them, he always says 'in a year or two'. I'm sure he means that and is only insisting on you staying here quietly to keep them safe.'

'I hope you're right. If it isn't safe, he would find it so much easier than I would to set us up in a new life somewhere. I'm so ignorant about the world.' After a pause, she asked, 'Do you think I'm right to stay here?'

'At the moment, yes. My main worry is that he might die before he acknowledges them. From things he's said, I think he worries that the lawyer might say something to Godfrey if he changed his will. Lawyers are supposed to keep such things confidential, but Mr Seaton doesn't seem to trust anyone these days.' Rhoda paused and added, in a tone of foreboding, 'And then there's his nephew taking advantage of the situation. Apparently when Mr Seaton fell ill, he went to the yard and tried to poke his nose into how the business is run, but your father refused to obey him.'

She hesitated. 'Maybe you should consult a lawyer yourself about the children's position, find out whether they'll be entitled to inherit anything if he doesn't put them in his will. They're more closely related to him than the nephew is, after all.'

155

Kathleen took the kettle off the hotplate and brewed a pot of tea. 'I'm beginning to wonder whether I want my children to inherit anything if their grandmother is unfriendly and Godfrey Seaton hostile.'

'Speak to a lawyer about it.'

Kathleen shook her head. 'If Mr Seaton found out I'd consulted a lawyer, I think he'd be very angry indeed. I'm not certain of much but I am certain of that.'

She poured them cups of tea and they sat at the kitchen table sipping it slowly. 'What I need is somewhere the children and I can flee to at a moment's notice if anything happens to Mr Seaton, just in case Godfrey is as bad as you seem to think. I've been wondering where I could go, but it's not easy to find somewhere truly safe.'

'I may be able to help you with that. The ladies I'm working with are going to do something to help women who need somewhere to take refuge, just as you may do. There is some money available and we're going to look for a house where they'll be safe. It'll probably be a few months before we can pull everything together. In the meantime my advice is to stay here, but be ready to leave at a moment's notice. You could run down the lane to my house, if necessary. And I'll tell one or two of the neighbours to come running if you call for help.'

'Oh, I wish I could be certain what the right thing to do is.'

'I feel sure you should wait until we see how Mr Seaton goes on and perhaps by then our

156

refuge will be ready.'

Kathleen thanked her and decided to follow Rhoda's advice. Her friend was older and knew more about the world than she did. She could only pray Mr Seaton didn't die suddenly.

But she had to get ready to flee, that at least she could do.

Her first action was to take ten pounds out of her savings and sew it into the lining of her old leather shopping bag. She then hid her bank book carefully inside a book standing in the shelf in her front room. She had to cut the middles out of the pages to do that and it upset her to damage a book, but her children's safety was far more important.

At least if you had money you were not totally helpless, as she'd felt before she ran away from home and rushed into marriage with Ernest.

13

It was three more months before Mr Seaton sent word that he was fully recovered and during that time, in May, King Edward died, which went to show that no one could avoid death, Kathleen thought, no matter how rich they were.

The papers reported that the King's funeral at the end of the month had brought more royals together in one place than the world had ever seen before. She'd never heard of most of these small countries, and didn't care who they were anyway. All she really cared about at the moment was keeping her children safe.

Rhoda had been to see Mr Seaton a couple of times and said he'd aged a lot lately, but he insisted he was feeling better all the time. She didn't say so but she was clearly worried about him. Kathleen wondered if he was fooling himself about how well he was, but people could tick along in poor health for years, she'd seen it happen, so she had to hope for the best.

She felt on edge now in her cosy little cottage, which had seemed so safe before. She was forever watching over her shoulder, wondering what to do if there was trouble.

The children protested about her fussing but did as she asked most of the time, which was always to walk home with other people, always to keep the outer doors locked and never to sleep with bedroom windows open.

It was another month before her father-in-law was driven over to visit them and Kathleen was shocked by how much older and frailer he looked. It was one thing to hear from Rhoda that he'd aged a lot, quite another to see him shuffle slowly into her house using a walking stick like a man of eighty.

Even his voice had lost its mellifluous tone and he spent more time complaining about how motor cars and omnibuses were taking away his trade than in discussing her situation.

Eventually, since he didn't raise the matter, she asked, 'What shall I do if anything happens to you? You were going to think about it. I'm really worried about the children's safety.'

He sighed. 'I'm worried too. When my head stops aching so much, I'll see my lawyer and make some plans, get things drawn up legally. The trouble is, the carting business isn't bringing in as much money as it used to so I have to go carefully, make the money spin out. Lawyers are expensive.'

He fumbled in his pocket and brought out a money pouch, taking out four five-pound notes and handing them to her. 'I brought this, just in case.'

'In case of what?'

'In case you need some money suddenly. How should I know what you might need? Put it away safely. I doubt you'll have to use it, but it's always wise to have something to tide you over.'

He took his leave soon afterwards, leaving her more worried than ever. He had been so vague, talking as if there was no real hurry to do anything. She'd known there wasn't a lot of time left as soon as she looked at him. She understood what that fragile, almost transparent look meant for an old person. Well, it was obvious that he was on his last legs.

That evening she sat the children down and explained the whole situation and its implications to them in more detail than ever before, telling them all she knew about Godfrey Seaton. 'We may have to flee at a minute's notice and if so, you must do exactly as I tell you.'

At eight and seven years old they shouldn't have had to face this, but since it was a distinct possibility, she wanted them to be properly prepared, so that they wouldn't do anything stupid.

Finally, she tried to make them understand that they mustn't tell anyone except Rhoda about this, not a word to their friends. 'Not — one — word,' she repeated emphatically. 'Promise me.'

They asked several questions till they understood the situation, clever questions, too, for such young children. Then they went very quiet, with Christopher taking his sister's hand, something he'd normally scorn to do.

'Are you sure we'll have to move away from here?' he asked at last.

'I'm fairly sure it'll be necessary one day. I just don't know when. But if we do have to run away, well, it'll be to save our lives, so we'll have no choice and I want no fussing and complaining.'

'We won't. And I promise I won't leave Elizabeth on her own on the way back from school ever again.'

She didn't comment on what that remark had given away.

'*You* mustn't be on your own either, Christopher. And you must neither of you trust strangers. For instance, if anyone tells you they've come with a message from me and are going to take you to me, it'll be a lie. If there's a problem while you're at school, I'll come to get you myself.'

'What if you couldn't come? What if you really did have to send us a message to tell us to meet you somewhere?'

She didn't dare cut off any avenue of possible action, just in case. But how would she make a message safe?

Her son brightened up suddenly. 'I know. In the past few *Comic Cuts* some boys are having an adventure. It's so exciting and they use a password to make sure messages aren't tricks. We could do that.'

She was dubious but didn't want to destroy his eagerness to help. 'I doubt we'll have to go to those lengths, Christopher.'

'But we might. And you always say it's good to be prepared. Let's plan it now, Mum. I know it'll work.'

She gave in. At least this might make keeping a secret more exciting, though she doubted a password would ever become necessary. As for *Comic Cuts*, she thought it a very silly little magazine, but her son was mad for it, so she and another boy's mother bought the two lads a copy on alternate weeks. 'Very well. What password shall we use?'

They were all silent for a moment or two, then Christopher clapped his hands together. 'How about Timbuktu.'

'Isn't that too hard a word for Elizabeth to remember?' Kathleen worried.

'No, it's not,' her daughter said. 'I'm sick of the sound of it. Those in the senior class at school have been reading about the stupid place and they all keep chanting the name.'

'Then they'll all know the password, so that won't do.'

Christopher grinned. 'We could change it to Timbukthree, though. They won't know that and it'll be easy to remember.'

Elizabeth clapped her hands, smiling and entering into the spirit of things now. 'That's a good idea.'

The children still didn't appreciate the deadly seriousness of their situation, Kathleen realised, but she'd done as much as she could think of for the moment. And even if they treated it like a new sort of game, they'd do as she told them, which was what counted.

Another worry was preying on her mind. What was she going to do with them during the school holidays, which were fast approaching? Normally they played out with their friends, roaming the woods and paths near the village, but she'd be terrified to let them loose on their own in the countryside at present.

Later that day Rhoda came to report on another visit to Mr Seaton. 'I asked him if he'd come up with any ideas about how to keep you and the children safe. I'm afraid he spoke sharply to me. But oh, dear, he looked even more unwell than when he came to see us. And him barely sixty!'

The Seatons didn't seem long-lived as a family, Kathleen thought. She hoped her children would grow up stronger and healthier than their father and grandfather. They would if it was up to her.

* * *

A couple of weeks before the end of the school term Kathleen heard that her mother had died suddenly and was thrown into a quandary as to whether she should attend the funeral. Her conscience said she ought to, even though she'd not been close to her mother. Her brain said she'd be a fool to risk going openly into Swindon.

When a shabby little pony and trap stopped in front of her house and a man got out, she didn't recognise him at first. Then he turned towards the house and she realised it was her father. He was looking careworn.

She couldn't refuse to let him in, but was relieved to see Rhoda hurrying along the street to join them. Her friend's nosiness was comforting rather than annoying these days, making it feel as if someone was always keeping an eye on her and the children. Today it was a godsend to have someone else there and she waited till Rhoda arrived before she took her father into the front room.

'We'll not be needing someone else poking her

nose into our business,' he said at once. 'No offence, missus, but this is for the Keller family to sort out.'

'Rhoda's my best friend and she helps me a lot. I'll feel better to have her advice.'

His lips tightened to a straight line for a few seconds but he didn't make any further protests. 'You've heard about your mother?'

'Yes. I got a letter from Mr Seaton.'

'He said he'd let you know. I want you there at the funeral. I want all my family there, showing respect for Deirdre.'

Without thinking, she blurted out, 'I'm worried about the danger.'

'What danger? What do you mean?'

As she hesitated, he added sharply, 'How can you be in danger, all comfortable in this cottage with Mr Seaton keeping an eye on you and paying you decent money every week? You have an easy life, my girl, and should be on your knees thanking God for it morning and night.'

Annoyed by this, she explained the situation to him. He hadn't heard any details about the threat posed by Godfrey Seaton, but didn't seem all that surprised at how eager the nephew was to inherit.

'I knew he was jealous of Mr Ernest being born to money, well, everyone did. Most people are guessing that Mr Godfrey will inherit one day now that Mr Ernest is dead, but I doubt it. Mr Seaton doesn't like him at all. You can tell. Only . . . surely Godfrey won't commit murder to get hold of the money?'

He was silent for a few seconds, then added,

'That explains why Mr Seaton gets all het up whenever his nephew comes to visit. I don't know why he doesn't just tell Mr Godfrey to stay away.'

'He likes to keep an eye on him, I think,' Rhoda said. 'And Mrs Seaton gets on well with Godfrey. You'd think he was *her* blood relative, not her husband's.'

Fergus frowned, and began drumming his fingers on the chair arm, an annoying habit he had. 'Anyway, the Seatons are not the point today. It's your bounden duty to come to your mother's funeral, Kathleen, and don't try to deny it.'

'Who's doing the funeral?'

'Mr Godfrey's funeral company.'

'Oh, dear! He'll know about my mother, then, and be expecting me to be there.'

'You surely don't think he's going to attack you at a funeral with your father and brothers there to protect you! Anyway, he doesn't do the cheaper funerals himself, so I doubt he'll be in attendance.'

'Why did you go to such an expensive firm?'

'Mr Godfrey sent me word he'd reduce the price on account of me working for his uncle, so I agreed. I thought my Deirdre deserved a better send-off than I could afford, and that includes all her children being present, Kathleen Frances.'

Most likely her father had been easily tempted because he wanted to show off to his friends. But still . . . he was right about one thing: it was a daughter's duty to attend her mother's funeral and she'd never forgive herself if she didn't do that. 'If I come, it'll have to be in disguise. I'll wear a veil, hide my face, stay at the back of the church.'

He sat frowning, then said, 'I suppose you could do that. I can always tell people afterwards that you were there. Make sure you come, though, I'll see you regret it if you stay away.'

'There's no need to make threats. I *want* to attend Ma's funeral. Where is it?'

'Where do you think? At our church, of course, and your mother will be buried in the churchyard.'

'How will Kathleen get there, Mr Keller?' Rhoda asked. 'It's a long way from here, much too far for her to walk.'

He frowned, thought for a minute then said, 'I'll send a motor car to fetch her.'

'A car?' Kathleen looked at her father in amazement. How could he afford that?

'I'm after learning how to drive one of them stinking machines, because anyone can see that's the way of the future, not horses. My friend Bill owns a car and he's teaching me. It's not all that hard. He uses the car as a taxi cab and he'll give me a good price on your fare.'

He grimaced. 'I wish the damned things had never been invented but I swore when I left Ireland that I'd do whatever I had to so that my family would never go hungry again. And I meant it. Mr Seaton may think he can still make a good living from his business but it's been going steadily downhill for years, and more so since he took ill. I can see the writing on the wall: horses and carts are going to be gradually replaced by lorries and cars, and *he* isn't going to make old bones, anyway.'

He stood up. 'So I'll be sending my friend Bill to collect you in his taxi and he'll bring you back here afterwards. The funeral is on Wednesday at one o'clock in the afternoon.'

When he'd gone she looked at Rhoda. 'I don't want to take the children. Can they come to you after school on Wednesday?'

'Yes, of course, dear.'

14

Kathleen got out the heavy mourning garments she'd worn for her husband's funeral and gave them a good shake. They looked too fine for her family's funeral and they'd be rather warm on a sunny day like this, but they were all she had and she was sure her father would be offended if she didn't wear some sort of mourning.

Bill arrived on time with the car. He proved to be a quiet man, friendly enough but not inclined to chat. Which suited her just fine.

When he dropped her off at the church, he said, 'I'll collect you from here after the burial.' He didn't wait for her answer but drove away.

She felt vulnerable as she walked inside the building and uncomfortable at the thought of Catholic rituals after years of worshipping in the Church of England.

She took a seat at the rear of the church, but a man walked down to her from the front and said, 'There's a place for you in the family pews unless you're too fine these days to sit with your brothers and sisters.'

'Patrick? Is that you? I didn't recognise you.'

'And no one would recognise *you*, dressed like an old crow with your face hidden from the world.'

She flinched from his sharp tone. 'I arranged with Da that I'd wear a heavy veil and sit here at the back, so as not to be recognised. There's someone I don't want to see me and now you're drawing attention to me.'

'Well, I reckon that's just an excuse to stay away from your family and I'm not having it. Think you're better than us, don't you? Well, you're not!'

He grabbed her arm and pulled her to her feet. He was as strong as her father and she could do nothing about it without creating a scene, so whispered, 'Let go. I'm coming.'

Until then she hadn't noticed the sharp-faced man staring at her from the far end of a pew on the other side of the aisle, but she did now and quickly realised she'd seen him somewhere before. She couldn't remember exactly where and that worried her. She was sure he didn't live anywhere near her. She knew everyone in Monks Barton by sight and most of them by name too. So who was he and why was he staring?

Keeping her head down, she took her place near the front. Her brothers and sisters edged along to make room, but none of them spoke to her. Her father looked round and nodded once, as if satisfied.

She felt angry that he hadn't kept his word to let her sit at the back. It was typical of him. Patrick would have obeyed their father if he'd said to leave her where she was, because from the way he'd behaved with her, Fergus still ruled his family, and probably the men who worked under him as well, with a rod of iron.

The service was brief and what the priest said about her mother didn't sound at all like the Deirdre Keller her daughter had known. But then, people rarely spoke ill of the dead; they told kind lies to comfort the bereaved relatives.

When the service was over, Fergus and his sons helped carry the coffin out and Kathleen's sister whispered, 'That's Godfrey Seaton walking in front of the coffin. He looks as if he eats well.'

Kathleen stared at the man who was causing her so much trouble. She'd seen him in the distance before, but never up close, nor had she ever spoken to him. His resemblance to Ernest upset her once again.

Everyone filed out behind the coffin and Kathleen stayed in the middle of her family. But when they got to the grave she felt a shiver run down her spine as she saw Godfrey Seaton staring at her from across the gaping hole. Did he know who she was? He was looking at her as if he hated her, so he must. More important for her peace of mind, did he know where she lived? If he did, she might have to leave secretly.

The grave was at the rear of the church in the untidy corner where they buried the poorer folk. Her father's desire to show off hadn't stretched to a fancy grave plot nearer the front and there were no marble monuments back here.

If he hadn't been offered a cheap price, he probably wouldn't have made such a fuss about the funeral. He and his wife had shared a house and created children together, but they'd never seemed loving towards one another. In the final few years before Kathleen left home, her mother had always seemed too tired for anything but struggling on.

Well, she was a fine one to talk, Kathleen

thought guiltily. She'd not loved her husband, either.

She glanced round as the words of committal ended. And there he was again, the sharp-faced man, not standing with her parents' friends and neighbours, but half-hidden behind a tombstone at the corner of the church. He was looking towards Godfrey Seaton, nodding, as if he was ready to do something.

Suddenly she remembered where she'd seen him: driving a pony and trap with Godfrey Seaton in it. Her heart fluttered in her chest. What if he followed her home? What if he attacked her children?

As her father stepped back from the open grave, she edged forward to join him, tugging his arm. 'Da!'

'What's wrong? Can you not even stand quietly while your mother's being laid to rest?'

'Da, there's a man following me. I *told* you it'd be dangerous for me to come here. Look at the corner of the church but don't let him see you staring.'

He nodded, waiting a moment or two before twisting his head for a quick glance. 'Thin fellow, bald? I know him. He works for Godfrey Seaton, brings him to the yard sometimes.'

'Yes, that's him. He looked at me then nodded towards his master as if to say he was going to do something for him.'

'You're sure he's been following you?'

'Certain.'

'Godfrey's a wicked devil, so he is.' Fergus sighed and glanced at the coffin. 'I can't do

171

anything at the moment, Kathleen Frances. This is my wife's funeral, after all. And anyway, I don't want Godfrey to think I'm not ready to obey him. I don't want to lose my job as long as Mr Seaton is still running the yard.'

He moved forward to toss some earth on his wife's grave and seized the opportunity to speak to his eldest son. 'Patrick! Come here. There's someone following your sister. Bald fellow standing at the corner behind us. Can you make sure he doesn't go after her when she gets into the motor car with Bill? She doesn't want him to find out where she's living.'

'Isn't she coming to the house with the rest of us?'

'No. And she has a good reason for it. So do as I damned well ask and keep your eye on her.'

'All right, Da.'

As they walked out of the churchyard, Kathleen saw Bill waiting in the motor car and ran to get into it as quickly as she could. Huddling down in the seat, she glanced back to see Patrick barring the thin man's way. He was trying to get round her brother, and they were shoving one another to and fro. Godfrey must know where she lived, so why did this man want to follow her? Was he intending to hurt her or threaten her on the way home?

'What's wrong?' Bill asked.

She explained a second time, more briefly.

'I'll drive as fast as I can and keep an eye on the road behind us. But I have to get back to your place on time, because a cousin of mine has arranged for me to pick up a young fellow in

Monks Barton and drive him home. Barty usually picks him up, but something's come up and he can't do it today.'

'Is it someone I know?'

'Shouldn't think so. This is a fellow from Malmesbury who likes going for long walks at the weekends. He arranges for my cousin Barty to pick him up somewhere in the afternoon so that he can go further afield and explore new areas. I don't know why anyone would want to do that, but he pays good money to be driven back and I don't want to keep him waiting.'

'As long as I get home safely.'

He repeated confidently, 'Don't worry. I'll make sure of that.'

But she did worry. She had thought Godfrey would wait for Mr Seaton's death before he did anything. Why had this man wanted to follow her?

★ ★ ★

Bill got her home but her heart sank when she saw a man waiting near her house. 'Someone else is there, another stranger. Please don't leave me till we find out who he is.'

He looked at the man and laughed gently. 'That's my passenger, Mr Perry. He must have got to Monks Barton more quickly than he expected. I'll introduce you, then you won't worry if you see him again. He says there are some grand walks round here and he'll be exploring it on fine Sundays for a while and asking me again to pick him up. Rather him than me for all that walking, but I hope *he* carries on with it.'

After helping her out of the car, Bill beckoned to the young man. 'Mr Perry, this is Mrs Seaton.'

He smiled. 'I'm pleased to meet you.'

'I've just brought her back from burying her mother.'

His smile faded. 'Oh, I'm so sorry. My condolences.'

'Thank you. I hope you had a good walk.'

His face brightened again. 'Yes, I did. I love exploring the countryside. I work in an office and I try to get out into the fresh air on Sundays whenever the weather permits.'

As she nodded and turned to go into the house, he moved quickly to open the gate for her.

'Thank you.'

'You're welcome. You have a lovely garden, Mrs Seaton.'

She only realised as she closed the door behind her and locked it that she hadn't even thanked him for his compliment. She couldn't resist peeping out of the front window and watching the two men chat for a few moments. Then they got into the car, laughing, and drove away.

Mr Perry wasn't good-looking, not with that large nose, but she'd liked his face because he had such a warm smile. And she'd liked his enthusiasm about his walks.

She envied him. She wished she had the freedom to go out exploring the countryside, or simply to wander round the shops in Swindon.

Her children were growing older and more independent, preferring to play with their friends rather than go out walking with her, but at the moment she always needed to be nearby to keep an eye on them.

She'd wished for all sorts of things over the years, and not got them all. You had to cope with what life did to you, not what you dreamt of.

Sighing, she went upstairs to take off her black clothes and put on her everyday garments. As she tidied her hair, she decided she wasn't even going to wear a black armband. She hadn't been close to her mother and she wasn't going to pretend to be heartbroken. Anyway, none of her family would see her.

When she was ready, she nipped along the back lane to Rhoda's to pick up her two children, locking the back door carefully behind her, something she wouldn't even have thought of doing a year ago.

Back to a life of waiting and wondering, she thought.

How long could this go on?

The thought wouldn't be suppressed: it'd go on till Mr Seaton died. And then who knew what she'd have to do or where she'd wind up?

15

A few days later Kathleen was surprised to hear something fall through the letter box in her door and drop to the hall floor, because the post had already been delivered. She'd noticed the postman stopping at Rhoda's.

She heard someone running away before she could see who had hand-delivered the letter. Why hadn't they knocked?

She picked it up and studied the envelope, which was addressed to her in rough printing, using capital letters only. Not liking the looks of it, she slit the top of the envelope and read the message quickly, gasping in shock at the words.

TAKE YOUR CHILDREN AND MOVE AWAY FROM WILTSHIRE, YOU BITCH. YOU'RE NOT WANTED HERE. YOU WOULDN'T WANT THEM CHILDREN TO GET HURT, WOULD YOU? OR YOURSELF? WE'LL BE WATCHING YOU, SO LEAVE QUICKLY! DON'T COME BACK. NEVER, EVER!

Shocked rigid, she let the piece of paper slip out of her fingers and it was a few moments before she felt calm enough to pick it up and reread it carefully. That was enough to fix the exact words in her mind and fill her with anger . . . as well as fear.

Her first instinct was to burn it, but she

decided it would be better to keep it, in case she needed proof of the threat.

Her second instinct was to show it to Rhoda and ask her advice. She locked the doors and ran round to her friend's house.

Rhoda stared at the paper in shock, then examined the envelope. 'Hand-delivered. Your father, do you think? You said you'd seen him watching the house.'

'I don't think he hates me that much. This seems . . . full of hate.'

'You can't always tell.'

'Well, it doesn't seem the sort of thing he'd do. He'd be more likely to turn up and thump me. Anyway, it isn't at all like his handwriting. It's too neat and even. He can't write straight unless there's a line ruled on the page. He confuses capitals and small letters when he writes, and as for apostrophes and exclamation marks, he never even tries to use them. I noticed the ones in the letter are all correct.'

She hesitated then asked, 'Can this be from Godfrey Seaton, do you think? Would he do something like this?'

After Rhoda had read the letter again, she said in a low voice, as if afraid, even in her own home, of someone overhearing, 'He'd be the most likely sender, I should think. Unless you have other enemies I don't know about, and I'm sure I'd hear about it if anyone in the village took against you.'

'Of course I don't have any other enemies.' She tapped the piece of paper. 'This has upset me and I can't seem to think straight. What should I do? I felt so sure he didn't know where I lived.'

'Wait till Mr Seaton gets better and show it to him. He'll know how to deal with it.'

'But what if Godfrey hurts the children in the meantime? They're too old now to be with me all the time, and there's the long walk to and from school. Maybe I should do what the message says and move away?'

'No. It never does to give in to threats. Anyway, I think it'd be easier for him to kill you in a place where you're not known.'

'Kill us!'

'How else can he inherit legally when Mr Seaton dies?'

Kathleen couldn't speak at this terrible thought; she could only stare at her companion in numb horror.

'If you ran away, I doubt you'd be able to hide where you went, not if someone with the money to pay for a search really wanted to find you. A pretty woman and two children would be easy to follow. No, better to rely on Mr Seaton protecting you.'

'But he's been so ill, and he still isn't well.'

'We'll all be very careful. He's getting better now and he'll know what to do better than either of us.'

She didn't contradict Rhoda, who was fond of her former employer, but what if Mr Seaton didn't get better? What if he died? Her children's safety was at stake, so she ventured to say, 'He's not his old self, Rhoda, and probably never will be.'

The older woman bent her head and began to fiddle with the braid on her skirt. 'I know he's not been in good health for a while, and . . . well, this illness has aged him greatly. I don't think he'll make old bones, but he's got the money to look after himself and *I* think he'll live for a good while yet. I visit him regularly so I'll see if he's taken a turn for the worse and be able to warn you. I do think you'll be safer near him . . . for the moment. No, he's not at death's door yet. Not Mr Seaton.'

'Well, if nothing else happens, I'll stay here as long as he's alive, but I'm ready to run away at a moment's notice and I'll do it if anything else happens. Mr Seaton's money isn't nearly as important to me as the children's lives.'

'Oh, my dear.' Rhoda took hold of the younger woman's hand and held it tightly. 'If you feel threatened, come to my house at any hour, day or night. You have a key. If I'm away on one of my little trips, just let yourself in.'

'Thank you.' But one small old woman wouldn't be much help in protecting them.

'I'll choose my moment and tell Mr Seaton what happened today. Could you make a copy of that letter to show him? I'm sure he'll have some good advice for us.'

Kathleen didn't have much faith in her father-in-law, or in Rhoda's present advice. But where else could she turn? No one would believe her if she accused Godfrey Seaton of plotting to murder her and her children? He was a respected member of the community, working at the biggest undertakers in the area.

And people would be even less likely to believe her if she was a stranger who had just moved to another town. No, better to stay here, where people knew she was a decent woman, a good mother, where the neighbours would come running if she shouted for help.

They sat together for a few moments then Kathleen went home to get on with her daily chores.

But she couldn't settle. She was too upset about this sudden twist in the situation and too uncertain of what to do for the best.

★　★　★

After some thought Kathleen wrote to Mr Seaton about the anonymous letter, letting Rhoda take a copy of the horrid thing to give him on her next visit to her former employer.

He'd read it, frowning, Rhoda reported, and told her he'd have to think about it. She'd asked him about his will, but he'd told her to mind her own business.

They hadn't heard a word from him since.

Something made Kathleen hide the original letter away carefully with her marriage certificate and the children's birth certificates in the secret drawer of the little desk.

She didn't see her father in Monks Barton again, but Rhoda saw him sometimes at the yard. 'I can see why you're afraid of him. He's such a big strong man.'

'My father will be plotting something, I know he will. He always has plans and you can't blame him after his dreadfully poor childhood. In some ways he's done really well for himself. But he used to accuse my mother of holding him back. And she did, she was such a poor manager. He probably thinks I might be useful to him. So if anything happens to Mr Seaton I have two people to worry about, Godfrey *and* my father.'

'Well, at least your father won't be trying to *kill* you. If it came to a choice and you had nowhere else to turn, you could seek his aid.'

'I'd have to be utterly desperate to do that. If he got me in his power, he'd order me around and find ways to make me do everything he asked. And I won't have my children growing up as I did, terrified of angering him.'

She studied the local and national newspapers carefully from then on, learning as much as she could. She looked at adverts for jobs, small businesses for sale, anything that might offer her a way to make a new life for the children. Thank goodness she had a decent amount of money saved. Now she had to learn what to expect if she went looking for a business of her own. They paid women only about half of what they paid men, so she decided against looking for a job. No, it had to be a business of some sort. And she was inclined towards running a boarding house.

The questions that began to pile up in her mind seemed endless.

Should she emigrate to Australia? To America?

How did you change your name officially?

But most of all, how could she get away from Monks Barton in the first place without being seen? If only there was a railway station in the village. That would have made it so much easier to escape.

And how could she carry enough luggage? They'd need clothes, all sorts of things.

But she had to prepare for the worst, so took what steps she could. She sewed some banknotes and coins into a new wide belt, which she wore all the time, and she kept her savings bank book on her, in a flat pouch tied round her waist under her clothes.

Her children had grown nervous, picking up on her mood even though they still didn't fully understand the gravity of the situation.

★ ★ ★

It was another two months before Kathleen heard from Mr Seaton again, or rather, from his lawyer, Mr Morton, who wrote to say that sadly his client had passed away suddenly and had wished her to be informed immediately if this happened. Mrs Seaton was organising the funeral, with the help of Mr Godfrey Seaton.

Kathleen went running to show the letter to Rhoda, who burst into tears and was of no help.

The lawyer had said nothing about the children, let alone them attending their grandfather's funeral, so she waited to hear. Surely Mr Seaton had left them something? Surely they should at least be invited to his funeral?

But she didn't hear a thing. Rhoda received a message not to go to the funeral from the lawyer on behalf of Mrs Seaton, who wished to confine attendance to their family and friends. That upset Rhoda greatly.

Kathleen bought the local newspaper, the *Swindon Advertiser*, every day and when she saw an announcement about the funeral, she wondered how to get in touch with Bill, so that she could hire him to drive her and the children into Swindon.

But before she could arrange this, she had another visit from her father, who had come openly this time, driven to Monks Barton in his friend Bill's taxi.

He came striding up the path to her front door and hammered on it with his usual impatience.

She heard him try the handle as she went to open it and that annoyed her. She gestured to him to come into the front room. What a pity Rhoda was out! She would have preferred not to be alone with him.

He didn't speak for a few moments, staring round as if cataloguing every item she owned, then he looked across at her. 'You'll have heard from the lawyer about Mr Seaton dying?'

'Yes.'

'Mrs Seaton's queening it and pretending to weep for her husband. As if *she* cares for anyone but herself! She's brought Mr Godfrey in to help her with the business *and* to organise the funeral. He's staying at the house and you'd think he was her *son*, the way he's behaving.'

Kathleen couldn't think what to say.

He continued as if he didn't expect an answer. 'It was him who sent me to see you today.'

Her heart lurched and she found it difficult to breathe for a moment or two. 'Godfrey Seaton did? What does he want?'

'Yes. He says to tell you his aunt doesn't know about you and the children, and he doesn't want her to know, because it'll only upset her. If you keep out of sight, he'll see your rent is paid and give you a pound a week for your keep. If you try to attend the funeral, he'll have you locked away as a madwoman and your children taken from you.'

Kathleen plumped down on the nearest chair. 'He couldn't do that, could he?'

'I reckon he could. His firm does the funerals for the workhouse and the infirmary, so he knows all the officials there. He could probably get you certified quick as that.' He snapped his fingers to emphasise his point.

'I don't know what to do, Da.'

He gave her a long, thoughtful look, then nodded as if acknowledging their relationship and his wish to help her.

'Do what he says, for the moment. It gives you a roof over your head and money to put bread on the table. But don't, whatever else you do, push your children forward as Seatons. I don't think they stand a chance of getting any of the old man's money, more's the pity, so be grateful for what Godfrey gives you.'

She nodded. That was fairly obvious.

'And you should be very careful what you say and do. Don't even mention his name or the relationship in public. He can be a nasty sod if you cross him. You need to remember it's my job that's at stake as well if you cause trouble.'

'I'll try not to upset him. Only Da, do you

184

think I should run away? I don't feel my children and I are safe here any longer. They may stand between him and an inheritance when Mrs Seaton dies.'

'Don't do anything for the moment. She's put him in charge so I'm working for him now. *She* doesn't come near the yard or the office, never did. Too dirty out there for her ladyship. Blood is thicker than water, so I'll keep my eyes and ears open. I can send Bill to get you away quickly if I think you're in danger. For the time being, just do as he asks and we'll all see how we go.'

He eased his collar a little as if uncomfortable asking the next question. 'You did get married properly, didn't you?'

'Of course I did.'

'I never saw the marriage certificate. Have you got it handy?'

'No. I keep it at the bank with my children's birth certificates, for safety.' She didn't know why she'd said that, when it was in the secret desk drawer near him at this very moment, but she didn't trust her father completely. Oh, he'd not let anyone kill her, she did believe that. But if he saw a way to make money for himself out of her awkward position, she doubted he'd hesitate to use her and the children.

And he was working for Godfrey Seaton now, wasn't he?

She watched him chew the corner of his lip for a moment or two, as he did when undecided about something, then he nodded. 'Wise of you.' He got up and moved towards the door, then stopped and said, 'I nearly forgot. He says he'll

185

come and see you when everything's settled.'

'When?'

'He didn't say.'

And with that, her father was gone. He hadn't asked to see the children, who were *his* grandchildren as well, and he'd left her with a lot to think about. She'd wait to see what happened, but thank goodness Godfrey and her father didn't know about her savings.

She went to study the little desk that Ernest had been so fond of. It was rather battered now but must have been a fine piece of furniture when first made. The secret drawer was fiddly to open, but she couldn't think of a better place to hide her documents.

They were all playing a waiting game now.

But if she had the slightest doubt about her children's safety, she'd be off.

⋆ ⋆ ⋆

A few days later she read about Mr Seaton's funeral in the newspaper. It sounded to have been a very grand affair, with the coffin carried in a glass-sided hearse drawn by four black horses. The body had been kept in the new 'chapel of rest' that the funeral company had built recently, to fit in with the modern taste of not keeping a dead body at home.

The widow had worn an elegant black silk mourning gown with a black jacket edged in jet beads, and a hat with a wide brim sumptuously trimmed with black feathers. Mrs Seaton had gone to London to buy these garments in a

186

mourning warehouse in order to do her beloved husband credit, the report said, then it went on to list the guests who were entertained at the house afterwards and to say what some of the more important ones wore, too.

After that, Kathleen made sure to keep one of the old carpet bags that had belonged to Ernest in each bedroom, so that clothes could be grabbed from the drawers and stuffed into them quickly. She even made the children practise doing it.

To think she'd nearly thrown Ernest's old bags away when they first got married, they looked so worn and dusty!

But she still wasn't sure where to go for safety. London, she supposed, or Manchester. Easier to get lost in a big city and they could go there by train if she managed to get them all to Swindon without being seen.

16

Godfrey Seaton turned up without warning two days later and would have walked straight into her cottage without knocking if Kathleen hadn't still been keeping the front door locked.

She and Rhoda were chatting in the kitchen when they heard a motor car pull up outside, so she went to peep out from behind the net curtains. She knew who this was because she'd seen him officiating at her mother's funeral. Godfrey always looked rather puffy in the face, as if he ate too richly, and he was now wearing Mr Seaton's gold watch and chain. She'd recognise it anywhere. By rights that should have gone to her son.

Worst of all to her, Godfrey had a strong resemblance to his cousin Ernest, which made her feel uncomfortable.

He hammered on the door for a second time, so impatiently she went running to open it. She didn't need her father's warning that it wouldn't be wise to offend this man.

'Mr Seaton. Please come in.'

He didn't move, studying her in a way that made her feel very uncomfortable, as if she had no clothes on. Men did that occasionally, which disgusted her, but not so-called gentlemen, usually.

Rhoda called from the kitchen, 'Who is it, Kathleen dear?'

'Is that old biddy still poking her nose in where it's not wanted?' he asked scornfully.

'Rhoda's been a good friend to me.'

'Well, at least you're not entertaining a male friend.'

She drew herself up. 'I don't have a *male friend* in that sense, Mr Seaton. I'm a widow.'

'And see that you don't take up with anyone or I'll cut off your allowance and throw you out of this cottage.'

'There's no need to threaten me. I'd never even think of doing that. Would you . . . um . . . like a cup of tea? We've just made a fresh pot.'

'No. What I'd like is to see how you live and check that you're keeping it all clean. You can go home, Rhoda. Mrs Seaton will be safe with me.'

When her friend had gone, he asked, 'Are the children at school?'

'Yes, of course.' He looked at her *that way* again. If he tried to touch her, she'd kick him in a very tender place.

But he made no attempt to take liberties. 'Make sure they study hard. They're going to have to earn their living once they leave school. I won't support them past the age of fourteen, or you from then on, either. So you should think about finding a job for yourself then as well.'

'My children are already good scholars, Mr Seaton. Christopher came top of his class last term.'

He didn't even comment on that, but started walking round her house, opening and shutting drawers and investigating their contents. She had to dig her fingernails into the palms of her hands

189

to prevent herself from telling him to stop that at once.

When he'd inspected every room, every drawer and cupboard, he went back to the front door. 'You understand that you are not to show yourself in Swindon, or make any claims on Mrs Seaton. She's too old to be upset by finding out about you and your brats.'

'Yes, I understand.'

'See you stick to that if you want to keep your weekly money.' He left the house, leaving the front door swinging open, and she stood a little way further back in the hall to watch him being driven off before she moved to shut it.

What was all that for? He was indeed a horrible man, checking up on her like that. Why, he'd searched her whole house.

Then she had a sudden thought. Had he been looking for her marriage certificate? Someone must have prompted her father to ask about it. What if Godfrey demanded she hand it over to him?

She had to sit down for a few moments to recover from her unwelcome visitor.

After that, the year seemed to drag on for ever, but to her relief nothing bad happened to them.

She never stopped worrying, though. Not for a second.

* * *

One frosty day towards the end of December, Kathleen came home from changing her books at the library in the next village and stopped dead in the doorway, sure that someone had been in her house. It smelt different and it *felt* different, too.

She checked all her cupboards and drawers, and although most things were in their usual places, a few weren't quite as she'd left them. Ernest had always said she was a creature of habit, but the old saying 'A place for everything and everything in its place' seemed a good way to organise your home.

She checked every single drawer and cupboard for a second time, but nothing had been taken. She was sure this search had been arranged by Godfrey Seaton, because who else cared about what she owned? Was he still seeking her marriage certificate? Did he want to destroy it? That was the only reason she could see for the search.

Should she take everyone by surprise and leave tonight? Was it time to tear her poor children away from all they knew?

Only . . . Godfrey hadn't harmed them, had he? If he had, she'd have run away the same day.

The time to leave was coming closer, though. She knew it.

Not yet, though. Not quite yet. She wasn't sure why she felt that, but she did.

And oh, she wanted the children to live a normal life for as long as possible, to grow a little older before their lives were disrupted, and at least to finish this school year.

★ ★ ★

The following year came in without a lot of fuss from Kathleen. She was in bed by ten o'clock as usual on New Year's Eve and lay there thinking about the year to come. Would this be the year they had to flee from Monks Barton? Probably.

But at least the children were a little older now. Christopher would turn nine in 1911 and Elizabeth eight. They were strong enough to walk a long way if they had to vanish into the night.

Where had the last decade gone? It seemed only a moment since her children were babies.

As the months passed she read in the newspapers about things happening in the wider world, but most of them seemed to have little effect on life in their small village.

King George opened his first parliament in February, but of more concern to some of the thinking people she chatted to occasionally was that Germany had increased the size of its army by half a million men. That number was far beyond her comprehension. What did that many men look like if you lined them all up? She had no idea.

In April her father turned up after school was finished for the day and asked to meet the children. He congratulated her on their rosy good health.

Why had he wanted to see them? Was she being suspicious about nothing, or had Godfrey sent him, hoping they would be sickly?

In May Lloyd George introduced the new National Health Insurance Bill. Now that seemed a really good idea to her. Poor people were always so worried about how to pay doctors' bills. If she'd had a vote, she'd have voted for a government who looked after people's health.

She read in the newspapers about plans for the new king's coronation, which would take place at the end of June. You couldn't help being interested. He was their king, after all. She still wasn't used to saying King George and as for Mary, it seemed a woefully ordinary name for a queen.

The coronation was going to be very grand, with thousands of guests. They were closing Westminster Abbey a few weeks early to fit it out for the ceremony, she read. What a waste of money that was! Couldn't royal people and lords and ladies sit in wooden pews for a couple of hours as other people did? It'd have been more economical to provide them with cushions.

And every month since Mr Seaton's visit, her father came to see her, bringing her housekeeping money and asking if everything was all right.

What did he expect her to say? Of course it wasn't all right! Godfrey Seaton was a shadow looming over her life.

The weather was glorious, the best spring and summer she could ever remember. Too sunny and dry, according to farmers.

In June, just before the coronation, her father seemed in a friendlier mood. He talked about his life as a widower, and mentioned a woman he'd been seeing.

'Would you mind me marrying again, Kathleen Frances?'

She was surprised he'd even bothered to ask

her. 'No, of course not. It's what most men do. They need someone to care for them and make a home.'

'It's not that. I have a woman coming in to keep house for me and she's a good worker. It's the company I miss, in bed and out of it. Now the children are grown up, I'm on my own of an evening. Mr Seaton doesn't like me going to the pub and warned me he'd not employ a drunkard.'

He scowled down at his feet, then sighed and looked at her. 'He still keeps an eye on *you*, you know, not just through my visits, either. He sends men to watch what you're doing from time to time. He doesn't want you marrying again, says he doesn't want a husband causing trouble for him and his poor aunt.'

'I don't want to marry again. It's probably the only thing he and I agree about.'

Her father frowned. 'He's got something planned for your future, I know he has. Don't ever let your guard drop, my girl.'

'I won't, Da.'

That was probably the longest chat they'd ever had and the most concern he'd ever shown for her.

Was it a ploy to gain her confidence or was it genuine concern?

17

Twenty miles away from the village where Kathleen lived, in the large old house called Greyladies, Harriet Latimer donned her coat and hat, and went outside to the motor car that was waiting for her, a shiny-clean Austin Landaulette. Barty, from the village, ran a taxi service taking people into Swindon or wherever they needed to go, or even just out for drives in the country.

This service, with all the novelty of it being a motor car not a horse-drawn vehicle, had been very successful, partly due to the fact that Barty had had a telephone installed, one of the first in the village, so that his customers could contact him more easily.

It was only people like her, with money to spare, who used taxis, of course.

She nodded to him and settled into the front seat beside him. There weren't side windows or doors in the front but at least the driver and his passenger had a windscreen to protect them from the rushing air as the car travelled so quickly along the roads. And canvas blinds had been fitted at the sides for added protection. The weather was good today, so she didn't mind an extra dose of fresh air. The back seat always felt like a glass-walled box to her.

She'd have liked to take someone with her today to get another opinion on what she was thinking of doing. Unfortunately she hadn't expected to hear so quickly about a suitable house being up for sale and her husband had gone up to London for a couple of days by the time she received the phone call. And the ladies she'd asked to help her with this charitable venture weren't wealthy enough to have telephones in their houses.

But she had to go because she didn't want someone else snapping up the house if it was as suitable for her purpose as it sounded. It was being sold by Perry's, unfortunately. She'd met Mr Perry before and hadn't taken to him. He was patronising and treated women like mindless idiots. He'd told her when he phoned that a gentleman had been very interested in the house but had apparently decided at the last minute to buy another one instead.

So she was going on her own to look at Honeyfield House. Silly of her to be charmed by its pretty name, but it seemed like a good omen. She murmured it again and turned to smile a farewell at her own house as Barty cranked up the motor. Greyladies was such a beautiful old place. She hadn't expected to inherit it and never took it for granted: it was such a privilege to live here.

Honeyfield House was several miles away from Challerton, with Malmesbury as its nearest town, only a small market town, but the charity committee had decided it would be better to buy a house in a quiet country area and she fully agreed with them.

She would be using money from the

Greyladies Trust Fund to purchase a house, but as usual, would do that anonymously. That was the way things had been done for the several centuries the trust had existed. The chatelaines of the big house always tried to stay out of the limelight, made anonymous 'bequests' and appointed other ladies to run the various ventures.

Since Challerton was a small village, people seemed to know everyone else's business, so she'd drawn her committee from a wider area, using a network of acquaintances and their friends to find suitable members. This project was to provide asylum mainly for women in danger from violent husbands, so there was an even stronger need for secrecy.

They turned off the main road north of Malmesbury, heading east now into the Cotswolds. This was an area she didn't know very well and she thought it pretty, with small farms set on gentle slopes, and an occasional orchard or market garden. It was wonderful how motor cars were opening up the world for people. Trains had made a beginning with that seventy years before, but with cars you could travel as an individual and set your own destinations.

A sign said they were approaching the village of Honeyfield and she looked ahead to see a pretty little hamlet. However, Barty turned right before they got there. She would explore the village later if the Trust bought the house.

A battered old sign with a pointing finger on the end said 'Honeyfield House' and they turned right again along a narrow winding lane between high hedges. There were no cottages along the lane, which was good considering her purpose. The lane ended suddenly at what were presumably the gates of the house.

Barty stopped the car, saying in satisfaction, 'I reckon this is it, Mrs Latimer. There isn't a name but it's the only house along this lane here and they wouldn't put up a sign for nothing, would they now?'

'You always seem to get us where we wish to go.'

Barty rolled his shoulders in a big stretch, clearly ready for a brief pause and chat. 'Them new road maps you got me are a wonderful help. That's progress, that is, making maps like that for anyone to buy. And when the maps don't tell me the details, well, I've still got a tongue in my head, haven't I?'

'I hope you managed to find out how to get here without telling anyone where we were going. This is one of my special trips.'

He chuckled. 'So you said. I haven't let you down yet, have I?'

'No, Barty, you've always kept my secrets. What's more, you're an excellent driver. I feel very safe with you.'

'Well, you bought me the car after the accident on the farm, didn't you? Gave me a way to earn a living even with a gammy leg. Got me a telephone, too. It's surprised me how often my car is called out by someone phoning me. I won't never forget what you did, Mrs Latimer. No, never.' After another pause, he added, 'Strange coincidence that I don't never seem to

198

be busy when you need me, though.'

'We've been lucky, haven't we?' Sometimes strange things did happen to Greyladies and its occupants, but strange in a positive way. She wasn't going to discuss that so contented herself with, 'I was glad to help you, Barty.'

'You do it quiet-like, but I reckon you've helped a lot of people round our way over the years.'

'I do my best.'

'How many years have you been at Greyladies now?'

'Six, I think. Or is it seven now?'

'Well, you're still young so we'll look forward to having you as the lady of the house there for a good few years yet, I reckon.'

'Chatelaines don't always stay on at Greyladies, you know. We don't own it — we're only given the right to live there.'

Silence, then he asked, 'Are you thinking of leaving, then?'

'It just seems to happen sometimes. None of us plan it, exactly, but I feel, and I've always felt, that I won't be chatelaine there for my whole life.'

She blinked her eyes to clear the tears that always came into them when she thought of leaving the wonderful old house. It wouldn't happen yet, though. She sensed that she, her beloved husband and her children still had some time left to enjoy living there. She couldn't imagine what would take them away, because Joseph had older brothers to inherit the family estate, so he had no responsibilities to his wider family. But something would happen, she was sure.

Many Latimers had this strange extra sense about the world. Not harmful, just . . . as if they could see things differently, sense the future.

Barty stared round. 'Lot of wild flowers round here, it being so sheltered. Real nice to see them.'

She looked at the hedgerows on either side of the gates. There were plenty of flowers at this time of year and she could see bees buzzing in and out of the blossoms. She'd always thought bees such comfortable, busy little creatures. The sight of them comforted her. You could almost say that she lived the same way, keeping busy, doing what came to hand. No use fretting about what might happen one day.

The wrought-iron gates were standing open and she could see why. One of them had a hinge missing, which had caused it to hang drunkenly to one side, and the other was propped open by two bricks around which grass had grown.

'Shame to let that gate hang there all skew-whiff,' Barty commented disapprovingly. 'Would only take a few minutes to fit another hinge and straighten her up, then it'd just take a bit of sandpapering and a lick of paint to get rid of that rust. You'd think people would look after their house, wouldn't you?'

'You'd think so. Could you stop for a few moments when the house comes into view please, Barty? I want to study the outside of it.'

When he stopped, he said, 'I suppose they ought to keep the lawn mowed, but it looks like a pretty meadow with all the wild flowers growing so free. Must be lots of happy bees round here. Do you think that's why it's called Honeyfield House?'

'Could be.' She studied the building at the end of the drive. 'How strange! It looks like a much smaller version of Greyladies.'

It was built in beautiful Cotswold stone, with a steep roof of stone slabs on which patches of golden lichen had found a home. High gables seemed to stand guard at each end of the building, which was two storeys high, three if you counted the attics whose windows were set in small gables in the roof.

'She could be a pretty house, couldn't she?' Barty said after a while. 'But she's looking sad and weary.'

Harriet liked the way he personalised objects. And yes, this house did look like a 'she' somehow. 'If I like the interior, Barty, the trust fund I'm representing will be able to set things to rights.'

'Who are you going to help this time, Mrs Latimer, if you don't mind me asking?'

'We'll take in anyone who's in trouble or danger and needs somewhere to stay hidden for a while, which will be women mostly, hiding from violent men. But keep that to yourself. If I buy it, I'm going to tell people it's a convalescent home.'

'Sounds like a good idea. If I had money to spare, I'd help other folk as well.'

'I did hear that you'd been doing some repairs for old Mrs Watley.'

He flushed. 'Well, she couldn't do them herself, could she, not at her age? And that son of hers is a proper townie who don't know one end of a hammer from the other. Selfish, he is. Hardly ever comes to see her. She don't complain but I know that upsets her. There are too many selfish people in this world, and that's a fact.'

'And too many violent people as well, who take pleasure in hurting those weaker than themselves.'

'Ah. I never could abide bullies.'

'Well, we'd better get going, Barty. I can see another motor car parked at the side of the house, so Mr Perry must be waiting for us.'

He was an accountant whose firm had a sideline selling property. He had spoken to her on the telephone, explaining that the previous owner had been dead for several years and the house now belonged to the lady's son, who was stationed in India.

Looking at Honeyfield House with its faded, peeling paint and dirty windows, Harriet felt that the son should have done more about maintenance, if only to keep up the value. She'd mention that when they discussed the price being asked.

She already *knew* she was going to buy it, had done as soon as she clapped eyes on it. And that strange other-worldly intuition was never wrong.

She'd already set up a small trust to buy and then run the home. There was always enough money in the main trust for such projects and if more was needed, a dividend would come in or an investment suddenly increase in value, or one of the people who'd been helped and were now comfortably circumstanced would make a donation.

How that happened in such a timely fashion, she had no idea. She was just glad that it was part of the conditions of inheriting Greyladies that the chatelaine used this money to help people, usually other women but sometimes men like Barty. It gave such a satisfying purpose to her life.

She'd *known* what Barty needed too, and look how valuable he'd become to her and the work of the trust.

★ ★ ★

Felix Perry waited impatiently for his client to arrive. He was a little early because the roads weren't busy today and his driver had driven over from Malmesbury without let or hindrance. He pulled out his watch and studied it again. His time was valuable and he didn't always go out to show clients round the houses, but his son was busy today showing a client round another property.

Nathan had been working in the family firm for some time now, doing quite well. He never made a mistake in his accounts and seemed to enjoy getting out and about. He claimed it was stuffy in the office.

Well, it'd have to stay stuffy. If you opened the windows, the papers would blow about. No one else had complained.

From the time he started work, Nathan had insisted on walking to the office in all but the most inclement weathers. Now he'd taken to going for long walks in the country at the weekend, missing church and refusing to change his ways. He even arranged sometimes for a man with a motor car to pick him up at an agreed spot at the end of the day so that he could go further afield. What a waste of money that was!

But you couldn't put old heads on young shoulders. Well, not so young. Nathan was twenty-seven now and seemed to have no intention of finding a wife, for all his mother's efforts to introduce him to suitable women during the past few years. She said there were no other suitable unmarried women of the right age living nearby. But they'd have to find him a wife somehow.

Felix frowned at the nearby woodwork. The house was in desperate need of repainting, but the absentee owner was an officer in a regiment stationed out in India and he didn't seem to care about the place. Major Marshall had said at first that he would keep his mother's house for his own family's use when he left the regiment and they returned to England. He'd therefore been happy to pay for any maintenance necessary to keep the house weatherproof, because a leaking roof or broken window pane might damage the fabric of the building, but beyond that he wasn't prepared to go.

After the first year Felix had suggested hiring a gardener now and then to tidy up the grounds, but since there was no one to look at the gardens the major considered that a waste of money, too. He'd bring things up to scratch when he could see with his own eyes what was needed.

To make matters worse, the fellow had now decided to settle in India after he left the regiment because he preferred living in a warm climate, so he'd instructed Felix to sell the house as quickly as he could. And look at the garden, like a damned meadow it was! How was he supposed to sell it as a gentleman's residence looking like that?

Two buyers had been interested and one had nearly bought it then changed his mind when he worked out how much there was to do to bring it up to scratch.

Ah, that was a car coming down the drive. It must be his client. Thank goodness! He was definitely going to hand over all the house sales to Nathan. It was a waste of time for him to hang around like this.

When the vehicle stopped, the driver went round to open the door for the lady passenger. She was sitting in the front seat, which was unusual, but then this lady had sounded rather strange on the telephone. She'd demanded secrecy in their dealings, warning him that she'd not buy the house if word got out that she was involved.

Now why would she want that? You'd think she was doing something against the law, but he'd sent Nathan to check up on her, because his son was good at finding things out, and he'd reported that she was very highly respected in charitable circles.

Perhaps she was just shy? No, it couldn't be that. She was so independent in her ways, Felix had thought at first she must be a widow, and a capable one at that. But it turned out she was married with two sons. Why hadn't she brought her husband with her, then? After all, buying a big house like this would take a very large amount of money, more than a woman should deal with, if you asked him.

When he'd suggested she should bring her husband, she'd spoken very sharply, saying she was looking for a house on behalf of a charity trust *she* was in charge of, not him so why should her husband get involved? Which wasn't the point, but something about her tone made Felix drop the matter.

He didn't believe in wasting money pampering the poor, but if she bought the house, his client would be delighted and he'd get a substantial commission. So let her do whatever she wanted.

The lady had stopped a few paces away and was studying the house, so Felix moved forward. 'Mrs Latimer? I hope you had a pleasant journey here?'

'I did, thank you.' Harriet hadn't liked his patronising tone on the telephone and he was still speaking to her like that. Even his appearance was unattractive, as he had mean little eyes and a large nose which gave a predatory look to his face.

She had to choke back a laugh and turn it into a cough when she realised that he bore a distinct resemblance to a vulture — an overweight one which had just stuffed itself with a dead animal.

206

'Shall we go inside, Mrs Latimer?'

'I'd rather walk round the outside first and get an idea of the surroundings, if you don't mind.' That was important because privacy was a very key consideration in whether she purchased or not. However strong her intuition about this being the right place to buy, she would make sure it was suitable in every way before she paid out good money. She always did.

His tone was weary. 'As you please, ma'am.'

She set off walking at a brisk pace, amused to see that her companion was soon panting slightly. Taking pity on his plumpness, she slowed down a little, glad that he wasn't a chatterer, at least.

Honeyfield had once been a gentleman's residence, she thought, not a farmhouse and it hadn't been a rich person's home, either. Just a plain, comfortable dwelling, which sat on a couple of acres of land bordered by high brick walls.

'Are there farms all the way round the house?' she asked.

'Yes. Three farms border your land.'

'That's good.' From an elevated part of the garden she could see that the nearest farm was far enough away not to overlook the place. Even better.

The rear of the house reminded her of a pretty woman who'd grown older and not taken care of herself. Harriet pointed out the many things in need of maintenance as they moved on, amused to see her companion becoming increasingly tight-lipped.

The house had a secretive feel to it, as if it was hiding from the world. Which was exactly what she needed. Sadly most of the women who came here would need to hide for a while, not only to recover their health but to build up their confidence, or simply to stay safe.

She had met and talked to other ladies doing this sort of work over the past few years, discussing the best ways of keeping the people they were helping safe. She'd learnt a lot from them about what to expect, also what sort of people to hire to run the place. Her predecessor at Greyladies hadn't opened a new house for a while, and had closed one down when its purpose became too well known.

One lady she'd spoken to had suggested that when the house opened, she make sure one employee was very strong physically in case a violent person tried to get in and harm a resident. The diaries of previous chatelaines of Greyladies said the same thing. Those diaries were so helpful. Every lady who acted as chatelaine was encouraged to keep one. Some were more interesting than others.

As a collection, the diaries painted a fascinating picture of several hundred years of charity work. Sadly, however, they also showed there had been a need for shelters for women right from the middle of the sixteenth century, when the Dissolution of the Monasteries had thrown many poor nuns out into the world penniless and bewildered.

But the supply of shelters had always lagged behind the need for them.

When they reached the front door of the house, Mr Perry gestured towards it. 'Shall we go inside now, Mrs Latimer?'

She followed him, stopping to stare round a small hall with a dark wooden floor and far too many pieces of old-fashioned furniture standing sentry round the walls. 'Has no one ever dusted the interior or cleared away the cobwebs?'

'I'm afraid the owner wouldn't pay for that.'

'Hmm. And what about all this furniture? Is he taking it away?'

'It goes with the house. We checked the place years ago for him and he selected the pieces he wanted to keep. There is nothing valuable left here now but some items may be of use, especially if it's for a charity. That's up to the purchaser.'

'Hmm. I'll think about it.' That would be an advantage and save the trust buying furniture, but she wasn't going to say so in case he put up the price. She'd make sure the contract specified that everything left behind belonged to the trust.

'Shall we go into the parlour first, Mrs Latimer? I think — '

'Just a moment.' Something was drawing her towards the rear of the hall.

18

When she went into the kitchen and servants' area, Harriet noticed that the back door was slightly ajar and dried muddy footprints led across the floor towards the back stairs.

'Goodness me! Someone must have broken in!' Mr Perry went to examine the door. 'The lock isn't damaged so how did they manage to get the door open? The house is always kept locked.'

There was a sound upstairs.

'He's still here. Quick, let's go outside again. Your driver and mine are stout fellows and will be able to protect us, if necessary.'

But she didn't get a sense of danger, not at all. She got a sense that someone was in pain, so she hurried up the stairs, leaving her companion squeaking out a protest.

'No, really! You mustn't risk — Come back, Mrs Latimer.'

She ignored him.

The sounds were coming from one of the bedrooms at the rear and when she opened the door, they continued unabated. There was definitely no danger here because the woman lying on the bed was in what appeared to be the final throes of childbirth.

Harriet flung her handbag on to the dusty dressing table and stripped off her gloves, tossing them after the bag, then unpinned her neat straw hat and cast that aside, too.

Mr Perry stopped dead in the doorway and turned pale, gulping audibly. A quick glance told her he wasn't going to be any use.

'Shall I fetch the village policeman?' he whispered.

'No, of course not. This poor woman needs help, not locking up. Fetch my driver.'

He stood looking at her in puzzlement so she gave him a push.

'Hurry up! Unless I'm very mistaken the baby is about to be born.'

'But she's broken into the house.'

'And as I'm likely to buy it, I can tell you that she's very welcome to seek shelter here. Now *fetch — my — driver!*'

She went across to the bed and the woman looked at her in mute misery, as if expecting to be shouted at.

'I think you're nearly ready to have the baby, dear. Am I right?'

'Yes, ma'am. And I'm sorry for breaking into your house, but I didn't have nowhere to go and it was raining and I knew the baby was coming.'

'You're welcome to have it here.'

'I am?'

'Yes. Now, let me help with the birth.' She looked round but could see no sign of luggage of any sort. 'Have you any clothes for the baby?'

'No, ma'am. They took them off me.'

'I'll just go and find some clean linen to wrap the baby in, then you can tell me all about it.'

The woman began sobbing helplessly, as if the kindness was too much for her. Then another

211

pain struck and she stopped weeping to grunt and strain.

Harriet ran along the landing and yanked the dust covers off the bed in the next room, relieved to find clean sheets still on it. She dragged them and the pillowcases off and ran back to the next room with them just as Barty came pounding up the stairs. Mr Perry puffed his way up more slowly behind him with a sour expression on his face.

'My driver's waiting just outside, in case he has to go for the police.'

'There's no need for that.' She turned away from the accountant to explain the situation to Barty. 'Can you light a fire and boil some water, then find me something to tie off the birth cord, do you think?'

'Yes, of course.'

'I got some string,' the woman panted. 'There.' She jerked her head in the direction of the bedside table. 'But I ain't got no clothes for the poor little thing. Them officials from the workhouse took everything what I owned, but I wasn't going to let them lock me in there, so I run off. I can't stand to be shut in, missus. I can't *breathe* if I'm shut in.'

'Some people are like that, I know.'

'An' I'd been saving my money, too, for the baby. Even though I hadn't much, I wasn't a *pauper*. I could've managed, but them officials took my money as well.'

Harriet didn't bother asking for more details because another contraction took away the woman's ability to speak coherently. When it was over, she said soothingly, 'We'll find some clothes

212

for the baby later. Let's get it born now.'

She threw off her jacket and rolled up her sleeves, tucking a pillowcase into her waistband in lieu of an apron. The baby was crowning already. It wouldn't be long.

Barty pounded back up the stairs with a ewer of water and nudged Mr Perry. 'You're in the way . . . *sir.*'

'Oh. Sorry. Um . . . what do you want me to do, Mrs Latimer?'

She hid a smile at the way the accountant had remained as close to the door as was possible without actually being outside the room.

'Please go away till the baby's born, Mr Perry. Then I'll join you and we'll discuss the price I'm willing to pay for this house. If you want to help, you can get a fire going in the kitchen.'

He glanced incautiously towards the bed, flushed bright crimson and hurried out on to the landing without another word.

Barty handed Harriet a big apron and a ewer of cold water. 'I can't get you no hot water till I get a fire going, so I brung you some cold to be going on with and I shook most of the dust off this old apron.'

'Well done. If you see to the hot water, I can manage here. Oh, and don't hesitate to ask Mr Perry for help.'

He grinned at her. 'I doubt that one would be willing to get his hands dirty. You sure you can manage here, Mrs Latimer?'

'Yes. I've assisted in births quite a few times.' She turned back to the bed. 'What's your name, dear?'

213

'Sal.'

'Well, Sal, here comes your baby.'

But the woman was too busy to answer, bellowing with pain as she pushed out her child. The infant began wailing even before it was fully delivered.

'A girl,' Harriet said. 'She looks nice and healthy, too. Well done.'

Sal lay back, panting, eyes closed.

Harriet laid the baby on the mother's belly and waited for the afterbirth. She'd never been in sole charge of a birth before but the actions seemed to come quite naturally, and she soon had the umbilical cord tied off.

Footsteps thumped up the stairs again. 'Thought you might need these.' Barty dumped some scissors and a sharp knife on the bed. 'I washed 'em as well as I could.'

'You're a treasure.'

He flushed with pleasure and gave her a nod.

Harriet cut the cord, then wrapped the baby in a pillowcase. She wasn't risking washing it in cold water. 'Here you are, Sal. Your new daughter.'

The woman's broad, heavy-featured face was suddenly transformed into near beauty as she gave the baby a glowing smile and a kiss, then cuddled it in her arms.

Harriet had seen this before and never tired of the utter love most new mothers seemed to feel instinctively for their babies. 'Is it your first child?' she asked gently.

'What? Oh, no, ma'am. I've already raised four, and lost two others. This one came as a surprise. I thought I was past having any more children.'

'Where's your husband?'

'He died a year ago. This one comes from some men forcing me because my husband owed them money and I couldn't pay it with my wage earner gone, could I? I could have fought one man off, two maybe, but not four of them at once. I hope they rot in hell for what they done to me.'

She sniffed back a tear. 'Afterwards they took everything I owned out of the house, except for my clothes. Said they were being generous leaving those, the devils.'

'Did the police do anything to get your things back?'

'Told me they couldn't find the men. Probably they were relatives and not willing to shop them. I got a job in another village. I didn't know I was expecting then. When I found out, the woman I was working for let me stay on after I explained, but she told them officials from Malmesbury workhouse where I was yesterday because she didn't want me giving birth on her.'

She paused to smack another kiss on the infant's cheek. 'I don't care now who fathered her. She's mine. I'll find another job somehow and raise her myself. They're *not* taking her away from me. I like children.'

When no one spoke, she looked fiercely at Harriet. 'I'm a hard worker and I'll manage somehow. But if you could let me stay for a few days, ma'am, it'd be a big help. I'll clean up the place in return once I've had a bit of a rest. I can do washing, do anything in a house. I promise I'll work hard.'

'Oh, we can do better for you than that,' Harriet said. 'I can offer you a job here. I'm about to buy this house and I need someone to look after it for me and act as caretaker. Later on, you can help the warden set the place in order and go on working here as a cleaner, if you and she get on all right.'

Sal blinked at her in shock and seemed to need a few moments to take in Harriet's offer. Then she burst into loud noisy sobs, rocking the baby to and fro. 'Oh, ma'am, yes. Yes, please. You won't regret it.'

Harriet felt a sudden warmth as if someone had put an arm round her shoulders, though there was no one else in the room. She'd experienced a similar feeling at Greyladies where the family ghost kept watch over her Latimer descendants. Perhaps Anne Latimer had come with her, or maybe this house too had its invisible guardian. Who knew? If so, the resident ghost seemed to be in favour of what she'd just done.

She washed her hands, helped Sal to wash herself, then gave her a clean sheet to wrap round herself in lieu of a nightgown.

'I'm a bit shaky on me pins,' Sal said. 'Sorry. I'll be all right tomorrow.'

Since the new mother was a large, muscular woman, Harriet had to call for Barty to help get her and her baby into another bedroom.

Then she did a quick inspection of the upstairs rooms and attics before going downstairs and checking the rooms there as well. All perfect for her purpose.

Only then did she go in search of Mr Perry, who was sitting bolt upright at the kitchen table. He was in a distinctly tetchy mood at being kept waiting, barely managing to speak civilly to her.

'The baby was a girl,' she said cheerfully. 'And I've offered Sal a job.'

'Well, I hope you won't regret it. Now, about the house.'

'I've just had a quick look round.'

'I heard you. I'd have preferred you to wait for me.'

'And I preferred to look on my own.'

She argued with him about the price for quite a while and finally managed to knock what he was asking down to an amount she considered reasonable.

This time she had the sensation that someone had given her a quick kiss on the cheek, a butterfly touch that had her fingering the spot. She hadn't imagined that, she knew she hadn't.

'You'll send someone to my office to complete the formalities and arrange payment?' he asked stiffly.

'I'll come myself tomorrow morning. The money is waiting in the bank. It's a bequest to charity, and I'm in charge of setting up the trust fund. I've done this before, so I have a document already prepared. We'll call this trust after the house and village, I think: *The Honeyfield Bequest.*'

He wrote the words 'Honeyfield Bequest' in his notebook and asked once again, 'You're sure you have the freedom to spend this money as you choose?'

'Not as I choose. It must be used for the benefit of people in need, not for myself or for anything frivolous.'

His expression was sour, as if he didn't approve of her having even this much financial freedom. 'Very well. I'll see you in my office at ten o'clock tomorrow morning. Will you be all right if I leave you now? I do have other appointments.'

'We'll be fine. I'll send Barty into the village for some food and we'll come back here tomorrow after I've seen you, with proper clothes for them both.'

'It doesn't do to spoil the poor, you know.'

'*Spoil?* That poor woman and her newborn baby are without food or clothing, Mr Perry. In fact, I'd like to ask your help in finding the officials who took all Sal owned off her, including her money. They had no right to do that and must give her things back. She was *not* a pauper.'

'I shall have to charge you for doing that.'

'All right. If you must. But sort it out as quickly as you can.'

'Is that all?'

'Yes. You can tell me how you're going on with it when I come to see you tomorrow. There's no time to waste. Sal has no clean clothes for herself, and no clothes at all for her baby.'

He drew in a deep breath, looking at her sourly, but not arguing.

The house felt brighter when he'd left.

She felt a glow of pleasure at this unexpected turn of events. Honeyfield House was already serving as a shelter for a woman in need. And fate had provided a strong woman to act as their caretaker.

Now they only had to find a capable woman to manage the place and a strong man to guard it. A big dog might come in useful too.

★ ★ ★

When his father came back, he looked furiously angry. Nathan was summoned to his office very soon afterwards and the situation at Honeyfield House was explained.

'So can you please visit the local poorhouse and get that woman's clothes back before this Mrs Latimer changes her mind about buying the house?'

'Yes, of course. What's the woman's name?'

'Sal Hatton. Start work on it today. That woman has nothing to wear.' He shuddered at the memory of her huge fleshy buttocks. 'Oh, and you'd better deal with Honeyfield House from now on. You can find its information in our records. I've written down the details of the lady in charge of this trust, including her phone number.'

Latimer! That was one of his mother's family names, the family line from which his strange abilities came, she'd told him. Could this woman be a distant relative? He'd never mentioned anything about that to his father but he'd never forgotten it, either.

His father was scowling at the piece of paper. 'It felt strange to have a woman give me her phone number. I wonder why her husband allows her such freedom, I do indeed.'

'Very well. I'll be happy to take over. Will it be all right for this poor woman who's had a baby to stay there in the meantime?'

'As long as Mrs Latimer can prove she has the money to buy the house, my client won't care who is staying there. Anyway, she's offered this woman a job as caretaker.'

'I'll deal with it all, then.' Nathan was glad his work on property sales got him out of the office. Glad to help this poor woman, too. His father was far too harsh on poorer people, too strict with his employees as well.

He hoped he'd get a chance to meet this Mrs Latimer.

He walked briskly across town and confronted the man in charge of the poorhouse.

'I remember the woman you're talking about. Sal Hatton should be in here, not out walking the streets. She's destitute with nowhere to live. Has she had the baby? Did it live?'

'Yes. And it's a fine healthy girl, apparently.'

'It won't stay healthy with no home to live in.'

'Well, a lady has given her a live-in job, so all's well that ends well. Sal now needs her possessions back.'

'They've been put into the common stores.'

'Then they must be pulled out of the stores.' He saw a refusal building. 'If not, you could be charged with theft. And there's her money too. That must be returned as well.'

With a scowl the man picked up a handbell and when a severe-faced woman in black answered it, he explained the situation, ending, 'See to it, if you please, Miss Topham! I'll get that woman's money out of the safe. It'll be ready for you when you leave, Mr Perry, with a small deduction for our expenses, of course.'

'I would regard any deduction as unlawful, since she didn't ask for your services.'

Silence, then, 'It's irregular, but I think we can waive the charges this once. Kindly go with Miss Topham now.'

He was glad to leave the arrogant fellow. Heaven help the inmates here with someone like that in charge. 'I'm Nathan Perry, ma'am.'

'The accountant's son. Yes, I know. I used to see you in church. You haven't been there much lately. This way.'

The storeroom was large and well supplied with piles of second-hand clothing and bedding, everything immaculately clean.

'I'll just call Betsy in and we'll sort those things out for you.'

'You know which they are? The poor woman can't afford to lose any of her clothing.'

'I know every item here, believe me. Only the money is kept in the office.'

Nathan left the storeroom with three unwieldy pillowcases — badly stained with frayed edges — full of clothing and miscellaneous extra items for the baby, about which he was to say nothing.

He was taken back to the man in charge, who counted out the money in small change. He was deliberately being awkward about this refund, Nathan decided, but he didn't comment, merely asked for an envelope to put the money in. Even that simple request caused a lot of humming and hawing about stationery expenses.

Since the bundles were awkward to carry, he beckoned to a lad in the street and asked him to find a cab, holding out a threepenny-bit temptingly. It was getting late, but it'd be easier to take the things over to Honeyfield tonight.

The office would be locked up now and only his father and the head clerk had keys. He could imagine his father's annoyance if he took the bundles home with him.

★ ★ ★

A mellow summer twilight was beginning as Nathan arrived at Honeyfield House with a cab driver who was happy to earn extra money by waiting for him. To his surprise, he found a car there that he recognised and when he knocked on the kitchen door, Barty answered it.

'Hello, Mr Perry. I didn't expect to see you here.'

'My father sent me to retrieve the clothes belonging to the woman and child staying here, so I thought I'd bring them over straight away. She must need them desperately.'

'She does. I was here earlier with Mrs Latimer and I've come back to help Sal. It's a bit hard to manage on your own after you've just had a baby in such circumstances.' He reached for the bundles.

'I'll help you take them up,' Nathan said. He was not only curious to see this woman but also needed to ensure that the clothing and money

222

went to the right person. Not that he didn't trust Barty, of course.

Sal was lying in bed, dozing, with the baby in a makeshift cradle made out of a drawer set on top of a chest of drawers beside the bed.

'This gentleman has brought your things, Sal,' Barty said.

She jerked fully awake.

'I'm Nathan Perry. Mrs Latimer asked our firm to retrieve your clothes.' He set the pillowcase stuffed with baby clothes on her bed and Barty dumped the other bags beside her.

'Oh. I never expected to see them again.' Tears trickled down her cheeks as she pulled out some tiny baby clothes and held them against her face for a moment.

'Someone sews beautifully,' Nathan commented.

'I made them and embroidered them too. I love sewing.'

'Could you do a quick check that everything is here, or are you too tired?'

'I'm not too tired to check, nor do I own enough things to let any of them go missing.' She rummaged through the clothing, muttering under her breath, then lay back on the pillows. 'It's all there. Every blessed thing I own now, plus a few extra baby clothes. How did you persuade them to give it all back? And do I owe anyone money for the extras?'

'The matron was happy to help and she knew where everything was. The extras were from her, no charge.'

'Only fancy,' Sal said, her voice weaker now.

223

'It's like a miracle, it is. That lady who's buying the house was kind too. I never had a miracle happen to me before.'

When he was leaving, Barty came to the door with him and Nathan told him he'd be dealing with the sale from now on and it was all right for Sal to stay on.

'That's good.'

'I'll come back tomorrow to get to know the house a bit better.'

Nathan treasured the memory of Sal's blissful expression all the way home.

Even his father's annoyance at him spending so much money on a taxi didn't take away the pleasure he'd felt at helping.

One day not too far away he'd find another job, one that suited him more than keeping accounts, one where he helped people preferably. He'd never lost his old skill at finding things. Surely he could put it to good use?

19

Kathleen had been feeling uneasy all week, but she couldn't work out why. Other people were excited about the coronation, which would take place at the end of June, while she was worried because she'd seen a man watching her. But when she turned a corner and nipped back suddenly to try to catch him out, there was no sign of him.

Had she been mistaken?

No. She had good eyesight and little got past her, as her children had found.

On the following Sunday she took the two of them round to Rhoda's house, as she had done a few times, then went off for a long tramp across the fields. She knew all the paths you were allowed to walk on. Just an hour or so of peace, she told herself. It was an indulgence but the children would be safe with Rhoda and she did her best thinking while walking on her own.

Why had she been feeling uneasy today? She couldn't work it out. No one had threatened her, there had been no messages from Godfrey Seaton for a while, and her father wasn't due till next week with the money. It was all very strange.

She looked round and realised she'd walked further than usual, feeling annoyed with herself for losing track of time.

As she began the long walk back to the village, feeling tired now, a car stopped beside her and for a few seconds her heart thumped in panic. Then she realised it was Bill.

'You're a long way from home, Mrs Seaton.'

'Yes, I was lost in thought and walked too far.'

'Want a ride back to the village?'

'Oh, would you? That'd be such a relief. I am a bit tired, I must admit. Are you meeting Mr Perry again?'

'Yes, I am. I've never met such a keen hiker. But he pays good money, so long may he continue.'

She asked Bill to drop her in the back lane, so that she could get the fire burning more brightly and put the kettle on before she fetched the children from Rhoda's.

As Bill drove away towards the street in front of her house, where he was meeting Mr Perry, she fumbled in her handbag for the key. It was a heavy old thing but the only one there was and she didn't dare leave it under a plant pot as most other people did.

When she opened the back door, the sight that met her eyes made her scream at the top of her voice and take a hasty step backwards. There was a dead fox in her kitchen. Well, she thought it was a fox. It was chopped into pieces and spread around the room. There seemed to be blood everywhere.

She screamed again as something swung towards her head and it proved to be a piece of the animal's innards hanging from the door lintel on a piece of string, which must have been released by her opening the door. It dripped blood on her face and hat before she could push it away.

Turning she ran out of the back door and screamed even more loudly as she bumped into a man.

Mr Perry stepped quickly back and held his hands out sideways, palms towards her, in a gesture that said he wasn't intending to hurt her. 'I was walking up the street towards Bill's car when we heard you screaming, so I came to see what was wrong.'

Pounding footsteps brought Bill to join them. 'I thought I'd better stop the car engine first,' he panted. Then he saw the blood on her face and gaped for a moment.

Shuddering with revulsion at the mess, she tried to wipe it off with her handkerchief, telling herself not to panic. She wasn't hurt, it was only an animal's blood. But she was sickened, utterly sickened by the sight of her kitchen.

Mr Perry put one hand on her shoulder and studied her face. 'You've got blood on your cheek. Where did it come from? Are you hurt?'

'No, I'm not hurt, but someone's broken into my house and left a dead animal in my kitchen. And a booby trap to cover me with its blood.' She pointed one shaking hand towards the bundle of guts swinging gently at the end of the string.

'Ugh. Perhaps you could go to a neighbour's while we check the rest of the house?' Mr Perry suggested. 'We'd better not clear up the mess till the police have seen it.'

'Police? What have the burglars done inside?' Bill asked.

'Go and see for yourself.'

He peered into the kitchen. 'Hell fire! Pardon

227

my language, Mrs Seaton, but there must be a lunatic on the loose.'

Kathleen couldn't stop shuddering and if Mr Perry hadn't put his arm round her shoulders, she'd have collapsed, she was sure, her legs felt so wobbly. It had been such a *shock*.

'Lean against me for a moment,' he said quietly. 'You've had a nasty surprise and you're white as a sheet.'

Some of her neighbours had come running out of their houses and were speaking to her, but their voices didn't seem to make sense and when Mr Perry guided her away from them, she let him take charge.

She didn't start thinking clearly again until she found herself sitting in Rhoda's kitchen, with the stranger explaining what had happened.

Kathleen's first thought was of her children and the need to protect them and prevent them running home. That helped her get control of her fear. 'I'm sorry, Mr Perry. I — it upset me.'

'A barbarous action like that would upset anyone.'

'I'll make you a nice cup of tea,' Rhoda said. 'Why don't you go and sit in the front room? You could lie down for a few minutes on the sofa.'

She brushed aside Rhoda's offer of her universal remedy: a cup of tea. 'I'll be all right. Where are the children? I don't want them seeing that horrible mess.'

'Mrs Dalton was going to her brother's farm, so she took them with her. Their cat's had kittens and you know how those youngsters of yours love baby animals.'

'Well, they're not having a kitten,' she said automatically. 'But thank goodness they're not back yet! I'll have time to clear up the kitchen.'

'Not till the police have seen it,' Mr Perry said firmly. 'An elderly gentleman has gone to fetch them, your next-door neighbour, I think.'

'Mr Polton?'

'I didn't catch his name.'

'Excuse me for asking, but how did you come to be involved, sir?' Rhoda asked when she came back with her best tea tray.

'Bill had arranged to pick me up in this street, which is the part of Monks Barton I know best. We were outside the front of the house about to get into his car when we heard Mrs Seaton screaming.'

Rhoda was nothing if not persistent. 'Why was he picking you up here? Have you been visiting someone in the village?'

'No. I work in an office and I miss the fresh air, so I go hiking at weekends. If I pay someone with a car to pick me up at an agreed spot, I can go for longer walks. You see so much more on foot.'

Rhoda was being her usual inquisitive self, Kathleen thought. She'd have been amused by that normally, but at the moment she was too upset and was still struggling to think what to do.

'If Bill knows you, that's all right, then,' Rhoda said.

'His cousin Barty's been driving me round for a few years. Bill takes over when Barty's busy.'

Even if Bill hadn't known him, even if he'd been a complete stranger, Kathleen would have trusted this man. He had a nice face, and though he had a rather large nose, his smile and kind expression stopped him from being ugly. A quiet, steady sort of man, she'd guess. She'd grown up with too many noisy people around her and she really appreciated a quieter, gentler approach to the world.

'Well, then. If the children aren't due back yet, I'll have time for that cup of tea, Rhoda,' she said.

Her friend bustled off to fetch another cup and saucer and Mr Perry sat down. 'You have a better colour in your cheeks now.'

'Thank you for helping me.'

'It was the least I could do.'

They heard someone knock at the back door and voices whispering in the kitchen, so they waited in a comfortable silence for Rhoda to come back. It was nice to have him there with her, Kathleen thought, and equally nice not to have to talk.

As if he'd understood what she was thinking, he smiled at her, so she smiled back.

Then Rhoda returned and the talking began again. What a pity!

★ ★ ★

The nearest policeman was in the next village and it took over half an hour for him to cycle over to Monks Barton after someone had phoned him from the village shop.

Once she'd finished her tea, Kathleen insisted on going back to her house with Mr Perry but

230

she went in the front way and sat in the parlour, unable to face the blood and guts again. She could smell them, though, and that made her feel nauseous.

'You all right?' Mr Perry asked.

'Mmm.'

He reached across to pat her hand a couple of times, a gesture that was comforting.

When the policeman arrived, it was Mr Perry who took him to see the kitchen.

As she listened to the men talking, she soon realised that the policeman was young and wasn't going to be much use at all. He did a lot of wondering who in tarnation could have done this, and wishing someone had tanned their backsides when they were young and taught them what was what.

As the words flowed on like a slow tide, she wondered how much he was actually examining in the kitchen.

In the end she heard Mr Perry take charge and went to peep as he walked round the kitchen again with the young policeman, prompting him to write this or that detail down in his notebook.

He sounded very capable so she left them to it.

They came to join her in the front room when they'd finished.

'I'll make a report, Mrs Seaton,' the policeman told her. 'And I'll ask around. Someone may have seen a stranger loitering.'

'Not if they used the back lane to get in and bent down as they walked to hide behind the hedges.'

'You're probably right. But I'll ask around all the same. And please be careful from now on, Mrs Seaton. Make sure you lock your doors carefully.'

'I did lock the doors and there's only one key to the back door that I know of, so I can't understand how they got it open.'

He looked puzzled. 'The lock hadn't been forced so there must be another key.'

Which didn't reassure her at all.

Smiling wryly, Mr Perry watched him leave. 'I gather you're a widow, Mrs Seaton. Is there anyone who can come and stay with you?'

'No one. I rarely see my family, and anyway, I don't get on with them.'

'Perhaps you should get the lock changed on the back door. That one isn't much use. I could pick it open myself.'

She blurted out without thinking, 'I'll not be staying here. I can guess who arranged to have this done. He wants to drive me away and he's succeeded this time.'

'Are you sure you know who it is?'

She nodded. 'Oh, yes. My husband's cousin, Godfrey Seaton. Others have warned me about him and he's been here and threatened me.'

'Tell me about it.'

And it all poured out, all her anxieties for the past year, the difficult position she was in, her worries about her children. 'I've been trying to work out how to get away without leaving a trail for him to follow,' she ended.

The clock on the mantelpiece chimed just then and she looked across at it in dismay. 'The children will be back from Mrs Dalton's soon. I need to clear up that kitchen.'

'I'll just go and have a word with Bill, then I'll help you.'

'I can't ask you to do that!'

'You didn't ask me, I volunteered.' He moved towards the front door. 'I'll be back in a minute.'

She couldn't resist a quick glance out of the front-room window and saw him gesticulating as he spoke to Bill. His face was alight with intelligence and life. He had a quiet way with him, but other men listened to him and let him guide them.

After slipping a coin into the driver's hand, he came hurrying back.

Taking a deep breath and telling herself she had to stay calm and dead animals couldn't hurt you, she moved towards the kitchen, absolutely dreading the task ahead.

Mr Perry moved past her and said gently, 'Let me get rid of the worst. Do you have any old newspapers to wrap the — um, mess in?'

'Thank you. I'm grateful. I'll get some newspapers for you.'

It felt strange to have help. She'd grown used to being independent and managing whatever needed to be done herself.

Just as she was finishing mopping the floor, there were voices outside. 'That's Mrs Dalton and the children.'

He took the mop out of her hands. 'I'll finish and get rid of the dirty water. Send her away then take them into the front room and explain what's happened.'

'And tell them that we have to run away tonight,' she said bitterly. 'They already know it's a possibility. Only I still haven't worked out where to go. I'll just have to go to London or Manchester or a big city like that, and find lodgings, then get work. I've got some money to tide me over.'

'You don't have any relatives you could go to?'

'Not that I'd trust to take me in and treat the children kindly. They'd be thinking how they could get money out of me.' She saw his expression of surprise and couldn't help wondering why she kept telling him things — or why he bothered to listen.

'I have a suggestion to make. After you've explained what's happened to the children, can you occupy them with something and discuss my idea with me privately? It may be the very answer for you.'

'You know somewhere we could go?'

'I think so.'

'I'll give them a glass of milk and a biscuit. They can sit in the kitchen now it's clean again. Christopher is always hungry. But I don't see — '

'You'll understand when I explain.'

So she did as he'd suggested. If he could help, they'd definitely leave tonight.

For some reason she trusted him absolutely.

★ ★ ★

The children were horrified when she told them what had happened, even more upset when she

234

said they'd have to run away that very night.

Elizabeth burst into tears. 'I don't want to go.'

'We don't have any choice, darling. This time whoever it was killed an animal. Next time they may ki — hurt one of us.' She had to cuddle Elizabeth for a moment or two before her daughter could stop sobbing. During that time Christopher sat like a statue.

When his mother looked at him, he said, 'I don't think adventures are much fun in real life.'

'I'm afraid not.'

'We were going to have a coronation at school,' Elizabeth said dolefully. 'I was going to be a lady-in-waiting. I'm going to miss everything now.' And she sobbed even harder.

'Stop crying, Elizabeth! *Stop it!* I'll get you both some biscuits and milk, then you can go and get out your spare clothes. Put them on the bed. When I've finished speaking to Mr Perry, I'll come up and check that you've got everything before we start packing. Choose one toy or book each. That's all we'll be able to carry when we leave. The rest must be clothes.'

Elizabeth was still crying, but silently now, tears trickling down her cheeks. There was no comfort Kathleen could offer because she too felt like weeping. Only what good would that do?

Instead she made sure the back door was bolted top and bottom, then gave the children a snack and joined Mr Perry in the front room. She couldn't think what he might be able to suggest, but she'd try anything sensible, or even half-sensible.

Nathan had heard the little girl sobbing and felt sorry for her, but it was the mother for whom he felt most sympathy. She hadn't complained or wept, and after the first shock had passed, she'd just got on with what needed to be done.

There was a lot to be said for getting on with things, in his opinion. Life wasn't always easy. His mother always made a fuss but left problems to her husband to solve. Which was what his father preferred. His father had to be king of the roost and he didn't want anyone to share that roost with him in any way. Not even his only son.

Mrs Seaton came to stand in the doorway. 'The children are occupied, Mr Perry. You said you had a suggestion.'

'Come and sit down. It'll take me a few minutes to explain.' When she was seated, he sat opposite her. 'I have to explain a few things first, so bear with me. There's a house called Greyladies further to the south and the owner has been left some money to spend on helping women in trouble.'

He told her about Honeyfield, where it was, the mess things were still in. 'But I think Mrs Latimer would be happy for you and the children to stay there. I met her when dealing with the house sale, because we found a woman there who needed help and I was able to provide it. Mrs Latimer is a very caring lady and I'm sure she'll help you as well.'

'Why would she?'

'Because you're in trouble and need somewhere

to go. That's what she is setting up the house for.'

He saw her flush and square her shoulders. 'I don't need charity.'

'I wasn't thinking of you asking for charity. She needs a housekeeper to run the place for her and manage women who will be doing a thorough cleaning from top to bottom. If you helped her and the other ladies on the committee to set things up, and proved your worth, she might consider you for the position permanently. It's near a village and there's a school within walking distance.' She was about to speak, but he held up his hand to stop her.

'In case you're wondering, I have nothing to do with the matter. I'm managing the sale of the house to the lady and taking an interest in the work she's doing, that's all.'

Kathleen looked at him. 'How did you know I was wondering about your involvement?'

'Any decent woman would.'

She sat thinking, wondering if this was the group Auntie Rhoda was involved with. But there wasn't time to ask her, because Kathleen was quite sure Mr Perry would be more efficient in helping her. And anyway, Rhoda might give something away if Godfrey questioned her.

She looked up. 'How can I find out if this Mrs Latimer is agreeable to such an arrangement?'

'I could telephone her. But not from this village or people might overhear me and find out where you were going. Look, you have to get away tonight, I agree absolutely. That mess was not the work of a sane person. So let's take a gamble on Mrs Latimer agreeing. I really don't think it's much of a gamble.'

'But what if she doesn't think I'm suitable?'

'I'll take you to a hotel in another town.'

'How will you do that?'

'Bill will take me home to Malmesbury and I'll contact my friend Barty from there. He's my usual driver and he's a lot more . . . ' he sought in vain for words and shrugged as he could only come up with 'capable and discreet than Bill. I know Bill has another person to pick up after me, so he won't do for your needs.'

'We couldn't walk far carrying our luggage, that's for sure.'

'Leave it to me. Barty and I will drive down the back lane. You can take as much as will fit into the car, instead of leaving most of your possessions behind.'

'That would be wonderful. But my neighbours will hear the car.'

'That can't be helped. That still won't tell them where you're going because we'll be changing drivers from Bill to Barty, who already helps Mrs Latimer from time to time. She told me once that she trusts him absolutely.'

Nathan watched her study him.

After a while she gave a nod. 'I don't know why, Mr Perry, but I feel I can trust you.'

'You can indeed. I'll leave now and come back after dark. I can't be quite sure of the time I'll return but make sure you don't open the door to anyone except me tonight.'

'I'll be very careful. And Mr Perry . . . '

'Yes?' He'd stood up to leave but he stopped

and waited for her to speak.

'Thank you. I don't know why you're doing this but I'm extremely grateful for your help.'

'I believe it's right for people to help one another. You can trust me to get you three out of here one way or another tonight and find you somewhere safe to stay.'

When he'd gone, Kathleen made sure the doors and windows were all locked, then packed as much as she could fit into their three shabby bags, helped by two subdued children. She wasn't sure how much they'd be able to fit into the car, but she intended to take as many other things as possible.

If Mr Perry came back for them.

No, he would come back. He would.

She paused in her packing as she realised that she couldn't seem to hold on to any doubts about him, let alone try to make other plans in case he didn't return, which even a half-prudent person would do.

Was she being a fool?

She'd soon find out. It was getting dark now and she still had a lot to do.

She kept a poker handy, though, in case someone tried to break in. A lot of women used pokers to protect themselves.

Who knew what she'd need in her new life? Her marriage and the children's birth certificates, obviously. And she had money safe in a special belt under her clothes, together with her bank book for the Post Office Savings Bank. She'd put all her money into her handbag. She'd not be penniless for a long time, thanks to

239

Ernest's savings and his father's present of twenty pounds.

But she'd be homeless and she hated the thought of that. Unlike her daughter, she couldn't give way to tears. She had to keep alert, be ready to deal with whatever happened.

20

There was a tap on the front door and Kathleen went to peer out of the window.

Rhoda. Of course. She'd want to know what was going on.

She let her friend in and told the children to come and kiss Auntie Rhoda goodbye, then lie down and rest, because they'd be up late.

Rhoda hugged each child for longer than usual and waited until they'd gone up to their bedrooms to ask, 'Are you really leaving?'

'Yes. It's no longer safe here. We're going tonight.'

'I saw those two men getting into the car in front of your house. They looked so serious and worried. And then you didn't pop round to see me to let me know what was going on, or send one of the children with a message.'

'I didn't dare send the children out on their own, or even bring them to you myself and leave the house unoccupied. And there's been so much to do.'

'Were you going to tell me at all?'

Kathleen couldn't lie to her friend. 'I thought it'd be easier for you to deal with Godfrey Seaton if you could tell him you didn't know we were leaving.'

'Nothing can make losing you easier, dear. Tell me where you're going, then we can write to one another.'

Kathleen shook her head again. 'Even if I knew, I wouldn't tell you. Oh Rhoda, *dearest* Rhoda, this is life and death. I have to disappear completely. No one must know where we've gone. *No one!* Not even you. I daren't take any risks. People know we've been friends and they might intercept your mail or threaten you, or anything.'

Rhoda sobbed, then pressed a handkerchief to her mouth for a moment as if to hold the grief in. 'How are you going to get away?' she asked in a voice choked with tears.

'Someone has offered to help us and I've accepted the offer.'

'That young man?'

'Not so young, though he's a little younger than me, I think.'

'It seems young to me. He has a kind face, though. I did notice that.'

'He's only taking us on the first stage of our journey. I won't be seeing him after that.'

Rhoda wasn't even attempting to stop weeping. 'But you'll write once you're settled, once it's all blown over, surely you'll write to let me know where you are?'

Another head shake was all Kathleen could manage or she'd be howling her eyes out. As it was, tears escaped her control and she managed to say in a choking voice, 'One day, when it's safe. Not yet.'

After a long silence, Rhoda mopped her eyes and blew her nose. 'It's probably wisest, but I'm going to miss you so much, so very much. Life can be . . . cruel. So . . . is there any way I can help you with the packing?'

'Thank you but only I can do that. I'm thinking what to take as I pack, pulling some things out again. We won't be able to carry much, you see.'

'Then I'd better leave you to it.'

Kathleen flung her arms round Rhoda and the two of them hugged for a long time. After that, her friend left, trying to hide that she was still weeping. It was a struggle not to do the same, but she didn't want to frighten her children.

She doubted she would ever have a friend as good as Rhoda, and until she felt safe, she wouldn't dare make any close friends. Well, she'd know no one in the place they were going to except Mr Perry. He was kind and he might — No, he was a busy man. He'd not have time to keep in touch with her and the children.

Oh, her thoughts were so scattered tonight, as if someone had tossed a handful of them into the air like pebbles. She had to concentrate, think very carefully about what to take with them. Be sensible.

She couldn't afford to give in to her grief.

★　★　★

It had been dark for over an hour before there was the sound of a car in the back lane. Kathleen had been starting to worry about whether Mr Perry would come back for them. He might *intend* to, but something outside his control might have stopped him.

But somehow she still *knew* he'd be back for them.

At the sound of the car, Elizabeth flung herself at her mother in terror and Christopher edged closer.

'Stay together near the kitchen table,' she whispered. 'I'll answer the door when they knock.' She picked up the poker.

She tried to look outside to find out for sure whether it was Mr Perry, but there were no street lamps in the lane and the moon hadn't risen yet. The light from her oil lamp made it harder to see outside, so she took it out of the kitchen and put it on the hall table.

When she went back and looked out again, she could see a car and two men, but she couldn't make out many details because her eyes weren't used to the darkness. One man was standing next to the car; the other was walking towards the cottage. He raised his hand to knock on the back door and she still couldn't see clearly enough to be sure it was Mr Perry, so didn't open the door. If he was knocking, he was coming openly. That was surely a good sign?

As if he'd read her mind, he went to stand in front of the kitchen window and tap on the glass to attract her attention. Then at last she could be sure who it was.

'It's him,' Christopher said. 'He's come for us like he said he would.'

'Yes. But stay where you are.' She opened the door and Mr Perry slipped inside, his eyes searching her face.

'Are you all right, Mrs Seaton?'

'Yes. I'm glad you could come or I'd not have known what to do.'

'I promised I'd help you. I always try to keep my word.'

'Yes. Of course. Have you . . . managed to arrange something?'

'I have. I telephoned Mrs Latimer and she's happy for you and the children to go to Honeyfield House. She thinks it's a good idea to have a sensible woman overseeing the cleaning and renovations, and will pay you a small weekly wage, plus board and lodgings for all three of you.'

Kathleen pressed one hand against her mouth to hold in a cry of relief. 'Oh, thank heaven for that! I won't let you down, I promise. Or her.'

'I'm sure you won't. Now, let's see how much we can fit into the car. We should be able to get you three and quite a few bags and bundles into the back section. This is Barty, by the way. He's a very good driver.'

She and the children got in and Mr Perry handed in all the bags she'd packed, then studied it and whispered, 'We can fit more in if you don't mind having things on your laps and round your feet. But you'll have to be quick getting them.'

She was already edging out of the car. 'I don't care how we sit, how uncomfortable we are, but these are going to be all our worldly possessions. Children, I'm just going to get more of our things. You wait here and stay quiet!'

'Don't worry. I'll keep an eye on them,' Barty said.

Her heart was aching for their white anxious faces, which showed clearly now that her eyes were more used to the dim light.

Mr Perry followed her inside and she said, 'Bedding.' So they took the lamp upstairs and he helped her fold all her bedding.

'Can I fit any more clothes in if I bundle them in sheets?'

'Yes, of course.'

'That'll be a godsend.'

In the kitchen he paused. 'Crockery is bulky and breaks too easily, but you could take your cutlery and metal things like pans.'

'The pans are such an awkward shape . . . '

'They can sit on the floor in the front by my feet. What else?'

It was an extravagance, but it'd lift her spirits once they were settled. 'A few of my books?'

'Of course. And grab any small items that can be crammed in, tea towels, tablecloths, whatever. I'll take the bedding out while you're doing that. We shouldn't stay much longer, though.'

He returned to help her carry out the rest and she looked round, mentally saying farewell to her home. When she slid back into the corner of the rear car seat, she was surrounded by bundles and had a shopping bag of cutlery wrapped in kitchen linen on her knee.

Mr Perry dumped everything else in around her feet anyhow and asked, 'All right?' When she nodded, he turned to get into the front of the car.

Barty said in a low voice, 'I think someone's watching us, Mr Perry. I'm sure I saw movement in this back lane. Can you see anything?'

Kathleen heard this and her heart started thumping in apprehension. 'Where?'

'Three houses along.'

'That'll be Rhoda, my friend and neighbour,' Kathleen whispered. 'She watches everything that goes on in the street. She's upset about us leaving.'

'I think it's more than that,' Barty said. 'There's someone at the far end of the lane as well. But there's only one way to find out for sure, set off and see if we're followed.'

'They'd have to have a car to do that. We'd hear it surely?'

'Once we start our engine, we won't be able to hear theirs. They won't dare drive too close behind us because their headlamps would show, but they'll be able to follow our headlamps because we'll probably be the only people out in the country lanes at this time of night. I'll stop later on and we can switch our headlamps off and watch out for them.'

'Good thinking, Barty. Swing that cranking handle and let's go.'

Kathleen was relieved when the engine started first time. She looked at the jumble of possessions around them and grimaced. Everything had been immaculate inside the car until they piled themselves and their things into it. She hoped Barty didn't mind the mess too much.

She felt something wet drop on the back of her hand, then more moisture, but didn't try to wipe away the tears because she didn't want anyone to realise she was weeping, especially the children.

The tears soon stopped. She never allowed herself to cry for long because there were children relying on her and she couldn't afford to give way to her troubles. She had somewhere to go tonight and someone to take her there, which was more than she'd expected. And possibly a job. She should be grateful for that. She was grateful. Very.

But still . . . she'd miss her home, her friends, her life in Monks Barton, miss them dreadfully, especially Rhoda.

Better not think of all she was losing. She'd had a little cry. That was enough weakness. She must look towards the future now.

She peered out of the car window but since it was a cloudy night with only a sliver of moon dipping in and out of the clouds, she couldn't see much.

Beside her, Elizabeth sighed and leant her head sideways on a lumpy bundle, settling into sleep in an awkward position. Not long afterwards, Christopher gave way too, leaning on his sister's back, one arm flung across her.

★ ★ ★

Nathan looked behind through the window between the front and back seats. Mrs Seaton was a brave woman, not weeping or complaining, just getting on with tearing her life apart.

He was glad Barty had had canvas sides made for the front so that the worst of the weather was kept off them, but he still found it a bit chilly, and though it was summer, could have done with gloves. Barty had made alterations to the window of the back compartment so that one half slid open across the other and the driver could talk to the people in the back. An enterprising man, Barty.

Mrs Seaton was still sitting bolt upright, wide awake, so Nathan slid the window open a little. 'Why don't you see if you can follow your children's example and catch a nap?'

'I don't think I could sleep. I was wondering where we were going.'

'To Honeyfield House, which is in a village of the same name on the borders of Gloucestershire and Wiltshire. I'll tell you more about your new situation when we get there.'

'It's a lovely name for a house.'

'It's a lovely house, with a meadow of wild flowers in front of it instead of a lawn because no one's been mowing it. That encourages the bees, I suppose. People around there are known for keeping bees to help pollinate their orchards and, of course, that gives them plenty of honey. I saw a lot of bees collecting nectar from the lawn of flowers when I went there.'

He waited and since she didn't ask any more questions, he repeated, 'See if you can sleep.'

He slid the window shut but glanced round a couple of times and saw her eyes close and stay closed, her whole body sag, in spite of her protests that she couldn't sleep.

'She's a brave woman,' he said to Barty.

'Yes. Must be hard for her to leave her home and friends, and so suddenly too. They seem a nice pair of children. Quiet, though.'

'It's a good thing they are, given the circumstances.'

'Mr Perry?'

'Yes.'

'While there's just you and me to hear this: I'm certain now that whoever was watching the house from the end of the lane is following us. I've caught sight of flashes of light in the distance when we've made turns at the top of slopes. The only thing that could be at this hour is their headlamps. And of course they can see ours.'

'Oh, hell.'

'If it's all right with you, I'm going to pull off into a carters' stopping place behind some trees about half a mile from here. I'll turn off our headlamps now and after we stop, I'll turn off the engine, too. Then we'll wait to see if anyone comes past.'

After they'd stopped, Nathan turned to check the three in the back and saw Kathleen jerk awake. He slid the window open. 'We've stopped behind these trees because Barty thinks someone may be following us.'

'Oh, no!' She glanced at the children but they hadn't stirred.

Barty got out of the car and went to stand behind a tree closer to the road to get a better view.

They could all hear it now, the sound of a motor car travelling along the road they'd just left. Gradually its lights came into view but the vehicle passed them without stopping.

Barty leant into the front of the car to tell them what he'd seen. 'Four men inside it, I think. I suppose it could be a coincidence that they seem to be following us. They could be nothing to do with Godfrey Seaton, but I doubt it. No one goes for joyrides at this hour of the night. I'm going to take a detour down a side road. If they're looking for us, we can't fight off four of them, but I bet I know more about the country roads round here than they do. I'll get us away, count on it.'

'They can't have any idea of where we're going, Mrs Seaton,' Nathan told her reassuringly. 'Once we get away from them, you should be safe.'

'But if they saw the number plate, they'll be able to trace you,' she said. 'I was reading about it in the newspaper a few weeks ago. With only two letters and four numbers, those plates are easy enough to remember and then anyone can find out who the owner of the vehicle is. The person writing the article was very indignant about that, said it was an intrusion on a person's privacy.'

Barty let out a snort of amusement. 'Don't worry, Mrs Seaton. I mixed up some mud and covered the number plates with it before we set off tonight.'

'What a clever idea!'

He looked up at the clear sky sprinkled with stars. 'Looks lovely, doesn't it? People are hoping the good weather is going to continue, but the crops and gardens need rain. Anyway that's neither here nor there at the moment. Trust me. I'll get you and your children there safely. I'm going to keep the headlamps turned off, though. I can see well enough if I drive slowly. The moon is up, even though it's only a quarter full.'

She nodded, but he hadn't waited for her

response. He crank-started the engine and got back into the car, driving out from behind the trees on to the main road again. A couple of hundred yards down the road he turned to the left. 'This is a roundabout way to Malmesbury and I know how to skirt the town. I'll light the headlamps again when we're nearly at Honey-field because it's up a narrow, twisty old lane and I don't want to land us in the ditch.'

When they stopped again at a slight rise, Barty climbed up a bank of earth and scanned the horizon in every direction. 'There's no sign of car headlamps anywhere and I couldn't hear anything either. They could have stopped to see if they can spot our lights, but there's nothing to see now. I think we're safe.'

Nathan turned to smile at her. 'There you are, Mrs Seaton.' He could see the worry still etched on her face so changed the subject. 'Your children are sound sleepers.'

Her face softened into a fond smile. 'Yes. Once they get to sleep it takes a lot to wake them up. It's better if they don't know about us being pursued, though. Elizabeth is a worrier.'

★　★　★

They seemed to travel for a long time. Barty stopped twice more, but he couldn't hear any-thing moving or see the lights of any other vehicles. Even the houses they passed were dark and silent.

Mr Perry told her softly at one of the halts, 'I doubt anyone will be awake to notice us passing through.'

'The only people out at this time will be poachers.' Barty chuckled. 'And *they* won't want to admit where they've been.'

They skirted Malmesbury, once again using country lanes, and only then did Barty stop to light the headlamps. Sure enough a short time later their light showed a sign with the village's name on it and Kathleen leant forward, trying to see as much as she could of what might be her new home.

'That's Honeyfield village ahead,' Mr Perry said, 'but we turn off to the right before we get into it. Honeyfield House is down a narrow lane and it's the only house there, so it's very private.'

'Good.'

The lane had high hedges and was rather uneven, so she could see why they needed the headlamps here. The children woke up as the car jolted in and out of ruts and branches swished and clicked against the roof and windows.

'What's happening?' Christopher asked, sounding anxious.

'We're nearly there. Shh.'

The house was a dark mass at the end of a short drive and there were no lights showing.

They drove round the back and Barty switched off the engine.

Kathleen let out a long sigh of relief. They'd got here.

'I think I should go into the house first and wake Sal,' Mr Perry said. 'Would you mind waiting in the car with Barty for a few minutes? If she heard the engine, she'll be worrying about who's arrived in the middle of the night. We haven't had a telephone put in here yet, so I had no way of warning her we were coming — but she'll recognise my voice.'

He took out a key and went into the house. She heard him call out, 'It's only me, Sal! Nathan Perry. I've brought a lady and her children who need a place to stay. Mrs Latimer knows about it.'

He lit a gas lamp in the kitchen and it shone out brightly across the darkness outside. It seemed like a beacon of hope to Kathleen. She had a sudden warm feeling as if being made welcome. How strange!

Barty got out and turned off the headlamps.

A voice was speaking to Mr Perry from inside the house and he was answering, but Kathleen couldn't hear what they were saying now that he had left the kitchen and presumably gone up the stairs towards the bedrooms.

When he reappeared in the kitchen doorway a couple of minutes later, there was a woman behind him, a very large woman who looked to be older than Kathleen, with a grey shawl round her shoulders and a mass of iron-grey hair streaming down her back.

His voice was louder than needed as he said, 'Sal, this is Mrs *Wareham*, who needs a place to stay. Someone has tried to hurt her and her children.'

Kathleen realised she should have thought up a new name for herself. She turned to wake Elizabeth, but the jolting had woken them both up. She needed to warn them about the name change. 'We're here now. Wait until someone opens the car door and helps you out. And I forgot to tell you that we'll have to change our name. Mr Perry has just said I'm Mrs Wareham, so that will be our new surname.'

'And can we call ourselves Kit and Lizzie?' Christopher asked at once.

'If you like.'

Elizabeth was still struggling through the mists of sleep.

'I never thought about having to change our names,' Christopher said. 'It'd have been more fun to choose a new surname ourselves.'

'Never mind that now. Just remember you're Kit Wareham. Now, we don't want our possessions falling all over the muddy ground so get out of the car carefully.' She wriggled out of her own seat, catching one of her bundles as it began to slide out after her.

She turned to help Elizabeth, who was yawning and still only half-awake, and found Mr Perry beside her.

'I can carry her, if you like.'

'Thank you. She's not fully awake yet and she's a bit big for me these days.'

'I'm afraid there's nothing ready for you here, but I'll help you make up some beds and you can sleep for as long as you like tomorrow.'

'It doesn't matter about things being ready,' she said. 'We've escaped from *that man* and there's a roof over our heads. Those are the main things we needed. I can't thank you enough for helping us.'

'Come and sit in the kitchen, while Barty and I unload your things. Sal, where can we put all

255

their bundles? We had to leave in a hurry so just threw as many of their possessions as we could into the car.'

'Put them in here, Mr Perry.' She opened a door and showed them a small dusty room with only a table and wooden chairs in it. She noticed Kathleen shivering and added, 'It's a good thing I always leave the fire banked up. I can get it burning quickly and warm you up. Tell me if you hear crying. My baby's upstairs.'

'Sal just had a baby, a little girl,' Mr Perry said with a smile.

Elizabeth brightened up at once. 'Oh, I love babies. How old is she?'

'Two days.'

'*Two days!* You shouldn't be looking after us, then, you should be resting.' Kathleen exclaimed.

Sal laughed. 'I've no time to lie around and I feel fine. I always recover quickly. I've had to. Who else will do the housework when you're married to a farm labourer who's out in the fields all day? He's dead now or I'd not be in this mess.'

As Kathleen started to get up, Mr Perry put a hand on her shoulder and pushed her gently back on the chair. 'You need to rest. Sal's got me to help her. What do we do first, Sal? You're in charge.'

She grinned at that and began giving orders. She was a quick worker and soon had a fire burning brightly in the kitchen range and a pot of tea ready. 'I'm sorry I haven't got anything to offer you to eat.'

'I've brought some bits and pieces of food. There's a loaf here and a jar of jam somewhere.'

Kathleen made sure the children ate something but didn't feel hungry herself. After that she kept her hands round her cup, finding the warmth comforting.

After they'd finished their snack, Mr Perry helped the two women make up beds for the newcomers, as Kathleen insisted on helping.

'I think you'll feel safer all sleeping together in this nice big bedroom, Mrs S — *Wareham*. Just get yourselves to bed for the moment. I'll try to come over to see how you are tomorrow — no, it's past midnight, so it's today, isn't it? — later today, then.'

'You don't think they could have followed us?'

So he repeated, 'Barty and I are both sure they haven't.'

She hoped he was right, wondering if she'd ever feel secure again. She felt much safer when he was with her, but she didn't say that. He had his own life to lead and was just helping a stranger.

When the men had driven away, she looked at Sal. 'I'm sorry to have woken you.'

'It's what Mrs Latimer wants this place to do, give shelter to women in trouble. I needed somewhere to go and she let me stay here. Well, she helped me birth the baby because you can't stop them once they start coming out, can you?' She laughed at her own little joke. 'She's a lovely lady. And now *you* need somewhere to live, as well as me, and she'll help you in any way she can, I know.'

She looked thoughtful, then added. 'Mind you, I take a poker to bed with me at night.

257

Makes me feel safer. You might like to do that too. Shall I get you one?'

'Yes, please.' Kathleen went into the next room to find the bags that had their clothes in. Then, with Sal and the children's help, she carried all of them up to the bedroom, leaving just the bundles of household items behind.

She and Elizabeth shared a double bed, and Christopher — no, *Kit* now — slept on a sofa. She was reminded of the old saying about falling asleep almost as soon as your head touched the pillow because that was exactly what her two did.

She envied them, was sure she'd never sleep, but when she opened her eyes again, it was light.

Flinging the covers aside, she got out of bed, wondering what time it was. Her little clock was somewhere among the things they'd brought. She'd find it before the day was through. She'd rolled up the marriage certificate and other papers she'd brought, and they were beside her bed inside one of the bags of clothes. She'd have to find a new hiding place for them today. Just in case.

Lizzie didn't stir when she got up. Her son turned over and sighed in his sleep as she passed the sofa. Sunshine showed through gaps in the curtains. It was going to be a lovely day. She'd take that as an omen.

This is my new life, she told herself firmly. *And I'm going to make it a good one for us all.*

★　★　★

When Barty dropped Nathan off at home, he asked, 'Do you want me to drive you over to

258

check that they're all right this evening?'

'It's a bit far for you to come.' Nathan fumbled in his pocket for his wallet and pulled out a five-pound note. 'Thank you for your help today.'

'That's too much, sir.'

'No, it isn't. You were risking yourself and your car last night and I'm grateful.'

'How will you get over to see them tonight, then?'

Nathan smiled. 'I've been thinking of buying a car for myself. I have a friend who wants to sell one. My father's very much against it, but I shall ignore that. I'm going to need one if I continue to help Mrs Latimer. I pass his house on my way to work so I'll tell my friend's wife to ask him if I can try the car out tonight. If it goes all right, I'll buy it.'

'Whoever invented cars did us all a service.' Barty patted the bonnet of his. 'I couldn't have carried on working on a farm after I got injured.' He grinned. 'And it's all turned out well, because I like driving much better than tending to cows.'

He leant closer to add, 'Mrs Latimer bought me the car and gave it to me — just gave it, can you imagine that? Her only condition was that I drive her whenever she needs to go somewhere. I'd do anything for her. I was in despair when she stepped in.'

Nathan made an encouraging sound, because he was finding this interesting.

'She and I live in the same village, so tomorrow I'll go and tell her how Mrs Seaton

259

and the children are and, if I know her, she'll want to come and meet them as soon as she can, to see what else they need.'

'She must be a wonderful person.'

'The ladies who inherit Greyladies always are, from what my grandfather and father have told me. Latimers have always been there at the big house in Challerton for as long as people can remember.'

'If you and Mrs Latimer do drive over to see Mrs Seaton tomorrow, perhaps you could leave a message at our office, to say whether my help is still needed for anything specific? Would Mrs Latimer mind stopping to do that?'

'I'm sure she wouldn't mind at all, sir.'

'I'll tell the junior clerk to fetch me if you turn up.'

It was only after Barty had left that Nathan remembered that Latimer was one of his mother's family names. How strange! He and this kind lady might even be related.

21

In the morning the maid had to shake him twice to wake him up.

'You'd better hurry, Mr Nathan, or you'll be late for breakfast.'

He grunted and opened his eyes, staring at her for a moment till he realised what she was saying. Then he blew out a long, weary breath and tried to work out what to do. He'd only had a couple of hours' sleep and felt in desperate need of more. 'Tell my father I'll not be coming down to breakfast today and I'll be late getting to the office, because I was out late last night helping a friend who was in trouble.'

She gasped and looked at him pleadingly. 'I daren't tell him that, Mr Nathan. He'd go mad at me and he might even dismiss me for not waking you sooner. You know how he insists on everyone in the house being punctual to the minute.'

To his *minute*, Nathan thought. His father insisted on the servants and his family showering attention on him and his routines, as if he was the only person who mattered in the whole world.

The muddy feeling was beginning to clear from his brain and anger was replacing it, but that wasn't the maid's fault. 'I suppose he will take it out on you. Sorry, Alice. I'll come down and tell him myself.' She'd been with them for ten years and he'd hate to get her into trouble.

He got out of bed and fumbled his way into his dressing gown, muttering, 'Him and his stupid rules!' as he tied his belt any old how. He was twenty-seven years old and the changes he'd been thinking about suddenly came together in his mind. The time had come to manage his own life. He'd saved some money and could well afford to rent and run a small home of his own, even though his wages weren't generous. So he was going to make a few changes.

And he wasn't going to allow his father to treat him like a child at work, either. He was good at what he did and could easily get a job elsewhere or even start up his own accounting firm. He'd dreamt of doing that, usually when his father was more tetchy than usual. It'd have to be in another town a long way away from his father, though, or he knew his father would blacken his name to people.

But the main reason he'd not made any changes before remained the same: his mother. Once he'd got enough money together, he'd stayed for her sake, because his father always took his ill humour out on her. She had a way of giving her son pleading glances, as if asking him not to upset her husband, and some of the things his father said made him feel desperately sorry for her. But it had been difficult at times to bite his tongue, very difficult.

His poor mother had been even more meek than usual lately and he'd been wondering why. What had his father been saying to her in private?

Even for her, Nathan couldn't go on like this any longer. If a woman without much money like Kathleen Seaton, with two children depending on her, could run away from her enemies and take a brave leap into the future, so could he.

He ran lightly down the stairs and walked straight into the dining room, where his father insisted they eat all their meals in some state, giving the poor servants a lot of unnecessary work.

Pausing in the doorway, he watched his father shake out the newspaper, pretending not to have heard him come in. His mother was staring across the room, her eyes vacant, waiting for her husband to signal the start of breakfast, not moving to serve herself yet.

Was it his imagination or did she seem to have done a lot of staring into space lately?

It was as if Nathan was seeing the scene for the first time. His father was doing what he wanted and his mother was taking care not to interrupt or disturb her husband. Neither of them seemed to care about their son's happiness, or anyone else's needs, come to that, just as long as their little domestic games were played out to his father's satisfaction.

At last his mother seemed to realise he was there. She shot a quick glance in his direction, her mouth falling open in shock to see him in his nightclothes still. She looked hastily towards her husband, who was still refolding his newspaper in precisely the same way he always did, then jerked her head as if to tell her son to go away and get dressed.

Nathan shook his head, leant against the door

frame and waited, unable to suppress another yawn.

Having got the newspaper sorted out to his satisfaction in precisely the correct folds, his father looked across at him. His mouth firmed to a thin line for a few seconds, then he spoke even more loudly than usual. 'What on earth do you think you're doing coming down in your night-clothes at this hour of the morning, Nathan?'

'I'm about to go back to bed. I just needed to tell you that I won't be coming into work until mid-morning. I was out helping a friend who was in trouble yesterday and didn't get back here until after three o'clock.'

'They had no right asking you to stay up that late. You need your sleep if you're to put in a good day's work. Your first responsibility is to me as your employer, sir, not to your friends.'

'This was an emergency. Anyway, I've no appointments until later, so I'll catch up on a bit more sleep and come in mid-morning.'

His father's voice was like a foghorn. *'You will come to the office at your usual hour!'*

As a child Nathan had been terrified when his father shouted at him. Now, he merely felt annoyed. 'I don't think there is any need for me to do that.'

'Then your pay will be docked for the whole day. And you can work all day Saturday to make up for it.'

This was getting more and more ridiculous. 'I'm afraid I can't accept you treating me like a child.'

His father made a few gobbling sounds at this,

though whether they were from anger or shock, it wasn't clear.

'I'll treat you in any way I wish. I am your father and you owe me your obedience for that, and I'm also your employer, so be very careful not to anger me further. Now, go and get dressed at once. You'll have to manage without breakfast this morning. I don't intend either of us to be late for work.'

'No.' It was a very satisfying little word sometimes.

His father made some more angry little noises, then snapped, 'If you don't come to work, I shall dismiss you, just as I'd dismiss any employee who didn't obey my rules.'

His mother let out a whimper of protest, but Nathan ignored that. 'I can find other employment, just as some of your employees have done over the years when they'd had enough of you shouting at them for no reason.'

There was dead silence at this. His father's mouth opened and shut several times, as if he didn't know what to say next, then he struggled to his feet, took a deep breath and roared at the top of his voice. 'I will not tolerate this disrespect in my own house.'

'And that brings us to the other thing I need to tell you. It's more than time I found myself somewhere else to live. A man my age doesn't usually live at home.'

'That's because a man your age is usually married. As I've told you before. Your mother has introduced you to several very suitable young ladies whose families we know and respect.'

'Well, I haven't met any lady with whom *I* wish to spend the rest of my life, however much *you* like their families, so that is no solution.'

Then his father said the same words that had threaded his life: 'I have said my last word on this. Kindly do as you are told.'

That sharp order added fuel to the anger that had been simmering for years, and it flared up even higher. Nathan was about to turn and leave when he noticed that his father's face had turned a dark red in colour, such an unnatural colour that he knew something was wrong.

His mother suddenly pushed her chair back and stretched her hand out to her husband. 'Felix dear, please calm down. You know what the doctor told you last time you had one of your turns.'

'Damn the doctor! And damn this ungrateful cub.' Felix tore at his high collar as if it was choking him. 'I will not — '

And in a sudden, abrupt silence, his hand dropped away from his collar and he began to topple sideways, slowly like a felled tree. He knocked a chair out of the way, then came to rest on the carpet, face down, one arm outflung.

Neither of the others moved, then his mother sank to her knees beside her husband. 'Get his pills!' She turned him over and finished loosening the tight shirt collar.

'Where are they?'

'In his desk. Hurry!'

Nathan rushed across the hall to his father's study, nearly bumping into Alice and yelling, 'Send for the doctor. My father's been taken ill.'

He found the pills in the top drawer and ran back to the dining room with them. His father hadn't moved and his mother was still on her knees beside her husband but she wasn't moving either.

'There you are.' He held the pills out to her.

'It's too late.' Her voice was a mere whisper.

'What?'

'It's too late. Your father's dead.'

Nathan stared at her, words choking him and refusing to be uttered. *Did I kill him? Why didn't he tell me he was ill? This is a nightmare. It must be.*

His mother began to struggle to her feet and he helped her up.

'I've told Alice to send for the doctor. He'll know what to do.'

'Felix — is — dead,' she whispered.

Then her whole body sagged and Nathan realised she was about to faint. He only just caught her, picking her up and lying her down on the sofa. He stared at her, not sure what to do next.

She was always pale and lately she had become so thin as to be ethereal. She was like a delicate flower, he'd thought when he was a lad, proud of how pretty she was compared to other lads' mothers. Her looks had hardly changed in the thirty years since her marriage. Her skin was only faintly lined, her complexion still good, and her hair frosted with grey only at the temples.

She had always spoken quietly in her husband's presence and that had grown more marked recently.

He was about to call for Alice when his

267

mother began to regain consciousness.

She stared blindly at him for a few seconds then sat up and stared at him, not speaking.

'I'll just check Father,' he said.

He made sure she wasn't likely to fall off the sofa and knelt beside his father, feeling for a pulse and finding none.

'You're right. He's dead.'

'Poor Felix.'

He couldn't bear those staring, slightly bulbous eyes, so closed them. He didn't know what to do next. Standing up, he turned to ask her, but she was staring down at her clasped hands now.

She wasn't weeping, though. And *he* didn't feel upset emotionally, because he hadn't loved his father, and didn't think Felix Perry had ever cared about anyone else, not even his wife.

'Mother?'

She turned to him. 'What must we do now, Nathan?' She was speaking in a quiet, almost toneless voice again, and it irritated him that she was waiting for him to tell her what to do, as she'd waited during her whole adult life for her husband to give her instructions.

His father had always been sure he knew the correct action to take, but Nathan couldn't for the life of him figure out what he should do next, let alone tell his mother what action to take.

'I don't know what to do,' he said baldly. 'We've both let Father dictate how our lives should be lived. Now we each have to find our own way.'

She looked slightly puzzled and he saw the moment when fear crept across her face. 'But I don't *know* what to do,' she whispered.

'Shall I send for your maid?'

But at that moment the front doorbell rang and he heard Alice open the door and greet Dr Chescombe.

Thank goodness!

'This way, Doctor!' Nathan shouted.

Dr Chescombe was older than his father but he was trim and energetic, well respected and liked. The contrast between the two men could not have been greater.

Nathan watched him kneel down by his father's body, but he knew what the doctor would tell him.

'I'm afraid he's dead. A seizure, I should think, from the look of him. Did he get angry about something?'

Nathan turned to his mother, but she was staring down at her own hands again, so he said it for her. 'Very angry indeed. I'd just told him I was moving into a home of my own and since I missed my sleep last night due to an emergency, I wasn't going into work till later.'

'He wouldn't like that.'

'No. I think I killed him.' He didn't relish the thought of that.

The doctor came across and laid one hand on his shoulder, a comforting gesture. Nathan couldn't remember his father ever touching him willingly, let alone offering comfort.

'No, Nathan, you weren't to blame. He killed himself, because he wouldn't moderate his behaviour, and refused point-blank to eat less, let alone refrain from flying into rages. I've warned him several times that this could happen, haven't I, Mrs Perry?'

'Yes, Doctor.'

He looked across at her and frowned.

'My mother fainted,' Nathan said. 'She seems a bit . . . well, almost disoriented.'

'She doesn't eat enough. You'll have to make sure she eats properly or she'll be following your father.'

Nathan stared at him. '*I* will have to make sure?'

'Yes. You're the only one left now.'

'But I shan't be here. I'm moving out.'

'Come into the hall.' Dr Chescombe led the way, closing the dining-room door behind him. 'Your mother is not a well woman. I'm sorry to have to tell you this on top of your father's death, but she's suffering from the early stages of senile dementia. She'll need watching carefully and looking after. She'll gradually lose the ability to remember and later, if she lives long enough, to speak or dress herself. It's going to be hard for you to watch her decline. I feel so sorry not only for such patients but for their families too.'

Nathan could only stare at him in shock.

'I explained all this to your father last year. Didn't he tell you?'

'No. He never said a word.'

'Well, he's dead now so it's no use going over that old ground. I can recommend a good woman as a nurse-companion, but *you* will be needed here to oversee things, Nathan. I'm sorry. Were you thinking of getting married? If so your wife can — '

'No. I was just thinking of getting free from him.'

'Ah. Well, you are free of him, but not free of your mother. I'll write out a death certificate for your father. I checked him only last week, because I insisted on seeing him before I would agree to prescribe any more pills. I have no doubt what killed him and it *wasn't* you.'

'I'm relieved about that.'

'I'll send a message to Broughton's about arranging a funeral, if you like, Nathan.'

'Yes, please. I must confess I'm very ignorant about what needs doing.'

'Put yourself in Broughton's hands. He's a very wise and caring chap, who looks after his clients in every way he can.'

Dr Chescombe gave Nathan a long, thoughtful look. 'You don't appear to be very well yourself.'

'I'm not ill. I had an almost sleepless night helping a friend.'

'Ah. Well, there's no need to rush through everything today. But you'd better let them know at the office what's happened, hadn't you?' He waited a minute. 'Are you listening?'

'What? Oh, sorry. I just realised something else. I'd promised the same friend to help again today. I'll have to send a message, find someone else to take my place.'

The doctor clapped him on the shoulder. 'You do that. Your place is here now. And you'll need to supervise the necessary changes at work as well. In fact, everything will be in your hands from now on, there and at home. But you're a capable young fellow. You'll manage all right.'

Nathan looked down at his hands. He could almost see the chains being clasped round his wrists, feel the chill grasp of the steel, and a pressure he couldn't fight against or escape from to remain in this house of unhappiness.

Just as he'd been about to seize his freedom.

⋆ ⋆ ⋆

The first thing to do, Nathan decided, was to go into the office and tell the staff about his father. From there he could phone someone to help Mrs Seaton. He had to make sure Kathleen and her children were helped to settle in at Honeyfield House and then helped to make new lives for themselves.

Who would be best? He could only think of Mrs Latimer, because if she couldn't do anything herself, she'd know someone else who could.

He'd have liked to have helped as well because he admired the young woman's courage and was rather attracted to her as well. Prettiness allied to character was rare in his experience. He wasn't the sort to rush in and make a fool of himself over a woman, but he'd wanted to get to know her better, he definitely had.

Well, there was no hurry. He could start to get better acquainted with Mrs Seaton after he'd sorted out whatever was necessary when someone died. The chief clerk would be able to help him reorganise things at work, he was sure. Mr Parkin was a capable fellow.

'We have to buy mourning clothes.'

He looked up to see his mother standing there, still with that rather blank expression on her face. He knew why she looked like that now and it hurt to see it.

'We have to buy some mourning clothes, Nathan.'

'We'll do that tomorrow.' He looked round and saw Alice hovering near the door. She seemed to be keeping an eye on his mother and must have been doing it for a while. He wondered if she'd make a better nurse-companion than a stranger, and on an impulse, he beckoned to her.

'Do come in, Alice. Perhaps you can help us? My mother needs to buy some mourning clothes but I can't attend to that today. Perhaps you could take her out and make a start on it?'

His mother drifted off across the room to straighten an ornament and he watched her, feeling very upset.

'The doctor told you, didn't he?' Alice said in a low voice. 'About your mother, I mean?'

'Yes. I hadn't realised. How did you know?'

'Your father said she was getting a bit absent-minded and asked me to keep an eye on her. But I knew what was really wrong. She's very clever at hiding it still, but that'll change eventually and she'll betray how confused she is.'

'You seem to know a lot about senile dementia.'

'My grandma went the same way. I was only nine, but I had to help my mother with her for two whole years.'

'It doesn't seem fair. My mother isn't even old.'

'Some get it younger than others, sir.'

'Look, perhaps we can find another house-maid and *you* could look after my mother full-time instead of us bringing in a stranger?'

'The doctor wants to bring Mrs Pakely in to look after her, but . . . ' Alice hesitated.

'Go on.'

'Well, she's very harsh with them. My friend works for someone who used her services. She sees they're clean and fed, you can't fault her on that, but they're not happy with her.'

He frowned then studied Alice, whom he'd known for years. He was seeing her with new eyes today as well. 'Could *you* manage to keep my mother happy if you had charge of her?'

'Bless you, yes. Your mother is no trouble at all. She has a sweet nature.'

'Then I think my first change here will be to promote you to a lady's maid and companion, and to raise your wages accordingly.'

She went pink with pleasure. 'Oh! Thank you so much. I won't let you down, Mr Perry.'

She'd called him 'Mr Perry' not 'Mr Nathan'. It seemed like a rite of passage. He was now head of the household.

His mother was about to go out of the room and he called, 'Mother? I thought you could have Alice as your maid from now on. Would you like that?'

She stopped and stared at him, then looked over her shoulder. 'Your father doesn't want me to have a maid. He says it's a waste of money and I should be able to find my own clothes.'

'Father died this morning, remember?'

'Oh. I'd forgotten. How could I forget?' She looked stricken.

'You were thinking of something else. We'll have to make some changes and you'll need more help without Father to . . . um, guide you. Would you like Alice to look after you from now on?'

'Oh, yes. She's always so kind to me.'

'All right?' He raised one eyebrow at Alice and she nodded.

'We'll need to find another maid to do the housework, sir.'

'Ah. Yes, of course. How do we do that?'

'You can go to a domestic agency or . . . Cook has a niece who's looking for work in Malmesbury to be nearer her family. You could talk to Cook and if her niece hasn't found a position, you could give her a try.'

'Shouldn't my mother do that?'

'Not any longer, sir.'

'Ah.'

Another shackle, he thought. Managing the household. And a very tight shackle too. He could see the sympathy in Alice's eyes. He'd do his duty, of course he would, but it was going to be hard to bear.

He went into his father's study, pausing in the doorway, still half-expecting to see his father sitting behind the desk. He'd have to clear this out before he could use it for himself. The desk was tidy and the drawers firmly closed and locked. His father would have the keys on his person, as usual.

With a sinking heart, Nathan realised that he'd have to go and get them.

The doorbell rang just then and it was the undertakers, so he had to drop everything to deal with them.

Mr Broughton was indeed helpful and tactful, and *he* found the keys. After that he guided Nathan through a list of decisions to be made.

'A lavish funeral? No, thank you. Just a quiet one.' His father had had enough fussing over in his lifetime.

'Are you sure about this?' Mr Broughton asked once they'd gone through the list of what he offered. 'A gentleman of your father's standing in the community would usually have a more . . . well, a more lavish send-off, with professional mutes, plumes and six black horses. Not to mention the best mattress and pillow for the coffin. We have some covered in the very best quality silk.'

'I don't want a big fuss made. My mother isn't well and I don't want to place too much of a burden on her.' He hesitated, then added, 'She's becoming very forgetful.'

Mr Broughton looked at him sharply.

'We have a maid who is looking after her and helping her, but she won't be able to cope with a big fuss, or even understand it very well.'

His companion nodded. 'Ah. I see why now. Definitely the right thing to do in the circumstances, a quiet funeral. I'm sorry you're having such troubled times, Mr Perry.'

'Thank you.'

He escorted Mr Broughton to the door when the first set of decisions had been taken. Alice was just leading his mother down the stairs, both dressed in their outdoor clothes.

'We're going shopping, dear,' his mother said. 'Will you be here when we get back?'

'No. I have to go to the office.'

He watched her walk out, her expression far beyond placid. In fact she had hardly any expression on her face. How had he missed that blankness? Why hadn't he noticed how vague she'd been getting?

He looked down at the heavy bunch of keys in his hand. Fancy carrying these around all the time. Had his father ever trusted anyone?

Well, there was no use procrastinating. It was going to be a long, hard day. He'd better make a start by phoning Mrs Latimer and asking her to help Mrs Seaton settle in at Honeyfield.

Unfortunately the maid who answered told him that her mistress had left suddenly and the maid wasn't sure where she'd gone.

He'd have to try again to contact Mrs Latimer later.

22

When Nathan arrived at the office just before midday, he went into his small office first and Mr Parkin came hurrying across the main room to speak to him. 'Is everything all right? It's not like your father to miss a day's work without sending word.'

'Um . . . no. It's not all right. Could you come into my father's office, please?' He knew the partition that divided off his office was not soundproof.

The older man gave him a sharp look, saying, 'Oh!' almost as if he'd guessed what this was about.

Nathan gestured to a chair and waited till the chief clerk had sat down before taking the big, comfortable chair behind his father's desk. 'I'm sorry to tell you my father died this morning.'

A quick intake of breath was his only answer for a moment or two, then Mr Parkin shook his head sadly. 'He'd been working too hard lately. And he hasn't been looking well for a while.'

'Yes. The doctor wanted him to take things more easily.'

Parkin hesitated, then said, 'He couldn't. There's a problem no one knows about but him and me, and now only me, so I need to tell you. I'm presuming you're the new owner?'

'As far as I know, yes.' Was he assuming too much? Surely not! Who else could his father leave everything to?

'The main problem is — '

There was a knock on the door and the office boy peeped in. 'There's a lady to see you, a Mrs Latimer. She's sitting in her motor car outside, says could you go out and speak to her for a moment, if you don't mind.'

Nathan went out to greet her.

He went across to Barty's car and found a lady sitting next to him in the front. 'Ah, Mrs Latimer.'

'Yes. And you must be Nathan Perry. I presume the lady and her two children were taken safely to Honeyfield House yesterday?'

'Yes. We were followed at first, but Barty managed to give them the slip. I was going to go out to see that everything's all right, but my father died this morning and things are a bit chaotic. I tried to phone you this morning to ask you to help Mrs Seaton settle in.'

'I'm so sorry to hear about your father. It's a good thing I came, then. I had a sudden urge to welcome the lady in person.' And had had one of her strange feelings that she was needed.

'I was going to ask you to take over organising things for the time being, because my mother's . . . um, not well, on top of everything else.'

'Let me take over, then . . . '

'Are you sure you don't mind?'

'Very sure. And one day we'll meet in happier circumstances and talk properly about ourselves. I think you have Latimers in your family tree and indeed, you have a look of my male ancestors.'

'How did you know that?'

'It's a sense I have whenever I meet another Latimer — well, one with certain gifts.'

He was startled by that.

She patted his hand as it lay on the edge of the car door. 'Do what you need to for your own family. It isn't time yet for you and I to work together more closely. Goodbye!'

He watched her go, wishing he could take the time to talk to her properly now, and find out what she meant by that, but he couldn't. From what Mr Parkin had said, something was very wrong with the business on top of everything else.

Taking a deep breath of the fresh air, he went back inside, calling, 'Someone open a couple of windows. It's very stuffy in here.'

★   ★   ★

Nathan opened the window in what he still thought of as his father's office, then sat down again. 'I'm sorry to keep you waiting. It was Mrs Latimer.'

'A very pleasant lady. Now, sir,' the older man leant forward and lowered his voice, which was completely unnecessary because the door was shut, 'I need to tell you about Mr Galton first.' He hesitated.

'What about him?' Nathan prompted. He didn't like Mr Galton, who had been working here for just over a year and was too friendly with everyone, with smiles that never reached his eyes.

'Your father thought he was stealing money.

280

He didn't have any proof and he didn't want to call the police in, but Mr Galton didn't come into work yesterday. Your father didn't know what to do, but we were going to see if he came in today and if not, look into his various accounts in more detail.'

That must have been why his father had been so urgent to get to work on time today. 'Why didn't my father want to call in the police?'

'He said it'd destroy the firm's good name. Um. I think we should check the cash boxes first. Your father was feeling unwell yesterday, so he said we'd look into it first thing this morning.'

'I see. We'd better do that straight away. Would you open the safe, please?'

Mr Parkin looked at him in surprise. '*I* haven't got the key, sir. Don't you have it?'

Nathan pulled out his father's bunch of keys. 'Will it be one of these?'

'Yes. That one. But you need the correct number for the combination lock as well, and I don't have that either. Your father could be rather secretive. Actually, I don't know how Mr Galton could have known the number, but small amounts of money were definitely going missing from the cash boxes every now and then.'

'I'm afraid I don't have the combination number.' Nathan wondered if this day could possibly get any worse.

'Oh dear.'

'Don't you have any idea, Mr Parkin?'

'Um . . . I think the number might begin with seven. I couldn't help seeing how Mr Perry started dialling because I used to pass him the cash boxes every evening as he opened the safe and he often started dialling before I was able to turn away.'

'Seven?' Suddenly Nathan was sure he could guess the first two numbers of the combination for their old-fashioned Milner safe. Perhaps the ability to guess things was related to the ability to find things. 'Our house number is 72. Could that be the start, do you think?'

It was a long time since he'd gone by his instincts for finding things and he wasn't even sure it'd work with guessing numbers, but he had no other way of finding the other two numbers needed. It was stupid of his father to start off with the house number, because it'd be an obvious possibility to anyone who knew the family's address.

Something was making his head hurt and he closed his eyes, rubbing his forehead to ease the throbbing. As he concentrated, a number seemed to whisper into his brain: his father's birthdate! Equally stupid choice, if that was so.

He swung open the picture on the wall that concealed the safe and tried the numbers 7216, then inserted the key. It turned easily and he opened the door. 'Thank goodness!'

He saw Mr Parkin staring at him warily and said, 'It was easy to guess: our house number plus his birthdate.'

'Oh, I see.' The older man relaxed.

His reaction had reminded Nathan yet again that people didn't like you being too different and doing things that weren't easy to explain. He must take care not to do anything like that in front of people from now on. But if he needed to know something, he'd do whatever was necessary in private. His father wasn't here to create a fuss now.

Mr Parkin joined him in front of the safe. 'Oh, dear! Look at that! The cash box is missing. Oh, and the petty cash box too. There was a lot of money in the cash box because, as you know, your father would only put money in the bank once a week.'

'Anyone who worked here would know that. He made quite a parade of going to the bank on Friday mornings, carrying the bag of money. Do you have some figures for what's missing?'

'Yes. Or at least your father does — did. They should be in his little black book. I hope the thief didn't take that! It's kept in the top drawer of this desk, and that's the key to it.' He pointed to a small key.

Nathan used it to open the drawer. 'His black notebook is here.'

'Thank goodness!'

'Have you any idea what's happened to Mr Galton?'

'I'm afraid not. And when I looked inside his personal drawer this morning, it had been cleared out.'

They stared at one another as the obvious reason came to mind.

'I think we'd better call in the police.' Nathan rubbed his forehead, which was still aching. 'Could you send someone to fetch them? Or do you think I should go myself?'

'No, no. You look weary, and no wonder with

283

what you've had to face today. We'll send the office boy. Tim is a good lad and I'm sure he won't say a word to anyone else. I'll call him in.'

While they were waiting for the lad to return from the police station, they used the black book to calculate how much money was missing.

Nathan stared at the figures. 'Over a thousand pounds! Why on earth did we keep so much cash on the premises?'

'It was from the sale of a house, the one you sold in Wayson Road.'

'Any sane person would have put that much money straight into the bank.'

The clerk's grimace said he agreed.

Since the police hadn't yet arrived, Nathan got Mr Parkin to help him go through his father's desk drawers, which were surprisingly untidy, and crammed with rubbish, as were the low cupboard by the window and the filing cabinet, both fitted with locks. It was as if his father had been afraid to throw anything away.

Nathan wondered how he could have worked here for so long and not known all this? But then, no one went into his father's office uninvited, let alone fiddled around in his drawers and cupboards — except Mr Parkin, who was going to be invaluable in sorting it all out.

And Nathan might be the only son, but increasingly his father had had him working on the house selling side, especially with the smaller properties, rather than doing the accounts for their various customers.

The doctor said his mother was going senile, but his father's mind must have been failing too.

This was a ridiculous way to run a modern business! Nathan was going to change a lot of things from now on.

If he still had a business to run!

Mr Parkin cleared his throat, looking even more unhappy, if that were possible.

'What else do you need to tell me?'

'There are debts. Your father hasn't paid some of our suppliers for a while. In fact, he's been waiting till the last minute to pay anyone. The accounting side of the business hasn't been doing as well as it used to. That's why you were selling houses a lot of the time. The commission from that side of things saved us more than once.'

Nathan closed his eyes, swallowing hard, then opened them again and asked, 'Are there any more shocks waiting for me?'

The old man was near tears. 'The insurance. Your father let it lapse. Said we didn't need it because we could look after the office ourselves.'

'Had he run mad? Why did I not notice?'

'I must confess that he had become . . . well, rather strange. Ever since he started being . . . not so well. I think he'd been working too hard.'

'That's putting it politely. As well as mismanaging the business, he disobeyed the doctor and refused to look after his own health, and he's been more bad-tempered than ever at home.'

'Here too.'

'I didn't realise he was doing such *stupid* things, though. Is that all the bad news?'

'I think so, Mr Na — I mean, Mr Perry. I'm

sorry. I didn't feel it was my place to tell you about it before, not while he was, um, coping.'

He could see the anxiety on the older man's face. 'It's not your fault, Mr Parkin, and of course you were right to keep your worries to yourself. I know better than most what my father was like. I want you to know that I value your hard work, and I hope you and I will work together happily for a good many years yet.'

'You won't . . . want a younger clerk to take charge, someone with more modern ways?'

'Definitely not. You and I will learn modern ways of doing things and put them into operation here together. At least we have a telephone, so we've got one useful piece of modern equipment.'

Mr Parkin pulled out a large handkerchief and blew his nose loudly. 'Thank you. I shall always do my best, I promise. Now, if you don't need me any more, I'd better get back to work till the police arrive.'

Nathan nodded and managed a half-smile. As he sat waiting for the police, he couldn't help wondering whether he'd been promising more than he could deliver. What if there wasn't enough money left for them to stay in business after they'd repaid this customer's house sale money and paid off the other debts? They'd have to pay back the money that had been stolen themselves if the business was no longer insured. And pay the tradesmen's bills, and whatever else was owing.

When word got out about the robbery, the firm's reputation would suffer. And it would get out eventually, one way or another. The question was, would enough people continue to use their services to keep the business running? People liked to feel sure about the safety of their money and the good status of the people who handled their accounts.

The sound of voices heralded the arrival of a young police constable, and when he found out how serious the burglary was, with a large sum of money missing, he insisted on going back to the police station and sending his sergeant to take over the investigation instead.

'Phone him from here!' Nathan said, very close to losing his temper. 'It'll be much quicker.'

The constable froze for a moment, then something about Mr Perry's expression seemed to galvanise him. 'Very well, sir. If you don't mind me using your telephone.'

The sergeant was there within ten minutes, which was one benefit of modern equipment, Nathan thought grimly.

He sent word that he'd be home late, and stayed on until eight o'clock that night compiling accurate accounts, with Mr Parkin helping him.

Only as he walked home did he allow himself to think of his personal life. There could be no question now of getting to know Mrs Seaton better. He'd have nothing to offer a wife for years yet.

But he would send her a letter explaining that his father had left the business in a mess and that he would therefore be occupied for 'a good long time' in sorting things out, so was sorry not to be able to help her settle in.

He might at least do that, because he didn't like to think of leaving her wondering why he was avoiding her.

★ ★ ★

During the next two weeks Nathan only took time off work to buy suitable mourning garments and to attend his father's funeral. He didn't invite guests to the house afterwards, because he knew his mother wouldn't be able to cope. Instead he told one or two rather gossipy people that his mother wasn't well, sure that information would be passed on.

He and Mr Parkin took on the work of Galton, thus saving one salary, and some of their old customers rallied round, though others sought the services of other accountants.

To his relief, Alice was as much a tower of strength at home as Mr Parkin was at the office.

His mother seemed to fade daily and was more like a ghost creeping round the house than the kind, smiling woman who'd raised him.

At least without his father bullying everyone, his home was a more peaceful place to be. But it was lonely, because his mother no longer contributed much to conversations, whatever topic he introduced.

Mrs Seaton wrote to him, offering her condolences and thanking him for doing her the courtesy of informing her of the reasons for his inability to help.

She had beautiful handwriting and he kept her letter, taking it out now and then just to touch the only tangible evidence of a might-have-been.

Life could take some choices away from you almost as soon as you found them.

⋆ ⋆ ⋆

As Harriet Latimer was driven towards Honeyfield, she thought about Nathan. She was sorry his father had died, though she hadn't liked the man, because death wasn't easy for those left behind, whatever the circumstances.

The weather was sunny again today. It was the most glorious summer she could ever remember. They didn't get to Honeyfield House until around eleven o'clock and she hoped poor Mrs Seaton hadn't been too anxious. She sounded to be a capable woman, from what Nathan had said. Harriet smiled. She'd been thinking 'young woman' but Mrs Seaton must be around her own age.

She found her new occupant giving the two children a snack in the kitchen with Sal sitting in a rocking chair nursing the baby in one corner. It was a placid, domestic scene to gladden the eye, even though it was taking place in a dusty, run-down house which desperately needed a thorough sorting out.

She went forward, hand outstretched. 'I'm so glad to meet you, Mrs Seaton. Or may I call you Kathleen?'

'Please do.' She looked across at Sal, who was staring at her in surprise.

'I thought your name was Wareham.'

'Oh, I'm so sorry,' Harriet said. 'I only know

you as Mrs Seaton and Nathan was in rather a hurry this morning. He didn't tell me you'd chosen a new name.'

Kathleen smiled. 'It doesn't matter, but I will use Wareham with outsiders from now on, if you don't mind. It'll be safer. Seaton's my old name, Sal, and my enemy's name too, so I hope you'll keep it to yourself and use only Wareham.'

'A-course I will. Good idea, changing names. I might do the same.' She winked at the children. 'You two can help me choose a new one.'

Harriet went across to peer at the baby she'd helped bring into the world. 'She's doing well, isn't she, Sal? A very healthy-looking infant. What have you called her?'

'Barbara, after my mother. But she'll probably end up being called Babs.'

'It's a lovely name either way. Now, Mrs Wareham, I have a message from Nathan. Could we go and discuss it in the sitting room? Sal, would you keep an eye on the children, please?'

'Happy to. Or else they can keep an eye on me and the baby.'

The children grinned, already seeming quite comfortable with her.

The sitting room was dusty and smelt of mice. 'I don't think I want to sit on this furniture till it's been thoroughly cleaned and the cushions beaten,' Harriet said. 'And we must set traps for the mice. Let's go and stand in the bay window to talk. It has a pretty view, or it will be pretty once we get the garden tidied up. I suppose we'll have to bring some men in to scythe that long grass.'

'It'd be a pity to get rid of the meadow, if you don't mind me saying so, Mrs Latimer. Wild flowers are prettier than grass and they're attracting lots of bees. We could get some beehives and produce our own honey.'

'What a good idea! We'll look into that later. I don't know anything about bee-keeping, though. Do you?'

Kathleen shook her head. 'No. I don't know what made me suggest it. The idea just popped into my head. It's because of the house being called Honeyfield, I suppose.'

'Well, I'm sure I've read somewhere that you can let other people put their beehives on your land and they'll give you a share of the honey in payment. That would work even better for our purpose. Now, first things first . . . Nathan. He's going to write to you himself because he was planning to come here later today to help you settle in. Only, I'm afraid his father dropped dead this morning so that isn't possible now.'

'Oh, how sad!'

Mrs Latimer gave her a wry smile. 'They were arguing at the time and they didn't get on at all well, so it's not as sad as it might be. Can you manage without his help for the time being?'

'Oh, yes, I'm sure I can. I've already been into the village and bought a few things to eat, as you can see. There's a very good baker there and a general store. And we can buy apples from some of the nearby farmers, I gather.'

'Good. I'll set up accounts at the village shops before I go home, because when Honeyfield House is in operation, you'll never know how

291

many people you're going to be feeding from one week to the next, and it won't be your responsibility to pay for the groceries. You'll need to keep careful accounts for the trust, though. Do you know how to keep accounts? If not, we can find someone to teach you.'

Kathleen smiled. 'I think I can cope if you show me what sort of accounts you want. I intended to become a secretary before I got married, you see, so I studied account-keeping and typing, among other things. Against my father's wishes, I might add. I'm like Mr Perry. I don't get on very well with my father and it wouldn't upset me if I never saw him again.'

'That's sad. But your knowledge of accounting will be helpful. I can see you're going to do well here. In fact . . . let me think for a moment.' She paused and looked round, closing her eyes as if listening to something.

Kathleen didn't like to disturb her, because she looked very peaceful, so waited, still enjoying the view.

Mrs Latimer opened her eyes. 'The house feels 'right' now that you're here. I can always tell. So if you want to take on the job of matron permanently, I'll be very happy to employ you.'

Kathleen was startled. 'Don't you want to see how I go first?'

'I don't need to. The houses our trust runs seem to acquire a warm, friendly atmosphere once we get the right person in charge. It always feels as if some kindly spirit is keeping an eye on the houses and giving approval of the new matron and her helpers.'

'I know what you mean. Last night I felt — '
Kathleen flushed and hoped she wouldn't sound
silly, 'as if someone kissed me goodnight.'

'Exactly. Our friendly spirit. And Sal seems to
fit in here too. Would you be happy to work with
her?'

'Oh, yes. We already get on well and she's
good with children. There's only one thing
worrying me. What if Godfrey Seaton finds me
and attacks this house? There's no one close
enough for us to shout for help.'

'We shall employ a strong man to look after
the grounds and maintenance, not just for you
but to protect anyone who's staying here. It's
usual to do that in places of refuge like this.
Some of the women we'll be helping will have
violent men pursuing them. We may get a dog, as
well, to help keep watch.'

'It would be a relief to have a strong man to
turn to, I must admit, and the children would go
wild with delight to have a dog.'

'So you'll work as matron here?'

'Yes, please, Mrs Latimer. It's such a peaceful
house.'

'Let's walk round the gardens together, then,
and discuss what needs doing and in what order
you should do it. I'd love to stretch my legs.
Then we'll go into the village together and set up
those accounts at the shops. Will you be happy to
leave the children with Sal?'

'They'll be fine, but should I not keep out of
sight while you're organising all this?'

'No. That would look suspicious. But we
definitely won't take your children with us into

the village yet. If whoever has been trying to harm you comes to Honeyfield, they'll be asking about a lady with two children, not two ladies.'

She looked thoughtful and added, 'With the baby, there will be three children here, which may further confuse the situation for anyone looking.'

Kathleen didn't know what to say to that. Indeed this whole experience was like something from a dream. A good dream, though. She had never believed in ghosts, or spirits, or whatever you called them. Not till she got to Honeyfield.

But she was disappointed that she wouldn't be seeing Mr Perry until after he'd buried his father and gone through the necessary formalities to take over the family business. That could take months. Would he still bother to come and visit her? She hoped he would, because she'd taken a liking to him, felt truly comfortable with him, far more comfortable than she ever had with Ernest.

That was strange, because she hardly knew Mr Perry.

She sighed. As if a gentleman like him would be interested in someone like her, a nobody from an Irish background.

Honestly! You'd think she'd have stopped building castles in the air at her age.

23

For the next two months all went well at Honeyfield House. Mrs Latimer insisted a matron wasn't there to undertake the heavy cleaning and employed a woman from the village to help Sal with that.

It quickly became obvious that Sal actually enjoyed scrubbing and cleaning. She would call 'Matron' to come and look every time she and her helper finished another room, and stand beaming both at its cleanliness and the praise given her.

She also kept the baby clean and happy, singing softly as she fed and changed little Babs.

Mrs Latimer hadn't yet found a strong man to help at Honeyfield, but she'd had the telephone installed, which made Kathleen feel a lot safer. At least she could call the village policeman for help now.

When she went to the shops, however, she still kept a wary eye open for strangers in the village and made sure she reminded the children regularly to take care who they spoke to.

Then Kit, as her son was now called, came running home from his new school one day with Lizzie pounding after him. 'There was a man waiting outside our school today, Mum, so I took Lizzie back inside and we climbed out over the back wall of the yard instead. I don't think he saw where we went.'

'We ran and ran!' Lizzie corroborated.

Kathleen's heart began to thump with apprehension and Sal stopped what she was doing to listen.

'Had you seen the man before?'

'I think it was our Irish grandfather.'

She closed her eyes for a moment and tried to work out what to do. 'We'd better keep you two home from school tomorrow. Maybe he'll go away if he doesn't see you again. I don't think anyone from the village will tell him where we live, not now Sal's put the word out that there's someone trying to hurt us.'

But she didn't feel easy and in the end she telephoned Mr Perry and explained her worries. 'I'm sorry to trouble you, but if you could just advise me . . . '

He was silent for a few moments then said, 'If you like, I'll speak to your children's headmaster tonight and warn him about the man. He'll probably take it more seriously coming from me.'

He didn't say 'because I'm a man'. He didn't need to.

'It's a lot of trouble for you. Only, Honeyfield isn't on any railway line and I have no means of getting away quickly.'

'It's not too much trouble because I have my own motor car now and it only takes about twenty minutes to drive over. I know where Mr Fleming lives and I've met him a few times on a church committee. I'll telephone you afterwards.'

'Thank you so much. I shouldn't ask your help because you have enough on your plate, but I don't know who else to turn to.'

'You're always welcome to ask my help. Always.'

He had better telephone Mrs Latimer about this as well, he decided, and make sure she knew what was going on.

Harriet Latimer was shocked. 'Oh, dear! And we still haven't found a suitable man to act as a guard. I should have made more effort. I'll look into that straight away. Could you let me know what the headmaster says?'

'Yes, of course.'

Nathan might not be able to put himself into a position to get to know Kathleen better on a personal level, but he was certainly going to make sure he kept watch over her from a distance. And he'd ensure there were other people watching out for her too.

It seemed so unfair to meet a woman he found attractive at a time when it was impossible to offer her anything but debts and the decline of his mother's health and understanding.

And at a time when she might have to flee and go into hiding. How would he ever find her again if she did that?

* * *

Since there was no telephone at the school, Nathan telephoned a farmer whose accounts he did in Honeyfield and asked him to send his lad round to the headmaster's home with a note asking if it would be convenient for him to call on James Fleming that very evening to discuss an urgent matter relating to the school.

The farmer telephoned back saying Mr Fleming had suggested seven o'clock.

Nathan intended to take Fleming into his confidence about Kathleen — though he must remember to call her Mrs Wareham. He could never think of her except as Kathleen, though.

He was ready early, so left the car outside the shops and went for a short stroll round the village. He stopped in surprise at the sight of a man walking slowly along, staring at passers-by, muttering to himself.

Could that be Keller? Nathan studied him carefully. Kit had a look of him, something about the eyes and the way the man's hair curled.

Who else could it be in a small village?

Nathan slipped into a doorway and continued to watch, wondering what Keller was intending to do. Had he teamed up with Godfrey Seaton to trap his daughter? Would the man really sell his own flesh and blood, and risk seeing Kathleen and her children murdered? That went against human nature.

He watched Keller go into a pub. Perhaps he didn't know exactly where his daughter lived. Reluctantly, he decided not to follow him because he mustn't miss his appointment, so he got back into his car and drove to the schoolmaster's house on the edge of the village.

James Fleming took him into a small study and listened carefully as he explained the situation. 'Are you sure about this?'

'I'm very sure that those two children could be in danger. But whether from their grandfather or their father's cousin I don't know. Perhaps both. They saw their grandfather outside the school, and I've just seen a man answering to his description walking up and down as if searching for something. So, as there's little doubt that it was Keller lingering outside the school, I felt it wouldn't hurt to alert you to the possible danger.'

'May I ask why you're involved in Mrs Wareham's affairs?'

'My firm does the accounts and oversees the management of the house where Mrs Wareham is the matron. It's being paid for by the Honeyfield Bequest, money left by a generous lady to help women in trouble through no fault of their own. Such places can attract men of ill will.'

'Ah, I see. My wife would probably like to get involved with something like that if she can be of any assistance to you.' Fleming gave him a wry smile. 'She's a firm believer in equal pay and votes for women, though not, of course, in violent means of getting the vote like those Pankhurst females advocate.'

'I believe women should have a vote too,' Nathan said. 'In my experience they're no less intelligent than men. Believe me, the lady in charge of the bequest would put many men in the shade when it comes to handling money and running a business. And after all, what is a big charity like that but a type of business? A lot of men employ me to look after their accounts because they can't even cope with keeping the simplest of account books.'

James smiled. 'You sound like a man who shares our views of the world. My wife and I will have to invite you round to tea one weekend — and your wife too, of course.'

'I'm not married.' He managed not to sigh, but he wanted to. 'Nor am I likely to be able to contemplate it, much as I'd like to have a family. My father left his business affairs in rather a mess and it'll take me a while to sort them out. And my mother is . . . not well, and not likely to get better again.'

'Then you could come here on your own and the three of us will sort out the country's problems over tea and crumpets.'

'I'd really like that.' Nathan leant back in his chair, liking this man more and more. It was a long time since he'd had an intelligent friend, not since his schooldays. Heavens, how quickly the years had slid past! Was he really twenty-seven already?

'We might be able to sort out the problems here in England, but there's trouble brewing in Europe, unless I'm much mistaken,' James said thoughtfully. 'And now there's a second Moroccan crisis. Where is it all going to lead? Didn't we have enough with the Boer Wars? Major nations talk about peace but they don't seem to be able to settle into it.'

'I couldn't agree more. The German Kaiser in particular seems to have some very dangerous ideas, for all he's related to our British royal family.'

A clock chimed the hour just then. 'Goodness me! I hadn't realised I'd been here for so long. I mustn't take up any more of your time.'

'Well, I do have some marking to finish, I'm afraid. It's been a pleasure to chat to you. Do you have a card? Thank you. Here's mine. I'll be in touch with you about coming to tea. And as for the other matter, you can be assured that I'll keep my eye on those two children. I take my responsibilities as headmaster very seriously, I promise you.'

★　★　★

After a day at home, Kit and Lizzie — who both loved their new, shorter names — said they'd rather go back to school because they were missing their new friends.

'I'll come and meet you after school and we'll walk home together,' Kathleen said at once.

Kit groaned. 'Oh, Mum, do you have to? It'll make us look like babies.'

'Then you'll just have to look like babies. Do not leave the school yard until you see me. I mean that! Do not even go near the gates!'

She was so anxious about their safety she was waiting there as the final bell of the day rang, standing behind a group of women and watching the passers-by carefully in case her father was there.

But there was no sign of him, thank goodness. She hoped he'd given up looking round Honeyfield.

The three of them walked along the main village street, with the children telling her about their day. But as they turned off towards

Honeyfield House, her father suddenly stepped out from behind a cart whose horse was waiting patiently for his master.

She stopped dead, not knowing what to do.

'I'm not going to hurt you, Kathleen, but let's get out of sight of people who might,' he said in his gravelly voice.

The children stared at him uneasily and he stared back, his expression sombre, not giving away anything about why he wanted to see her.

She turned into the lane and then stopped. 'You can run off home now, children. We'll follow you more slowly.'

She watched them hurry off down the lane, relieved that Sal would be there at the house. Dear Sal wouldn't let anything happen to them. 'What do you want, Da?'

'I need to know where you are, and now that I've found out, I want to know what you're doing here.'

'So that you can tell your employer where to find me? Well, we won't be here by the time you get back, I promise you. I have friends who'll help me get away this very night.'

'There's no need to run off. I'll not be saying a word to *him* about you.'

He bent his head, fiddling with the hat he was still holding in his hands, then looked at her with a sad expression. 'He's worse than I'd thought, Mr Godfrey is, an evil man. It didn't take me long to find that out and I'm leaving Seaton's as soon as I find another job. He's cruel to the horses, that one is, expects too much of them.'

Her father had always cared more about horses

than people, she thought.

'It's always a bad sign that, folk who're cruel to their working animals. No need to make pets of them, but if you want them to work hard, you have to treat them right. The old master's wife dotes on Mr Godfrey and he takes care to keep *her* happy, because he wants her money, but he doesn't give a fig for anyone else and the men are afraid of him.'

She studied her father's face as he spoke. She'd learnt years ago that certain muscles in his jaw twitched slightly when he was telling her lies. They weren't twitching now. Was it possible he was telling the truth? Did she dare trust him?

No, she didn't dare, just simply couldn't after the years of harsh treatment. But it wouldn't hurt to listen to him, to find out if what he had to say was credible, see if she needed to flee or not. She looked along the lane. It led to nowhere but Honeyfield House, so there could be no disguising where they lived.

'You might as well come home with me, Da. I'll make us a cup of tea.'

'That'd be welcome. I've a powerful thirst on me. And a bite of something to eat, if you can spare it.'

'You always did eat and drink a lot.'

'I work hard. I need to feed my muscles, don't I? And now that I daren't go into a pub, I get more thirsty of an evening.'

She'd set off walking but stopped in surprise at this statement. '*Daren't go into a pub?* Whatever do you mean?'

'*He* said if he sees me in a pub, he'll sack me

303

on the spot, and the same goes for any of the men. Seems he's a teetotaller and wants the whole world to be as miserable as he is. It was a bad day for us all when Mr Seaton died. You're not the only one to lose by it.'

If her father was spinning a story, it was better than his usual efforts, she had to give him that.

'How come you've got time during the day to come hunting for me, Da?'

He shrugged. 'Work's slowed down because people don't like dealing with *him*. He's sent all the men home for three days without pay, except for one man to take care of the horses. How does he think we'll put bread on the table if we don't have any money?'

'How did you think of coming to Honeyfield? How did you find me? That's what I don't understand.'

'Barty mentioned the place he'd taken you to his friend Bill, who is also my friend. But he wouldn't give me your address, even though I told him I'd not be hurting you. He said the fellow who helped you get away lives round here, but has stopped going for walks at weekends.'

She should have remembered that Bill knew her father and not been tempted to live at Honeyfield House. It was too close to her old home.

'I hired a horse and rode over to see if I could find you. The fellow at the pub is keeping an eye on the horse for me. You see a lot when you're on the road on foot or riding a horse. You don't see nearly as much when you're in one of them tin boxes with your nostrils full of the stink of petrol. But the day before yesterday, almost as soon as I got here, I saw the school and thought I'd have a look at the children.'

'Sheer chance, then.'

'Nay, I had the wit to come to Honeyfield, didn't I? The wit to think that my grandchildren would be at school, with a mother so fond of book learning. Do you think you're the only one in the family with a brain? Well, you're not. Anyway, I recognised your two straight off, because that little lass has a look of you, and your lad looks like our Daniel did when he was a boy. Only they ran off and I couldn't find them.'

He shrugged. 'I knew then that you'd be living somewhere round about so I came back today. They weren't there. I was going to see the headmaster and ask him, only I saw you walking down the street with them.'

Blind chance had a lot to answer for, she thought bitterly. 'Well, come in.'

But he was staring at the house and then at her, frowning suspiciously. 'How come you're living in such a grand place? Have you got yourself a gentleman to keep you?'

'No, I haven't. I work here. I'm the matron. Or I was till you found me. Now I'll have to run away again and who knows where I'll wind up? I should have gone further away this time, if it weren't for being offered such a good job.'

'You've no need to up your sticks again. I'll not be telling *him* where you are.'

'Except that I don't trust you.'

He grabbed her arm and gave her a quick shake. 'I'm telling you the truth, Kathleen Frances.'

The kitchen door flew open and Sal hurtled out brandishing the poker. 'Let her go, you brute!'

He laughed, feinted and grabbed the poker, twisting it quickly out of her hand.

Kathleen pushed between them. 'This is my father, Sal. He's coming in for a cup of tea and a chat. Don't ever let him take the children away, though. I don't trust them with anyone else. Are they all right?'

'Yes. They came running in and went off to hide. That's what they think of their grandfather. I've got one grandchild now and another was on the way when I left. I'd be ashamed for them to be hiding from me, deep-down ashamed.' She scowled at Fergus.

He blinked in shock at this defiance and didn't seem to know what to say. His years with her meek mother hadn't prepared him for dealing with women who stood up for themselves, Kathleen thought. To her surprise she found herself smiling. She'd back Sal against anyone unless Sal was outnumbered.

'*And* you'll have bruised your daughter, grabbing her and shaking her about like that, Mr Keller. Shame on you. If you were *my* man, I'd wait till you were asleep and hit you good and hard with a big stick to pay you back.'

To Kathleen's further surprise, her father began to smile.

'I bet you would, too. Ah, come away in with you, woman. I didn't hurt Kathleen, nor does she need a watchdog barking at me. She's never been afraid to do her own barking.' He turned to his daughter. 'Does this woman know about you?'

'Of course she does.'

'Well, I'd still rather speak to you on my own.'

'And I'd rather Sal stayed with us.'

A baby cried from inside and Sal turned at once. 'She's hungry. I'll have to feed her or she'll cry the place down.'

'You've got a child?'

'Yes. But no husband because he's dead.' She set her hands on her hips for a moment and gave him a challenging stare, then went inside.

'She's a fine woman, that one,' he said. 'Got spirit. I like that in horses and women.'

That was news to Kathleen. Her father had always seemed to want a meek wife . . . .Or had her mother been meek by nature? That had never occurred to her. 'Sal's been a good friend to me. Come away in. I could do with a cup of tea as well.'

Her father didn't say much as he drank three cups of tea and ate some bread and jam. Then he began to fiddle with the cup and look sideways at his daughter. 'You can trust me, you know. Now I've had to give up drinking, I'm not feeling as . . . well, as angry all the time. My mind seems a lot clearer. And your mother didn't help. She used to drive me wild, the way she wasted my hard-earned money. I'll try to keep an eye on Mr Godfrey. I think you'd be safer here among people who know you than you would be wandering the country on your own.'

'You're not the first to tell me that. I hope you're right.'

Sal came back to join them. 'What we need is

a strong man to work here and help protect us. Haven't been able to find one yet, though. He needs to be able to look after a garden, do odd jobs and keep an eye open for intruders. Do you know anyone, Mr Keller?'

'I might.' He turned to Kathleen. 'You remember Brian O'Donnell? Well, he's looking to get away from Swindon. His wife up and died on him and the new baby with her. He's talking of going on the tramp, he's so desperate to leave. He was fond of her, was looking forward to having children.'

'I remember him from church. He was in the choir, wasn't he? Smiled a lot.'

'Yes. He doesn't do much singing or smiling now, though.'

'Give me his address and I'll tell the ladies who manage the charity about him. *I* don't have the power to hire anyone.'

He pushed the piece of paper back to her. 'I'll tell it to you and you write it down. You write a clearer hand than I do.' He did that then nodded at Sal and pushed his chair back. 'Thank you for the food, missus. I'd better be off now. That horse will want to get back to its stable.'

'Fancy you spending money on finding me.' Kathleen said.

His voice grew sharper. 'Spending it on keeping an eye on my family, more like. The others are all right at the moment but *you* aren't safe yet.'

'This is a new thing for you.'

'Aye. It is. Being on your own leaves too much time for thinking, and regretting.'

'What about your lady friend? What does she think of it all? Have you told her about me?'

'No, I haven't. When I decided I wasn't ready to marry straight away, she was quick to find someone else. And besides . . . she was a bit stupid-like. I've had one stupid wife. I don't want another.'

Kathleen had never thought how much it must have irritated him to live with Deirdre. Her mother hadn't been quick-thinking, to put it mildly, as well as being a very poor manager. Kathleen reckoned she took after their father, and so did her brother Daniel.

She walked to the end of the lane with him, not saying much. To her relief he made no attempt to touch her or kiss her. Well, he never had been one for 'mauling folk around' as he called it.

She watched him stroll back into the centre of Honeyfield village and go round behind the pub. She stayed watching, hiding behind a tree, till she saw him ride off on a horse. At least he'd told the truth about how he got here.

Only after he was out of sight did she walk slowly back to the house, finding it hard to sort out her thoughts. Did she believe her father or not? Was he protecting her or was he working for Godfrey Seaton, protecting his own interests? Should she leave now . . . or wait and see what happened?

She asked Sal what she thought but she wasn't much use because Sal thought her father was a 'fine figure of a man' and seemed dazzled by Fergus.

So Kathleen decided to telephone Mr Perry and tell him what had happened, and ask his advice again.

24

Nathan had worked out a rough outline of what had to be done to remedy his father's mistakes, calculating as best he could how long it'd take him to sort it all out and what he had to do first. His father's old-fashioned ways had probably led to some people going elsewhere for help with their accounts.

Broadly speaking, it would take a year or so to work through the financial tangles and pay off the debts, depending on how many of their remaining customers stayed with them.

And then it'd take a further year to build up their clientele again, so that his firm was making a decent profit. It would be a more modest profit than in their heyday because they'd lost some of the bigger farmers and certain country gentlemen who'd relied on them for many years to do the accounts or to check their other employees' accuracy.

On a personal level, he intended to work long hours at a job that he only admitted to himself he didn't enjoy and never had done. At home, he'd live frugally, keeping only the servants necessary to look after his mother and using only the rooms they actually needed. His social life wasn't going to be very full because he was too busy, but he would accept a few invitations from family friends and people useful in business.

He soon realised that the local families now

saw him as an eligible suitor for their unmarried daughters. He wasn't, either financially or emotionally. He still dreamt about another young woman with lovely dark hair, clear blue eyes and the slightest of Irish lilts in her voice.

And he even dreamt occasionally, as he had in his youth, about following in the footsteps of the fictional Sherlock Holmes and becoming a detective. He didn't know why this had appealed to him so much, but it had — and still did. To help people right wrongs or to find things or people they'd lost would be much more interesting and worthwhile.

His mother's condition was known about now and apart from asking how she was, people no longer tried to invite her out to tea or dinner, or even send her messages. It was sad because although she was quieter than before, she still enjoyed a conversation about something simple. He was grateful for Alice, who was wonderful with her, looking after her devotedly.

Mrs Latimer had engaged Perry's to handle the accounts at Honeyfield, and that had helped him find one or two other customers. But he didn't intend to go out to the house himself to check the books every month. It would be too . . . distracting. Instead he would send the new accountant he'd recently employed, Jason Norcott. That young man had an excellent brain for figures, better than himself, Nathan suspected.

He would continue to sell houses for people in the area, something he quite enjoyed. He wished there were more houses to sell. Perhaps he should sell the accounting side of the firm and move somewhere busier to concentrate on house sales.

Who knew what was best? At present he had debts to pay and a mother to care for, a woman who needed to be in the same rooms at the same time of day, or to visit the same shops. The doctor said she would be greatly upset if he moved her away from her familiar home and advised strongly against changing anything at this stage.

He continued to watch and appreciate Jason's skill at work. His father would never have hired a man like that, would have considered him too 'uppity' with his employer and too friendly with the other employees. Nathan liked the way Jason got on well with everyone, including Mr Parkin, to whom he was always very respectful. The chief clerk seemed a happier man these days, had lost his anxious look and nervous mannerisms.

Nathan's thoughts drifted to Kathleen again. He still thought about her more often than he ought to. In his mind she was always 'Kathleen' now, not 'Mrs Wareham' or 'Matron'. But as long as he kept his thoughts about her to himself, he could let himself dream now and then, surely?

He'd seen her in Malmesbury once but she hadn't seen him and he'd turned down a side street to avoid an encounter, then wished he hadn't.

He'd run into her in Honeyfield a few days ago. She'd been approaching along the footpath and he hadn't been able to turn aside without being rude, so had raised his hat and stopped to exchange greetings. He still remembered every word.

'How are you keeping, Mrs Wareham?'

'I'm very well, thank you. You look a little tired, if you don't mind me saying so, Mr Perry.'

'I've been rather busy and my mother isn't in good health.'

'I heard. I'm so sorry.'

He hadn't been able to resist prolonging the discussion a little. 'I saw your children the other day coming out of the village school. They looked full of energy.'

She smiled. 'Yes. They love living here. You should see how much Kit eats these days. I think he's going to be a tall man once he's fully grown.'

'He's what, nine now, am I right?'

'Yes, and ought to be studying hard to get into a grammar school, he's such a clever lad. But you know how we're circumstanced.'

'It's such a pity. He'd win a scholarship, I'm sure.'

She forced a smile, but it faded almost at once. 'Oh well, you can't have everything. And Mr Fleming is a very stimulating teacher. Kit thinks a lot of him.'

'So Lizzie must be eight?'

'Almost. That girl has the most vivid imagination. She — Sorry, you can't be interested in such details.'

'I am interested. I like to hear about your children. I wish I wasn't so . . . um, busy.'

She flushed slightly, as if she'd guessed what

he really wanted to say.

'Are you going to continue sending Mr Norcott to look over our accounts?'

'Yes. He's very efficient and it's a straightforward job.'

She didn't say it, but her eyes said she wished it were him coming to Honeyfield House.

Nathan hadn't allowed himself to continue chatting. He'd only be torturing himself because every time he saw her, he found her more attractive. He'd tipped his hat to her, claimed an appointment with a client and walked on along the street, resisting the temptation to glance back at her till just before he turned a corner.

But she was still watching him, so he raised his hand and forced himself to walk on.

She was as charming as ever. And as lovely. He dreamt of her that night. He dreamt of her far too often.

★   ★   ★

One evening the telephone rang in his office and Nathan answered it since he was the only person left in the building. He often worked late. What was there to go home for?

'Mr Perry?'

He didn't need to ask who it was. 'K — Mrs Seaton. I hope you're well.'

'Not exactly. You know I had a visit from my father?'

'Yes.'

'Could I talk to you, ask your advice? I'm not sure whether to run away, you see. I've thought

315

and thought and I can't make up my mind.'

Her voice was tight with anxiety, and no wonder.

'Your father didn't . . . cause you any trouble, though.'

'No. He just wanted to talk. But what he said, well, I can't decide whether to believe him or not, whether to stay or to go. I badly need advice. I know how busy you are, and I'm sorry to impose, but perhaps I could come and see you? I can pay one of the farmer's lads to drive me to Malmesbury and — '

'No need. I have my own motor car now, remember? I'll come and see you at once in case the matter of your leaving is urgent.' If it was, did he dare offer her asylum in his own home? He would if necessary and hang what people might say. He wasn't risking her getting hurt. He'd heard rumours of Godfrey Seaton's ruthlessness more than once, especially since the fellow had taken over Seaton's.

He was away from the desk in seconds, not putting away the papers on it, only locking the safe and the outer door. The motor car was parked in the street nearby, for convenience, in case he had to go out to a farm. He had it started in a minute.

She had sounded anxious.

He didn't want her to leave the district. And he wouldn't allow anyone to hurt her.

It was only a fifteen-minute drive to Honeyfield, but it seemed longer.

316

Kathleen heard a car coming slowly along the deeply rutted lane much sooner than she'd expected. He must have driven quickly. She'd asked Sal to go to bed, so that she could talk privately with Nathan — no, she must remember to call him Mr Perry.

She opened the back door and cried out in shock as a man shoved it wider, holding it open, saying, 'This is the one he wants.' Then he grabbed her.

She screamed at the top of her voice and struggled against him, but he was taller and much stronger than she was and she could only slow him down as he dragged her towards the waiting car. Another man had taken the key out of the back door and locked it from the outside.

When she didn't stop screaming, her captor put his hand across her mouth, but she bit him good and hard.

He cursed and slapped her so viciously across the face she felt dizzy for a few moments, by which time he had shoved her into the car.

The other man slipped into the back seat beside them, saying, 'Go on!'

The driver set off and the two men held her down between them.

'Even easier than I'd expected,' one of them said.

'She's a pretty one with her hair all tumbled round her face like that.'

'Don't lay one finger on her. He'll find a way to make you sorry if you do anything except exactly what he's told you. He insists on his orders being followed to the letter. And he pays well, so it's worth it.'

'Pity. Do you think we should tie her up?'

'Wouldn't hurt to tie her hands together. It'll make it easier for us to handle her at the other end.'

'And easier for him too.' The other man tittered.

'Why are you doing this?' Kathleen asked. 'What have I ever done to you?'

'We've been paid to take you. Now shut up or I'll put a gag in your mouth.'

She shut up, but only to keep them from gagging her. If she saw any chance, she'd be screaming for help to passers-by. And she could still kick them, too, once they were out of the car.

Kathleen was given no chance to call for help because the car didn't stop. They nearly bumped into another vehicle coming towards them just outside Honeyfield and after that, they didn't see anyone else, but racketed along the country roads and drove across junctions, without the driver seeming to watch for other drivers.

She was sitting in the middle of the back seat so could see out through the front window. She heard dogs bark as they passed isolated houses and farms, saw foxes and badgers slink out of their path and once they hit some small animal, a rabbit she thought, which squealed just once.

Her heart sank when they arrived in Swindon and turned into a yard with a sign above the double gates saying 'Seaton and Sons, Carters'. The driver got out and shut the big gates behind them.

It was definitely Godfrey who'd paid to have

her kidnapped, then. Well, she'd guessed that. Who else could it be? Was he going to kill her? Was he really that wicked?

If anything happened to her, what would he do to her children?

She tried not to let her fears show in her face. Bullies liked to see that you were afraid of them.

But she was terrified.

★ ★ ★

Just before he reached Honeyfield Nathan had to brake and swerve suddenly as a bigger car coming the other way hurtled round the corner towards him. He just managed to stay out of the ditch, cursing people who didn't learn to drive properly. No wonder so many people were being killed in accidents with motor vehicles. They weren't used to vehicles that could go so fast, either as drivers or pedestrians.

That was the only car he passed. Well, you didn't see many cars on these country roads in daytime, let alone after dark. Cars were too expensive, far beyond the common man's purse.

He drove slowly and carefully for the last few hundred yards towards his turn-off, meeting no one else, thank goodness.

When he got to Honeyfield House, he found lights on everywhere and Sal peered out of the kitchen window then flung the door open. The children were behind her and Lizzie's face was streaked with tears while Kit looked angry. The lad had a rolling pin in his hand, brandishing it like a weapon.

'Don't switch off that motor, Mr Perry,' Sal yelled as soon as she recognised him. 'They've taken Kathleen. You have to go after them.'

'What? Who's taken Kathleen?'

'Some men. I'd gone to bed because she wanted to speak to you privately, but I looked out when I heard her screaming and I saw two men dragging her towards a car.'

'I came running down but I was too late,' Kit said. 'Why have they taken Mum away?'

'I don't know.' Nathan looked back at Sal. 'You've no idea who they were?'

'No.'

'Tell me what the car looked like.'

She stared at him blankly and it was left to Kit, a car enthusiast like most little boys, to describe the car. 'It was a Sunbeam, I'm sure it was. Four-cylinder with a side valve. Someone drove it in the reliability run and it went from Land's End to John O'Groats and back without an engine stop. And — '

'All right. I know the sort of car you mean. The one that nearly ran me off the road just before I got to the village could have been a Sunbeam,' Nathan said slowly, thinking aloud. 'In fact, now you mention it, I'm sure it was. I bet that was them. But they'll be long gone now and hard to find. Is there a village policeman?'

'Yes. But he's not much use.'

'Better him than no one. Does he have a telephone? No? Then tell me where he lives.'

'I'll show you,' Kit said at once. 'It's round the back of the main street. Let me come with you, please. I want to help catch those men who hurt

320

my mother. I can put my overcoat on top of my pyjamas.' He grabbed it from the hook near the back door.

Nathan nodded. 'All right. It'll be quicker. But afterwards you'll have to walk back here on your own from the main road, Kit. Will you be all right in the dark?'

'Yes, of course. I'll take this with me.' He brandished the rolling pin again.

Nathan looked at Sal. 'Keep the doors locked. Don't let anyone in unless you know them.'

'You'll find her, sir.'

'I'll do my best.'

'It'll be that Mr Godfrey who took over from her father-in-law. She told me about it all.'

'That's what I'm thinking. And I know where he lives.'

'I'd come with you, but my Babs is too little and there's Lizzie to keep safe as well.'

'Better you stay here. After I've left, go round and check that all the windows are locked. And don't answer the door to any stranger. Come on, young 'un.'

They set off again, but Nathan didn't dare drive too fast along the bumpy lane. He didn't want to damage his car. It was the only way he had of following her.

He was cursing himself for not taking better care of Kathleen and vowing that he'd get her back, whatever it took. If they'd hurt her, he'd make sure they suffered too. Oh, yes. And to hell with the law. He'd do whatever was necessary.

'Turn right after the pub, Mr Perry.'

He did as the boy told him and after two more

turns they found the village policeman's house.

Everything was dark and they had to wake up the plump young man who was the village bobby.

It took a while to make him understand what had happened and in the end Nathan shouted, 'Get dressed as quick as you can and I'll explain the details while we go. They've kidnapped Mrs Seaton and could be hurting her even as we speak.'

The young man ran inside, muttering under his breath, but came out again more quickly than Nathan had expected, brandishing a truncheon.

At the turn off to Honeyfield House, Nathan stopped. 'Out you get, young 'un.'

'Let me come with you. *Please!*'

'No! Out! You're delaying us.'

Sulkily Kit got out of the car, kicking the nearest tyre.

Just as Nathan was starting off again, a dog ran out of a garden barking and he had to brake hard.

Kit didn't hesitate. He ran forward and clambered on to the luggage rack attached to the rear of the car, the noise he made lost in the furious barking of the dog as its owner dragged it back into the garden.

The man called out, 'He don't like motor cars, sir. Sorry.'

But Nathan had already set off again.

Kit crouched down so that the men in the car couldn't see him through the rear window. There was a tarpaulin strapped to the rack and as the cool night air made him shiver, he unstrapped it,

322

not without difficulty, and pulled it over himself when the car slowed down.

As the car jolted along the bumpy country roads, he was grateful for the tarpaulin's shelter because it was cold riding on the back. He hoped no part of him was showing and that he just looked like a lumpy piece of luggage.

He prayed as he'd never prayed before that they'd get there in time to save his mother from that horrible, horrible man.

★ ★ ★

Fergus pretended to go home that night, but crept back into the stables. No one stayed on night duty now, so he was able to join the injured mare in her stall and bathe the nasty cut caused by careless driving by that new man, who treated horses like motor cars, which didn't need the rests the poor overworked horses did.

Things were going from bad to worse here. He'd have to find another job, even if it meant accepting a lowly one, because it was breaking his heart to see the animals so badly treated.

No, he couldn't leave yet. He had to keep an eye on Godfrey, damn his eyes! The fellow meant to harm Kathleen, so Fergus was pretending to hate his daughter. He thought he'd won his new master's trust, but hadn't been included in whatever was going on tonight, hadn't even found out what Godfrey was planning.

'There you are, my girl,' he murmured to Blossom, stroking her neck and lighting a small candle to check her injury.

It needed bathing again, he decided, and some powder putting on it. Why hadn't they used the powder the vet sold? It was cheap and effective against infections.

Penny-pinching on everything, that sod was. Except for the fancy motor car he'd just bought and his church duties.

It was then that Fergus realised: the motor hadn't been in its usual place under the awning at the end of the stables. He'd been so concerned about the horse that he hadn't noticed.

Mr Godfrey couldn't have gone out in it because Fergus had seen him through the window of the house, in the back sitting room, in a comfortable armchair chatting to his aunt. His wife didn't live here. No, just him. He'd moved in with his aunt and left his wife in their old home looking after his children. And for all his talk of abstemiousness, he and his Aunt Agnes lived in high old style.

Where could the motor have gone at this hour of the night, then? No one would have taken it without the master ordering them to.

Fergus decided to watch out for it coming back and see if he could overhear what they'd been doing. He put out the candle when he'd tended to Blossom and waited patiently.

An hour later he heard the sound of an engine and the gates clanking as they were dragged open.

Fergus went up into the hayloft to watch. It overlooked the place they kept the car, which was perfect for his purpose.

'Out you get, missus,' one man said, not a man Fergus recognised.

But he did recognise his daughter, with her hands bound, a bruise on her cheek and her hair all tumbling down as if she'd been in a struggle. Dear God, what were they intending to do with her? They'd roughed her up already.

And him on his own here! He couldn't rescue her from three men and Godfrey Seaton. He'd have to get help. But first he'd see if he could find out what they were about.

Silently as a ghost, he left the hayloft and crossed the yard. He didn't need a light, could have walked it blindfold. He stayed in the shadows, avoiding the brightness from the window of the back room, the place Godfrey sat most evenings. Mrs Seaton was no longer there, just *him*.

Unlocking the side gate, he slipped outside but hesitated, uncertain whether to call in the police immediately or continue watching what was going on through the window of the back room.

No, the police would pay more attention to what Godfrey told them than to him. He had to find out what they were intending to do with her, have something definite to tell them.

Unless Godfrey was going to kill her and then he'd just have to hurl rocks through the windows to distract them and yell for help. Surely someone from a nearby street would hear him and come if he yelled 'Murder'?

He went back into the yard, but left the little gate unlocked in case he had to get away quickly.

25

The men took Kathleen into the house. She didn't struggle because she wanted to fool her captors into thinking they'd frightened her so much she'd obey their orders. In a pig's ear she would.

Godfrey was waiting for them in the back room. He looked at one of her assailants and placed one finger on his lips. Before Kathleen could draw in the air to scream, one man had put a hand across her mouth.

So she didn't even wriggle, just stood there, her expression blank as it used to be when she worked in the café. At least, she hoped it was blank.

'I see she struggled when you captured her.' Godfrey stared down his nose at her. 'Even her own father speaks ill of her, says she's disobedient. I shall enjoy punishing her for that.'

She felt hurt, because her father had told her another tale entirely about how he felt about his new employer.

'How an Irish whore like her persuaded my cousin to marry her, I don't know. Anyway . . . ' Godfrey looked at the men and tossed a purse on to the floor. 'Gag her properly and tie her to that chair. I've left the ropes ready. Then you others can go home and forget what happened tonight. I just need Jack from now on. Jack, wait in the kitchen and leave her for me to deal with.

What happens to her is none of your business, so ignore it if she screams. I'll answer the front door myself when they come for her. You're just staying to make sure no one interferes. Her father might draw the line at what we're doing, so I don't want him involved.'

One man nodded and bent to pick up the purse. The other shoved Kathleen on to the chair and bound her feet and body to it with the ropes that were already in place. Jack was the largest of them all, a big brute of a fellow whose nose had been broken at some stage. He waited by the door.

She was afraid now, suddenly quite sure Godfrey intended to murder her. And she would be helpless to stop him. She'd never thought to die like this.

When the men had gone, he sat down and studied her. 'You're quite pretty, in a coarse sort of way. I expect you're wondering what's going to happen to you.'

She said nothing, staring in another direction, the only act of defiance she could manage now.

He walked across the room and slapped her hard across the face. 'Look at me when I'm speaking to you, bitch.'

If her mouth had been free, she'd have spat at him. As it was, she shut her eyes. Another slap rocked her head but she kept her eyes stubbornly shut.

'I'll tell you anyway because you can't shut your ears. I'm selling you into a brothel.' He chuckled. 'They'll keep you safely locked away and use your body till you're no use to man nor beast, till you've no defiance left in you, till you don't even care what I've done to your brats. And those two won't grow much older, by the way.'

Her heart twisted in terror.

'Of course I could just kill you, but I'd much rather know that you're suffering for years as a punishment for daring to marry a Seaton.'

He glanced towards the clock. 'They'll be here in an hour to collect you. Until then you and I can have a little fun.'

She was shocked to the core by what he'd said. What had she ever done to deserve such a fate? Or her children? Oh, dear heaven, please Nathan look after them when I'm gone. Don't let this madman kill them.

She was helpless to do anything, utterly at the mercy of this monster.

★ ★ ★

Outside Fergus breathed deeply to control his temper at what he'd overheard. How dare that hypocritical fiend treat his daughter like this? For all her unfeminine independence, Kathleen had always lived a decent life, he knew that.

He pressed himself into a dark corner and watched the men walk out of the yard. One of them turned to click the catch shut on the gate, then they went off down the street, laughing and joking about how easy that job had been.

The other man he'd seen was Godfrey's 'manservant' Jack. More like his tame bully, as far as Fergus could tell, because he looked more like a prizefighter than a manservant.

Luckily, since neither Jack nor his master had any skill with horses, Fergus had kept his job. But he knew that it was only a matter of time before he lost it because Godfrey hated the Irish. Some people just did, though Fergus could never understand why. Godfrey would replace him in an instant once he found a man more to his liking. Heaven help the poor horses then.

After making sure the gate was unlocked again, Fergus went back to the house. What he saw through the window made him want to throttle Godfrey, who was making free with poor Kathleen's body, enjoying hurting her and taunting her, while she was tied to the chair, helpless.

Fergus went to the back door and got into the house by using the key he'd never handed over to his new master after old Mr Seaton died.

In the old days, the servants would be sitting in here in the evenings. Now, even Mrs Seaton was encouraged to go to bed early and one of the maids had told him Godfrey was giving her something each night to make her sleepy. He'd reduced the number of servants, and those left were sent up to their attic bedrooms much earlier to save coal.

Fergus wasn't sure how to rescue Kathleen, but wasn't going to rush into it, because he didn't know where Jack was and he'd only have one chance to help her.

It was a good thing he'd entered carefully because, talk of the devil, Jack came clumping down the stairs to the kitchen.

Fergus only had time to duck into the scullery and watch through the partly open door.

Jack helped himself to a bottle of beer and sat at the kitchen table, shaking out the crumpled evening newspaper, which his master had finished with, and reading it by gaslight.

Damn him! Fergus thought. He couldn't do anything while Jack was around to turn a fight against Godfrey into Fergus fighting against two large men.

Jack was as strong as an ox and a dirty fighter too. Fergus had seen him in action. He had to deal with him first, then he could handle Godfrey on his own, he was sure. By hell, he'd make him sorry for what he was doing to Kathleen, not to mention what he was intending to do.

And how did a man who flaunted his Christianity at you know enough about brothels to 'sell' a woman to them? Only one way he could know them that well, the damned hypocrite.

Fergus looked round for something to throw to catch Jack's attention, but just then there was the sound of a motor car outside the house. He grimaced. Surely the brothel hadn't sent someone to pick up poor Kathleen already? Godfrey had said they were coming in an hour's time.

* * *

Nathan stopped the car at the front of the house and urged the policeman out of it. The constable hovered on the doorstep, not seeming at all anxious to force his way into a gentleman's residence.

330

Nathan hammered on the front door.

It was answered by Godfrey himself.

'I believe you have my fiancée here.' Nathan had told the policeman he and Kathleen were engaged to be married and it was as good a story as any for giving him a right to be anxious about her.

'No. She's not here. Why should she be?'

'I don't believe you, so we'll take a look round, if you don't mind.'

'I do mind.' Godfrey tried to close the door on them.

'We won't take long, sir,' the policeman bleated.

Nathan had already stuck his foot in the door. 'We'll take as long as is necessary, Seaton, because I know for certain she's here.' That inner sense that helped find what had been lost had kicked in as soon as he got to the house, had told him he was right and she was here.

There was the sound of footsteps and a burly man came hurrying from the back of the hall to join them.

'Ah, there you are, Jack,' Godfrey said. 'Get rid of these people for me, will you? And as for you, Constable, you should know better than to force your way into a gentleman's residence for no reason. I shall complain to the chief constable.'

'I'm sorry, sir, but — '

Nathan poked him in the ribs.

' — I'm afraid I must insist. We have information that Kathleen Seaton has been brought here.'

'The woman is *not* in my house, damn you!'

331

Under cover of the altercation at the door, Fergus crept up the stairs from the kitchen, pocketknife in hand. The others were so caught up in their arguments they didn't see him at first in the shadows at the back of the hall.

Then Nathan caught sight of him, so Fergus put one finger to his lips and pointed towards the room where they were holding Kathleen. He managed to creep along the side of the hall without any of the others noticing him and slipped inside the back room.

She was sitting there, tears streaking her cheeks. As quickly as he could, he cut through her bonds and then yelled at the top of his voice, 'She's here! They had her tied up and gagged.'

Nathan immediately tried to push past Godfrey and his servant, but they pushed back and the policeman was a bit slow to come to Nathan's aid.

A small figure bent down and wriggled past their legs, running across the hall shouting, 'Mum! Mum!'

Godfrey left Jack to bar the door and chased after the lad, catching hold of his coat collar.

Fergus helped his daughter to the door of the back room. She was moving stiffly after being tied up for so long but when she saw her son and Godfrey shaking him like a dog shakes a rat, she yelled a protest and went for the man's face with her nails, heedless of the fact that he was much bigger than her. So furiously did she attack him that she drove him back a couple of steps and he had to let go of Kit to defend himself.

Fergus had to leave her to help Nathan with

Jack, who looked as if he was going to murder his assailant.

As Godfrey stepped back before Kathleen's assault, the policeman also edged round the two struggling men and ran to help Kathleen, trying to get between her and Godfrey.

'Stop! Stop this minute, in the name of the law!'

As Kathleen fell back, he followed up with, 'You're under arrest, Mr Seaton, for kidnapping.'

Meanwhile Kit had picked up the rolling pin, which he'd dropped. He saw Godfrey punch the young policeman and send him sprawling to the floor, then grab his mother again.

But the man had forgotten about him, so Kit darted forward with the rolling pin raised and hit the back of the man's legs, and any other part of him he could reach. Kathleen managed to scratch Godfrey's cheek.

He yelled in agony at the double attack and Kathleen shoved him off her with a sudden surge of strength. As he staggered backwards into a hall table, he reached into his pocket and pulled out a flick knife, clicking the blade open.

'No!' The policeman jumped to his feet and as Godfrey moved towards her, knife raised, he pulled out his truncheon.

Kathleen grabbed her son and pulled him behind her, trying and failing to move back into the nearby room. Before the knife could strike her, the policeman used his truncheon, whacking Godfrey across the back of his head as hard as he could.

The yells cut off abruptly and the knife fell

from Godfrey's hand as he crumpled to the ground. He made no further sound, just lay there motionless.

Jack took one look at his master's still body and ran for his life, but Nathan dived for his legs and tripped him up.

Fergus slammed the front door shut and helped Nathan and the constable hold Jack down and handcuff his hands behind him, then the young policeman said, 'You stay there, if you know what's good for you, and don't try to get up or I'll charge you with . . . with resisting arrest.'

And all the time Godfrey lay without moving.

Kathleen took the rolling pin from her son's hand, still looking fierce and wild, as if she was prepared to take on the whole world in defence of her child.

With Jack subdued, the constable went back to kneel down and check Godfrey. He looked up, gasping in shock, 'He's dead.'

'He can't be,' Fergus said. 'You only hit him once. He's just unconscious.'

'See for yourself.'

Fergus bent over the body, putting his fingers to the pulse at the throat. But the pulse was still now, would be still for ever. 'You're right. He is dead. There's no mistaking that look.'

'I've never killed anyone before,' the constable moaned. 'What's the sergeant going to say about this?'

When Jack saw that his master was dead, he went very quiet, muttering, 'I had nothing to do with that. You can all bear witness. I didn't touch him.'

Nathan ignored him. 'It was an accident, which took place because he was trying to kill Kathleen. You were a hero, constable. You saved her life. A real hero.'

The young man gaped at him. 'Do you think so?'

'I do.'

'I agree. Well done, lad,' Fergus added. 'We'll tell your sergeant how it happened.'

'Oh. Right.'

There was a sound above them and they saw the rest of the servants standing in a cluster on the landing, staring down in horror at the chaos below and the body of their master.

'Is there a telephone in this house?' Nathan shouted up to them.

'Yes, sir.'

'Someone show the constable where it is, then he can phone his sergeant. On second thoughts, I'll go with him.' He wasn't at all sure the young fellow could explain things coherently. He looked up the stairs. 'Can you two young women come and help stand guard over this man. You can use this rolling pin on him if he tries to get away.'

Eyes brightening in anticipation, the two maids came down the stairs.

Nathan followed the constable out of the hall to a spacious study, where he spoke on the telephone to the operator, insisting she connect him to the police station immediately.

Jack didn't move but one maid kicked him in the ribs anyway, glaring down at him. 'I wish you'd been killed as well. Then you wouldn't hurt no other lasses.'

The other moved forward to join her. 'I'll hit him over the head for you any time you like, Mr Keller.'

Before Fergus could stop her, she kicked Jack in a very painful part of his body, making him writhe about on the floor in agony.

Fergus found himself smiling, something he hadn't expected to do after he'd seen a man killed. 'I didn't see you do that, but you'd better not do it again, lass.'

'Can I if he tries to move?'

'Definitely.'

Jack shrank away from them, curling up, trying to protect himself as well as a man with his hands bound behind his back could.

Fergus went across to his daughter. 'Are you all right, Kathleen Frances?'

'Yes, Da. Thank you for helping me.'

'I wasn't going to let them do what they'd planned to you, if I could help it. That son of yours is a brave lad. Well done, Christopher.'

Fergus turned back to his daughter. 'I'm sorry I couldn't get to you sooner. I was hiding in the scullery trying to work out how to rescue you, because there were four of them and only one of me. Good thing that new fellow of yours brought in the police.'

Nathan and the constable came back as he said this. 'The police are on their way.'

There was the sound of a car stopping outside and Kathleen gasped. 'It could be the people from the brothel.'

Fergus went to peer out of the front door.

'There's a car stopped. Come here, Constable. Let them see your uniform.'

The policeman joined him in the doorway and there was the sound of a vehicle driving off.

'That's got rid of them devils,' Fergus said in satisfaction.

But Nathan and Kathleen weren't listening to him. He was walking across to her, with eyes for no one else.

Fergus took a step backwards and winked at the policeman.

Nathan spoke to her as if the two of them were the only people in the world. 'Are you all right, Kathleen? He didn't . . . hurt you?'

'He humiliated me, and my face feels bruised. But no, that fiend didn't hurt me in the way you mean.'

'Thank goodness! Ah, hell, I can't do it, can't wait any longer.' He pulled her into his arms and held her close. 'I died a thousand deaths on the way here, worrying that he'd kill you before I could get to you.'

She shivered and glanced sideways at the corpse, which no one had touched. 'He had much worse plans in mind for me. I'm glad he's dead.' She huddled against Nathan, utterly exhausted all of a sudden. 'How did you find me?'

'Where else would they take you but to Seaton's?' He kissed her forehead, then her lips. 'I can't marry you till I've sorted out the mess in our family business, but if you'll wait . . . '

She pulled her head back a little, staring at him. 'You'd marry me?'

'Of course I would. It's what I want most in the world. Don't you feel how right it is when we're together?' He brushed her hair gently back from her forehead and kissed her nearest cheek. 'I love you, Kathleen.'

'Yes, of course I feel how right it is. And I love you too. But . . . you're a gentleman.'

'And you're a wonderful, brave woman. If you like, I'll court you slowly, but it'll come to the same thing in the end, if you give me even half a chance.'

Her lips curved into a smile. 'I'll give you a full chance, Nathan Perry.'

He pulled her close and kissed her again.

Kit rolled his eyes at the sight. Fergus smiled and bent to whisper to his grandson, 'Isn't that grand? They're going to get married.'

'It's not grand if they keep on kissing one another. It's soppy.'

'Let them be soppy, then. One day you'll feel the same about a woman.'

'Ugh! No, I won't!'

There were sounds outside. 'Ah, that sounds like the police.' Fergus tapped Nathan on the shoulder. 'You'd better stop billing and cooing, and talk to the police.'

The only person missing from this final scene was Mrs Seaton, and she was found later so fast asleep that no one could wake her properly.

'He gives her a drink every night, says it's a tonic, but it sends her straight to sleep,' a maid told the police sergeant. 'She'll do anything *he* asks.' Her eyes went towards the corpse, now decently covered by a blanket. 'I don't like her,

338

but that wasn't a fair way to treat her, was it?'

'Does she have any other family we can bring in to help her?'

'I don't think so. There's a lawyer comes sometimes, Mr Morton. He was helping her till Mr Godfrey moved in. Then Mr Morton didn't come here any more.'

'We'll be getting the lawyer back, then. Can you keep an eye on her for us till this Mr Morton gets here?' the sergeant asked.

'Yes, sir.'

'Now, will someone please explain exactly how this happened? No rushing it this time. Tell me every single thing you did, every step along the way. No, on second thoughts we'd better go to the police station and do things properly. We can lock that other scoundrel up safely there.'

It took several hours for explanations to be made and full notes to be taken. By which time they were all exhausted.

'I'll see to the horses at the yard till that lawyer comes,' Fergus said. He turned to his daughter. 'I hope I've redeemed myself, Kathleen Frances. I'm sorry I hurt you when you were younger. I think it was the booze. Godfrey was right about that, at least. For me it's the devil's brew. It puts a madness into me. And your fool of a mother made it worse the way she wasted the money I earned.'

She nodded, then said slowly, 'I'd rather you didn't tell the lawyer or Mrs Seaton about me and the children.'

He stared at her. 'But they're the heirs now. Of course she should know about them.'

'No. His wife can have all the money and do what she wants with it. I don't want my two bringing up in that unhappy house. Their father was unhappy here, their uncle Alex left home and hasn't been back. It just *feels* horrible the minute you go through the door.'

'You don't want them to have the money?'

'No. I want them to have a happy life. I'll give them a good education, make sure they can earn their own money.'

Nathan put his arm round her shoulders. 'I'll play the father's part, Mr Keller, and help them grow up into decent people, I hope. And we'll have enough to live in modest comfort.'

Fergus shook his head in bafflement. 'You're sure about this, Kathleen Frances?'

'Yes, very sure.'

'Then I'll not tell the old lady about you and the children. She's not very clever at the best of times and her wits have been further addled by what that sod had been giving her. She'll never know you exist.'

It felt as if a weight had fallen from Kathleen's shoulders. She turned to Nathan. 'Will you take me home now?'

'It'll be my pleasure. Come on, young fellow. I thought I'd left you behind.'

'I rode in the luggage rack. It was cold.'

'Well, you can ride back inside the car.'

Nathan put his arm round her shoulders and they walked out together, followed by Kit, yawning as he stumbled along.

* * *

Nathan drove slowly back to Honeyfield as dawn was lightening the sky in the east.

Kathleen sat in the front of the car beside him and they conversed in low voices, while Kit slept soundly in the back, sprawled across the fine leather upholstery.

'May I come a-courting you, then?' Nathan asked with a smile.

'I'd love it. I don't want to rush into anything. I want to savour each step along the way. I was rushed into marriage before.'

'That'll suit me too, because I like to do things properly. Besides, I have my father's debts to clear before we can marry.'

'It'll be good to get to know you better before we become man and wife. The little things, what you like for tea, who your friends are, that sort of thing.'

'Then we're agreed.'

'Yes. Only, will you kiss me like that now and then? It was wonderful. I've never been kissed that way before.'

'Didn't your husband . . . ?'

'He was a kind man, but slow-thinking and not . . . not a skilful lover. Ernest married me to save me from my father forcing me to marry a bully he used to drink with. I always felt I was more Ernest's mother than his wife.'

After a pause, she spoke her thoughts aloud, 'I'd really like to be just me, Kathleen, for a while.'

They didn't say much as they drove the last couple of miles, but they smiled at one another from time to time.

And Kathleen knew in her heart that this was her man, the one she was meant to marry, the one who would make her happy.

As for waiting a couple of years, no. That was too long. She'd see about that later, once this horrible incident was behind them. A few months, perhaps. She needed that time.

'It's going to be another beautiful day,' she murmured as they turned off the main road towards Honeyfield House.

'It's going to be one of the happiest days of my life,' Nathan said and, after he'd stopped, he kissed her senseless before helping her out of the car.

Of all the things he'd ever found, this was the most precious, the love of a wonderful woman.

Endnote

[1]Greyladies: This book is about people helped by the Greyladies Trust. Anna Jacobs has also written a three-part series about the owners of Greyladies, set in the early twentieth century: *Heir to Greyladies*, *Mistress of Greyladies* and *Legacy of Greyladies*.

We do hope that you have enjoyed reading this large print book.

Did you know that all of our titles are available for purchase?

We publish a wide range of high quality large print books including:
Romances, Mysteries, Classics
General Fiction
Non Fiction and Westerns

Special interest titles available in large print are:
The Little Oxford Dictionary
Music Book
Song Book
Hymn Book
Service Book

Also available from us courtesy of Oxford University Press:
Young Readers' Dictionary
(large print edition)
Young Readers' Thesaurus
(large print edition)

For further information or a free brochure, please contact us at:
Ulverscroft Large Print Books Ltd.,
The Green, Bradgate Road, Anstey,
Leicester, LE7 7FU, England.
Tel: (00 44) 0116 236 4325
Fax: (00 44) 0116 234 0205